GET UP

Reece Pine

Recently dumped (again) for being cold, Guy gladly accepts his publisher friend's request to go to a remote hut in wintry Nunavut to find out whether aspiring novelist Cam Campbell is a plagiarist. By agreeing also to help the eccentric ecologist survey wildlife for a month, Guy buys time to assess Cam's innocence and hear stories about Cam's late father—Guy's favorite fantasy writer and the man whose book Cam is accused of stealing.

Guy's investigation is soon biased by his attraction to Cam and the growing concern about Cam's odd behavior. At times, Cam dissociates and is icier than Guy could ever be, yet he's the only one who's ever recognized, at a glance, the emotions burning beneath Guy's surface. Guy knows he's the best person to help Cam abandon the dangerous wilds outside and address those in Cam's head, but he also knows that he'll lose the chance if he comes clean about his ulterior motives for getting close to Cam. How can he convince Cam to come in from the cold... and why are they both really out there anyway?

A NineStar Press Publication

Published by NineStar Press
P.O. Box 91792,
Albuquerque, New Mexico, 87199 USA.
www.ninestarpress.com

Get Up

Warning: This book contains sexually explicit content, which may only be suitable for mature readers, and scenes of graphic violence.

The sun himself is weak when he first rises,
and gathers strength and courage as the day gets on.
Charles Dickens, *The Old Curiosity Shop*

Chapter One

AT LEAST HE wasn't nervous about meeting the kid anymore. He'd stopped feeling anything at all besides dread and the wheels of the suitcase he'd slung over his shoulder bruising his numb ass with every stumble. Finally, Guy glimpsed smoke wisping from a rustic pipe chimney a hundred yards farther than the thousand miles he'd already come. His brogues, so iced over they looked like glass slippers, skidded on the porch's wooden boards. The leather-gloved hand he threw forward to balance himself rattled the doorframe with a thudding knock, sending ice shards showering behind him from the rafters overhead.

"Hell-lo?" he croaked. "Cam-meron C—"

The alluring burst of firelight that greeted him as the door opened was immediately extinguished by someone squeezing the swollen wood shut behind themselves as they stepped forth. Guy was suddenly too surprised to be awestruck over meeting Alessandro De Carli's son at last. He was glad his frozen eyelids couldn't blink, because the guy—the specter, presumably Cameron Campbell—might disappear if he did. For a second, he wondered if he'd knocked on the wrong gingerbread house door, only there was no other shelter for fifty miles.

Cameron Campbell was known to be even more reclusive than his late father, but he wasn't actually supposed to be mythic. The tiny guy blocking the door with sturdy, unlaced boots looked like a wood nymph. Eyes as blue as distant stars stared at him unabashedly. Maybe the reason no journalists had ever snapped pictures of the kid, and why he had no online presence, was because he couldn't be caught on film.

"Incredible." Cameron must have read Guy's mind, and he pressed rosebud lips together in exasperation. "Are you alone? Did you hitch here? There's no corpse in a cab parked on the highway I need to go rescue? *Insane.*"

Guy respectively nodded and shook his head, hoping the well-earned insult was aimed at the driver on his way west who'd dropped him at the side of a barely used road, far from the highway. Guy had considered himself lucky to thumb a ride at all out of the tiny settlement of Ipasila, built around a gas station, which was the closest town to Campbell and two hours' drive from the Hudson Bay hamlet of Arviat in southern Nunavut. In hindsight, the man had been almost as reckless as Guy himself had been for not driving him straight to the police. Instead, Guy had been let out of the relative safety of a truck armed with nothing more than the GPS tracker Guy had brought with him and prayed was accurate.

"C-Cameron..." *Not Cameron,* Guy revised. A *Cameron* was a strapping guy—like a Brad or a David—or a blonde woman. This pixie prince was either a *Cam* or a question mark. His eyes looked magnified behind the lenses of large glasses, the arms of which must have burned cold against his temples because Cam removed them—only for his naked eyes to be comically large. It was still possible he wasn't even De Carli's son, since he looked nothing like him. Wrote nothing like him either, which was why Guy was here. "You're C-Campbell, right? De Carli's s-son?"

It was Campbell's turn to draw back in surprise. "Are you from a newspaper?"

"Am I *s-selling subscriptions?*" Traipsing from cabin to cabin after dark? "D-does it matter? Let me in." Heat from indoors infused the porch floorboards and bled into Guy's damp soles, announcing itself as pain in his brittle toes.

"I don't do interviews about my father." Cam reached inside the hood of his puffy coat, just a shade lighter than his luminous, creamy skin, to pull a long coil of black hair forward. It hung like gossamer over the gray scarf around his shoulders.

He'd let down his hair, so now Guy could enter, right? "Do I l-look like a journalist?"

"Nah, you look too honest."

Guy's brows were too frozen to frown at the sarcasm. He knew damn well he had a poker face. That was the problem; now that he was literally incapable of moving his face he probably looked normal, not dangerously hypothermic.

"I'm with your p-publisher."

"You're from Ames? In that case, first, tell Claire she should be fired and charged with attempted murder for sending you. Secondly, and for the hundredth time, I canceled the submission for *Close to Home.* I didn't mean to send it to you guys in the first place. Third, stop hounding me about it."

"Fourth, f-fuck off," Guy anticipated his next order. "I c-*can't*. And I'm from F-Fairbanks Press."

"Ha! Are you guys even still publishing me?" Cam swept his bangs behind an ear, which was slightly pointed at its tip.

Of course, it is. "You're the one who n-never answers emails."

"Internet's intermittent out here. And there's nothing wrong with that manuscript that isn't Fairbanks' fault." Cam pursed his lips, which were tinging blue before Guy's eyes, and nuzzled his chin into his scarf. Guy was torn between thinking it served him right to be cold and wanting to offer his firstborn as passage to the gatekeeper who halted Guy's shuffle forward by holding up a gloved palm. "Uh-uh, no way. You ought to know the drill, New Yorker. You are, aren't you?"

Guy was as native a New Yorker as anyone who'd moved there in adulthood and would never live elsewhere. A load of the population was in the same burned boat as him, so yes, he could claim to be from New York, but that was irrelevant while the heat fleeing his eyes stung.

"S-so?"

"So the same rules apply here as there," Cam continued, as though this were a holiday home in Connecticut. "You know, I met a hiker from Texas here who'd never even seen snow before, but he knew enough about it to come in September, not March. Why do you think I can't get any volunteers to assist me at the moment?"

Because not only did this waif conduct questionable wildlife research in the middle of nowhere while purportedly editing a novel, but he also lived at the end of a spur trail a mile west of an icy road to nowhere.

Cam stamped his feet, blowing into hands he cupped over his mouth. "Come *on*."

What did the little sylph want? For Guy to roll a seven? Produce a magic key?

"For God's sake, guy, you need to *strip*!" Cam finally twisted the door handle behind him, spilling back into an amber glow. Guy tumbled in after, out of the deadly night air.

Instantly, his coat became the warmest bath Guy had ever had the pleasure of sinking into. Flames in the hearth curled into come-hither licks Guy's jellied legs couldn't obey. There was enough ecstasy to be had where he wilted against the closed door. The sensation wrenched him from numb to overwhelmed in a blink, and thrust him the closest to an imminent powerful orgasm he'd been since...he didn't want to know.

Cam busied himself over at a kitchen counter, ignoring Guy, who stood, shaking in the doorway, suddenly struggling with a boner that had sprung from pure physical shock, surprising and mortifying him. He had to admit he could see how post-hypothermia blood rushing around could cause such a phenomenon, but man, did it *have* to? Thankfully, melting into a hunch helped hide it when Cam reappeared in front of him wearing only a few layers of sweaters and brandishing two steaming mugs of coffee.

Its intoxicating aroma further confused his senses by going straight to Guy's cock. *Now,* there's *a new kink.* He failed to convince himself his hand quivering was an aftereffect of the cold, not the sight of the now gloveless, pale hand offering a chipped mug with the handle out for Guy to grab. Cam raised an eyebrow at Guy's taking it with his left hand.

"Oh, you're a lefty?"

"I guess," Guy said, distracted by just how fine Cam's fingers were...and how Cam's palm was apparently immune to the hot ceramic he held courtesy of calluses, frostbite, or immortality. "Looks nice...."

"Not too strong?" Cam asked, a smile curling the corners of his mouth.

"N-no such thing." Guy slurped half the treacly concoction before gasping, "Thanks."

"Sit." Cam nodded to a couch piled high with blankets resembling a laundry pile. There was nowhere to sit except on top of them. "And I wasn't kidding before. You need to strip, like, five minutes ago. Show me some skin."

"What?" *Skin?*

"And a business card."

Shit. Guy had no such thing—he should have made Huw make him a mock-up one before coming. If Cam was astute enough to ask questions like that, it might be hard to deceive him as planned. Plausible excuses whirled in his mind, but were as hard to grasp as the snowflakes he ruffled loose from his hair, stalling for time. He was surprised they hadn't melted, since his scalp was beginning to burn....

"Of course, I'd prefer skin first. And so would you," Cam said.

"I'm here to work," Guy retorted, reinforcing the lie to himself.

"How do you know De Carli was my father?"

Guy blinked. "Isn't he?"

"My pen name's Cameron Stewart. I know my real name's on the contract I signed with you guys, but *that's* Cameron Campbell."

"That's De Carli's son's name."

"It's also as common as mud. How do you know I'm him?"

"Because..." Heat surged through Guy's veins, and flashes from the fireplace in his periphery blinded him. Flames shot up his spine, turning his thoughts to smoke. His erection stirred as he willed it to subside. Instead, his heartbeat faded, which was a lot more alarming. "Because..."

Struggling to balance his tilting mug on the surging, damp footwell he slumped down upon, Guy bit at his glove to peel it from his roasting hand. It dangled from his lip, and he batted it away to better claw at his collar, trying to escape its stranglehold. Sweat made it slippery in his shaking hands, and he panted more feverishly than he had while staggering outside, where everything was white—as white as everything was turning now.

"Hey, stay with me, guy." Cam rose from his slouch against the back of the sofa, surrounded by a blizzard of stars that swarmed Guy's vision. He was warmth personified, the most enchanting thing in the dreamscape Guy had navigated to get here, and he was still miraculous, even now that everything had become a nightmare. His own sharp intake of breath echoed from afar as Cam lunged toward him through the static.

"I hoped you were him," spilled in a murmur from Guy without his control. Strangely, Cam seemed to slip farther away the closer he got, as Guy sensed himself falling. It looked like he wouldn't manage to save De Carli's son after all. Well, he thought as all light vanished, at least he'd managed to meet him. And he got to die in the arms of a beyond-beautiful man.

No, forget that, his consciousness broke through. De Carli's son was stunning, strange, and fascinatingly all the way out here. Never mind the fact Guy couldn't write, he was going to live and find out what made Cam tick if it was the last thing he did.

Chapter Two

I'M ALIVE.

Safe.

Alone? Where's Nick— Oh. Guy remembered Nick was a country away, if not a dimension, and probably in someone else's bed by now. They'd split up a month before. In consolation and maybe correlation, Guy's mind was working just fine after its flare-out at the hut's front door. He remembered catching planes and a ride from a middle-of-nowhere Canadian town to the barren fringe of Canadian nowhere, and then staggering through a frozen hell until his life depended on the very person he'd come to rescue.

Guy had been foolishly glad he hadn't printed out the manuscript that Fairbanks's owner and director, Huw, emailed him. He recalled reading it at home and thinking all it was fit for was kindling, which was all he had wished for earlier in the snow. The memory of his being cold was hardest of all to get a hold on, possibly because it was traumatic, but probably also because right then he was strangely warm. Hot bath warm. Shared bed warm. Afterglow warm... *Because...I'm naked?*

The assumption he was safe fell away, along with the musty blanket covering his chest as he jolted up in bed in a tiny dark room. He was naked and trapped at the mercy of a supernaturally pretty being in the next room, the son of a ghost, who was himself too much of a vivid apparition and just plain too short to have carried Guy in here. He must have been dragged—and drugged? What was in that coffee to make him overheat like that? And why the *hell* was he naked?

A dim golden glow from beneath the bed spilled across the wooden floor. Guy hung his head over the side of the thin mattress, half expecting fireflies or a chatty French candelabra or anything else fairy-tale-like. Luckily, there were no monsters—instead a cast-iron pan containing a handful of charcoals sat atop a steel tripod beneath the bed's metal slats. He had to admit its heating properties were a lot more efficient than a hot water bottle and more romantic, too, lending a candlelit glow to the room. Exposed beams overhead made him feel like Pinocchio inside a ribbed belly, and the marbled grays seen through a small window looked like a paused scene on a black-and-white TV.

He crept off the bed, folding the blankets so they were nowhere near the charcoal bowl, and padded on bare feet to the window. Shards of a thermometer glinted on the outside sill, having shattered from the cold. They displayed a temperature locked perpetually high, mocking his earlier trial by tundra.

His breath clouded in the wan light as he layered on clothing from his suitcase, which was propped by the room's door. A knitted red woolen sweater was folded on a rickety chair. He unfolded it to see a garish Christmas pattern emblazoned on its front, which he wasn't sure was meant to be ironically ugly or not. Since De Carli's son had already no doubt seen his cock at attention, which Nick had called the only warm part of Guy, he figured he shouldn't be vain, but he really didn't want to wear it, and really hated knowing better than to reject it. He couldn't help Cam if he collapsed from hypothermia again.

There's a reason I'm asking you and no one else. Huw's voice rang in his near-frostbitten ears. *Besides the fact you'll fit right in in the Arctic. You're 'castratingly cold,' after all, according to Nick's Facebook.*

Even after fourteen years' friendship, dating back to when De Carli's books began to ruin Guy for all other fiction, Guy's former college roommate, Huw, remained oblivious to all but superficially expressed emotions, so Guy had grunted to make his displeasure known. "I'm not cold."

"You're a bunny wrapped in an enigma, but me and Campbell need your judgmental stare. Well, he might like the bunny part, too."

"Campbell and I," Guy had corrected.

"Great, keep that up, editor." Huw had scratched the air, making quotes around the last word. "Anyway, Campbell's probably a Popsicle himself out there, so defrost him with all your actual warmth because I need his book okayed. How often do you get a sure thing in publishing? Never, that's how often, unless you've got, like, George R. R. Martin's kid's debut."

"He's De Carli's son." Guy had hated the comparison. De Carli was better.

Fairbanks had spent eight months wrangling Cam's debut, only to be served an injunction, lodged by his older sister, who claimed the manuscript was stolen from their father's estate. Huw had only ever communicated with Cam online, and not thought to connect his common real name with the uncommon phenomenon who had been De Carli. No one had. The publishing grapevine hadn't heard anything since Cam had been institutionalized for suicidal intent for a month after De Carli's fatal heart attack two years earlier, then disappeared upon release. Remembering that, Huw figured family bickering over probate wasn't something to spring on him from afar, especially when the injunction was suppression ordered, making its claim more than a little suspicious.

After eagerly—then less eagerly—skimming Cam's book, Guy had vouched it wasn't an authentic De Carli. If the kid had desecrated a stolen draft to pass it off as his own work, he'd done too good a job. Unfortunately, Guy's fanboy opinion wouldn't make great testimony, and even he conceded the manuscript bore some similarity with De Carli's, which could be due to their shared tastes or family history…but maybe not. Huw had convinced him to go covertly to uncover proof in the form of drafts, and judge Cam's authenticity, too.

In one of his very few interviews, De Carli had said, "*My son is a simple boy. He wants for nothing.*" Journalists interpreted that as meaning homeschooled Cam had special needs, so hadn't pried. It surprised Guy to learn Cam had earned a doctorate in ecology last year at the age of twenty-two, mostly completed online, and had then assisted with wildlife projects abroad. The few available scientists Huw had tracked down attested Cam was *competent,* code for *nothing else good to say.* In other words, he was probably a precocious little…handful.

That and the kid's current dubious rabbit search didn't make for a stellar start to his research career, but was nothing compared to what Cam would face if he was found to have plagiarized his father. It'd destroy not just his career writing books, but also science journal articles that were as dry as the wings of his PhD subject, moths. The articles he'd previously cowritten all conformed to academic templates, so there was no comparison with his fiction, no way to tell if he'd forged the latter.

The chance to escape social circles shared with his ex for the time being was icing on the cake. Nick had liked the mystery of Guy's *mask* enough to seduce him, then grown quickly bored of its not melting under his hand. The fact that Guy honestly *wasn't* mysterious was a secret he seemed cursed to bear. No matter how many times he assured the Nicks of the world that he really was just that calm, it wasn't enough, and that was about all that made his blood simmer. To be fair, it wasn't Nick's fault that all that made Guy's heart race was analyzing a good book or an interesting person. The chance to meet De Carli's son, who was himself a shimmering incubus with a shady past, had Guy almost trembling even before he'd hit the cold.

Exhaling deeply, Guy told himself now to *chill*, almost wringing a smile from himself as he entered the hut's main room.

CAM BROKE THE rubble of threadbare blankets on the couch with a single hand to mash a wireless game pad. A cut scene of a fantasy game played out on Cam's laptop, propped on a split log standing in for a coffee table between the couch and hearth. Dramatic dialogue filled the rippling air by the fire, over which Guy's brogues hung off the mantelpiece like Christmas stockings to match the sweater he wore.

The room was like a hoarder's den. Hiking gear, books, tools, eclectic artwork, and notes were embedded like shrapnel in the log walls after an internet search engine had exploded. Ancient nature magazines, tents, and a beaver's dam's worth of walking poles—the hut was a condensed hiking warehouse. Amid the oddities, patches of bare floor sparkled. The wooden walls were waxed, and the kitchen's chrome gleamed. At second glance, the clutter seemed arranged in sensible sections. So the elf constructed mazes. Was that how he trapped animals in the woods, too, or did he just ask them politely to meet in a pentagram-shaped glen for tea?

Cam's colossal headphones might have canceled out noise for him, but they broadcast to others what he listened to in a boom, so Guy was surprised when Cam shimmied free of the blanket nest and turned to face Guy standing behind him.

Of course. Guy was stunned anew at Cam's poetic features. *Angels have senses beyond the usual five.*

Cam paused the game and set the controller down on the log. "Morning, guy from Fairbanks."

"Is it? Already?" Guy stepped to the window and cupped his palm by the icy glass to make out light in the void beyond. Fog from his breath instantly blocked his view.

"Now is the winter," Cam said, hanging his headphones on his laptop's screen.

"You stripped me." Guy made no move to sit on the sofa as Cam slid to one end, curling his knees underneath the rolling sea of wool.

"You ruined your pants," Cam echoed his matter-of-fact monotone.

Shit. "That was invol—"

"By spilling coffee on them," Cam clarified, and Guy's shoulders fell in relief. "As for the boner, it was nothing I haven't handled before."

The oblique admission sank in. *Oh.* Was Campbell gay, then? Or was he referring to jerking off? The image of Cam stroking himself to climax on that very couch flashed in Guy's mind, causing him to grit his teeth. So what if Cam ever did? There wasn't much else to do here but read and play video games—and write, hopefully. Whatever Cam did apart from writing his book for Fairbanks was none of Guy's business.

"If you'd let me inside sooner, I wouldn't have collapsed."

"Like hell. I *told* you to strip. Going from that cold outside to room temperature is murder on your circulation. Be glad you didn't get a nosebleed, or your jacket would be wrecked as well. It's a nice jacket, for Lawrence Oates."

"I don't know that designer."

A smile flickered on Cam's face. "Speaking of designers, nice sweater."

"Yeah, thanks," Guy muttered, more thankful that it was warm enough in the living room that Guy could take the thing off and leave it folded on one of the book stacks.

"Aw. I don't know which I prefer, before or after. A or B," Cam mumbled in return, as if to himself.

The sight of Campbell's onyx hair draped over his fine shoulders reminded Guy to brush his own short locks back into place with his fingers while he perused the spines of one stack.

"Have you read all these?"

"Ha! They were just left by hikers lightening their load, same as everything here." Cam arced his arm to indicate the left half of the room. "I've only read the ones from here to the wall."

"Hundreds," Guy remarked.

"It was a long winter."

"So you prefer reading to writing? To doing your edits, I mean?"

"No, I love writing." Instead of elaborating, Cam watched Guy, waiting for him to make a move.

This *was* Guy's move, though. Passive observation. That was his normal modus operandi *and* the brief Huw gave him. He definitely wasn't supposed to be actively observing Cam's ridiculously large eyes, willing them to crinkle in a smile, unsure whether he was distracted by being near De Carli's flesh and blood or simply still thrown by how beautiful the man in front of him was. Wastefully beautiful, since he was stuck in the middle of nowhere, and dangerously beautiful to himself and others as long as he let just anyone in... For all Cam knew, Guy was an ax murderer. Guy *was* here as a wolf in sheep's clothing, technically.

Cam blinked and Guy started, disguising it with a glance at his watch. Seven o'clock. It was really late. Or early. Had Cam been messing with him about it being morning already? Or was it really the next day?

Worried at not having come around soon after fainting, Guy pressed his forefinger to his neck. His pulse beat normally. The warped glass windows didn't reflect the room accurately—*or this is a vampire tomb, what a surprise*—so Guy left to find the bathroom. Its light was too dim to assess pupil dilation in the mirror above its tiny sink. A showerhead on a tube ran from the faucet and hung over the side of a large barrel. It had no drain, so Guy assumed wastewater from it went into either the sink or toilet, which reeked of antifreeze.

Returning to the couch, he hid his worry. "How long was I out?"

"Relax, guy. You came from New York, right? So you were exhausted on top of being hypo, then hyperthermic. You're good now. I took your temperature when you were out, twice."

Orally, Guy hoped. He sat beside Cam and took Cam's hand in his, folding all but its index finger down, which he raised to his nose. He drew Cam's finger a couple of feet in front on his own face and moved it back and forth at eye level. No blurred vision meant no cranial nerve palsy.

"Do my pupils look okay?"

"Ha! You didn't hit your head." Cam's eyes were so large—*All the better to see through you with*—that it was hard to tell when they narrowed only slightly in annoyance. Guy guessed he was insulted by the insinuation he wasn't quick enough on his feet to have prevented Guy from getting concussed. Whether it was his pride as a biologist or as an omniscient fairy that was dented, Guy didn't know.

Cam quieted into a piercing stare, causing Guy's heart to twinge. He worried he had hypothermic arrhythmia until Cam's lips parted and his gaze flickered to Guy's mouth as he reached forward and cupped Guy's chin. His fingers were warm....

Guy pulled back, freeing himself. His heart wasn't misbehaving because of hypothermia, but proximity. *Get a grip.*

He winked one eye and then the other. Both saw Cam clearly, good. *Camera one. Camera two. Make that Cameron two.* Both perspectives were stunning... He brushed Cam's hand aside and turned to face the fire, ashamed of his attraction. First aid wasn't risqué; he was here on a job; he didn't know Cam from Adam or any other mythological creature; and Cam was ten years younger than Guy. He *looked* younger still. Guy's overreacting heartbeat was probably just a hangover from his crash and recovery, or a reflexive complex developed from being saved. Or it was due to Cam's De Carli connection, or the surreal surroundings. Maybe it was love for the coffee Cam had given him earlier, which Guy had downed almost entirely in one gulp. If single sips were worth the same as pomegranate seeds were in Hades, Guy thought, he'd be trapped here for at least one season. He didn't hate the idea.

"Got any more coffee?"

Cam leaned back, plucked a plastic water bottle off a book stack, and handed it to Guy. "No more diuretics, you're too dehydrated. Drink."

Realizing he was *parched,* Guy gulped the water. *Two seasons. Three seasons. One year. Fuck it.*

"Anyway, guy from Fairbanks. You're some shiny ball and chain for me to bat around?"

"No, thanks. Fairbanks respects its staff *and* authors."

"Seriously? By deploying a warden?"

"If you ignore emails, yes. Doesn't Ames?" Guy had suspected Cam's namedropping of Ames earlier was a possible delusion of grandeur, but right now Cam seemed more down to earth. Still cast down to earth, but he didn't seem to be lying. "You asked if I was from Ames Press, didn't you? Do you have something with them too?"

Cam drew his slim shoulders up. "Fairbanks doesn't have an exclusivity clause in our contract."

"Why not give Ames *Distant* too?" De Carli's old publishers could afford to market shoddy work based on Campbell's name alone once its tacit relation to his father's distinct name was made more public.

"Because I'm *not* with Ames, exactly. And I like Fairbanks's pop-psych books."

Guy sat up straight, taken aback. "That's not your genre."

"You'd be surprised."

Whoops. Guy pretended not to notice he'd stumbled into a minefield regarding Cam's hospitalization. "Look, I didn't come all this way to talk about pop-psych."

"The latest version of my manuscript is already okay enough."

"Are *you* satisfied with it?"

"That's not your problem," Cam parroted, but wilted, obviously discontent.

Yeah, I only had to read it. Thankfully, Guy didn't need to reread it. He just had to witness Cam writing something similar. "You don't have to specifically edit that manuscript in front of me."

"Then Fairbanks accepts it as is? It's already had two complete edits."

Guy mentally whacked his own forehead. "No, you still have to re-edit that"—*trash*—"piece, but if you're stuck or sick of it, try writing something else for the time being. A short story, poem, anything that'll motivate you to return to *Distant*."

"Even if I start now, a conservative estimate is that it will take six weeks to finish editing. Would be sooner if I had interns or volunteers, but trapping and data entry eats up most of my time."

"You mean the time you're not reading or playing games."

"Exactly. That's the most crucial part of the process. Finding inspiration."

"Well, if you want to talk editing strategies or go over notes, I'm here to—"

"Oh, my God." Cam leaned forward to latch onto Guy's forearm, firmly enough that Guy froze.

With dimples made deep by a wide grin, Cam breathed, "You can *help* me."

Chapter Three

CAM'S GAZE DARTED to rock-climbing gear hung from the exposed rafters, which resembled a bondage array. "That'll fit you perfectly."

Guy's heart was already pounding before he realized Cam was more interested in the crumpled backpack stashed alongside the harness. "What do you know about trapping?"

"A bit." Clearly not enough to avoid being caught.

"Okay, what do you know about wildlife research? Or any research?"

Guy cleared his throat. "A bit."

"Great! See, last summer I came here with some researchers surveying squirrels, and saw a rabbit I know isn't supposed to exist here. No one else did, so they went home but let me keep their gear. Once spring starts, I can go track just the rabbit again, but until then, I'm doing a small mammal survey of the area within five miles east of the hut."

"Why?"

"Because it's cool. If you help, I can finish surveying earlier every day, and I'll be less tired."

"You'd be less tired if you didn't stay up until three."

"Hey, I don't tell you how to do your job. But I'll tell you how to do mine."

Guy knew Cam was squatting in this hiking hut that should have been closed for winter. According to Huw, the university in charge of the squirrel survey had refused to accept liability for Cam's remaining alone all winter, so he'd gotten permission to trap from a Province authority that wasn't due to expire until summer. Town authorities also turned a blind eye to Cam whenever he surfaced to resupply, because a newly discovered rabbit would be a major tourist draw. It was unlikely that Guy would be arrested for anything....

It had been twilight at 5:00 p.m. when Guy foolishly stepped into the ethereal mist by the roadside and bird calls sang in the valley at the changing of the guard. At the moment, it was silent as a tomb. Snow outside dampened all sound but for the fire's snap, crackle, and pop. True, the hut was a fine sensory deprivation chamber for post-breakup contemplation. It was also potentially claustrophobic without, say, booming headphones. Or a buddy. *Poor guy*, he thought about Cam, then corrected it to *Poor Guy* as the recent memory of nearly freezing to death trickled ice down his veins. Day after day of going out into that abomination?

"You said six weeks?"

"If you're here, I can finish *Distant* in a month. It'll fly by, guy. Don't panic."

No one had accused Guy of panicking in his life. Being told not to panic was an invitation to be wary. That and the fact that although Guy knew he wasn't the kindest-looking person by a long shot, Cam regarded him eagerly, instead of cringing the way people usually did when they asked Guy for a favor, Huw excluded.

"Why me?"

"Because you're here!" Cam exclaimed.

Duh, Guy inferred. The subtext was *You ain't special*, delivered through perfectly straight teeth in a broad smile, bracketed by those two deep dimples. Who was supposed to be the wolf here again? Wow, so the pixie was actually even colder than Guy was accused of being. He didn't seem dishonest, rather the opposite, but the duality in his personality cast fresh doubt on whether or not he might be a plagiarist.

"Excellent." Cam's cheerful response to a nonverbal confirmation Guy knew he never gave made Guy peer at him harder. Was he undermining in order to manipulate him? Was that the elf's game? "I'll show you all the ropes."

Including a noose? On the other hand, Guy rationalized he'd get to snoop at his leisure, quickly prove Cam wasn't a plagiarist, and spend the rest of the time mining him for anecdotes about his father.

"All right. But first and foremost, I'm here about your book. That's my priority, not a rabbit."

"We'll have to agree to disagree, then." Cam turned to the mantelpiece a split second before an alarm clock perched upon it rattled an alarm, the force of its shaking nearly dancing it off the shelf and into the fireplace. Guy barely processed the din by the time Cam cast off his blankets and leaped to catch it before it fell.

Sentient suicidal appliances. Guess I'll learn what happens around here at the full moon in a couple of weeks, too.

"Boiler's done boiling. Do you want some bunny stew?" Cam giggled, setting the clock back down and rounding the couch to head for the small hallway. "Kidding. It's just for the bath. I'll go take one now. Help yourself to food if you're hungry."

Guy sat reeling through his ambivalent agreement for a moment, and exhaled slowly before rising and surveying the cozy room, his home for the next month. Besides the couch and books, it held a dining table with benches attached, and a kitchen counter above a bar fridge and cupboards. A gas stove on the counter had two hot plates, one reserved for a whistling kettle. Thank Christ that Cam didn't cook on the fire. The air was musty enough without the smell of smoked meals. The kitchen shelves were bare of nutrients, though not of foodstuffs. While Guy rued the lack of fresh food, he appreciated the absence of dust behind the cupboards' swollen doors. Everything was regimentally clean.

Guy could check off having investigated the kitchen. No manuscript draft lying around in there. Returning to the lounge area, he noticed the paused game on Cam's laptop was in fact running online. Huw had warned internet access was intermittent, but the phone Guy retrieved from the bedroom—his bedroom now—had service.

"What's the time difference there?" Huw slurred sleepily upon answering his phone.

"You tell me. How long have I been gone? Five minutes? Thirty years?" It should have been an hour behind New York, so Huw had no excuse for napping. "I think I've been enchanted."

"Oh, manly, is he? Rugged wilderness type?"

Huw's husband groaned in the background, and Guy ignored the suggestive slap as Huw shushed him.

The house was silent but for muted sloshing and pouring sounds and the snap, crackle, and pop of the fire. Cam might overhear, but Guy didn't care. He could sneak in some indirect chastisement. "He stripped me naked within five minutes."

There was a pop as Huw yawned. "Well, when your tongue's free, tell him to answer our emails that fast."

"So look, about his white rabbit. I said I'd help look for it for a month. *This* month. I'm...going to stay here for a while."

Huw was silent for a moment. "Sorry I was flippant about Nick picking you apart on Facebook. Oh, by the way, he did it again. Even though he's already dating some new guy."

"Did he? Is he?" Guy suddenly felt better about Nick's imminent deletion from his cell's contacts.

"Called you alexythmic."

Incapable of expressing emotions. "Wow," Guy said in a monotone.

"I'll beat him up," Huw's husband interjected, letting Guy know he was on speakerphone.

"Sean will beat Nick up," Huw repeated.

"Not Nick," Sean said.

"Hi, Sean, sorry to disturb."

"Yeah, it is late. But I hear you're late, late, for a very important date." Huw snorted.

"I'm not staying because of Nick." Guy stretched the truth. The hut *did* offer space for reflection on how he kept attracting and apparently fooling guys like Nick. "We're over, I know, and I don't feel too bad about that."

"Surely, it won't take that long to raid the place for notebooks."

"Well...it might. Campbell doesn't seem easy to deal with."

"That's why I sent *you*." Tension entered Huw's voice. Guy knew he was privileged to harangue this marketable little Titan in Huw's place, but the butterflies in Huw's stomach over Cam's theft allegations were nothing compared to the horde of clashing dragons battering Guy's brain out here at the edge of maps. "How strange is he?"

"I don't know yet," Guy replied.

"I thought you said his book was boring."

"It is boring. That's why it's interesting that he's not."

"His dad was crazy."

"But his dad could write," Guy said. "And please don't be ablelist."

"*You* try not to offend my new star author while you're ripping up his mental carpet, or probing him about De Carli. Or at least make sure you prove his innocence first."

"Star author? Good luck," Guy muttered.

"*Help him* with editing," Huw said. "Encourage him."

"I will."

"Want me to leave the tub full? You'd better hurry before it goes cold," Cam asked from behind the door facing Guy's room, his normal volume barely muffled. He'd no doubt heard everything.

"No, thanks." Like hell Guy was going to strip again. He didn't need to be reminded of his bad first impression.

"You could join me in here." A teasing lilt entered Cam's voice. "Just get naked again, like I left you in bed."

"A-*ha*. I see how it is," Huw said loudly, then continued, to Sean. "Never mind, Guy's fine after all. He just caught cabin fever off Campbell already." He returned to speaking to Guy. "All right, get cozy with him, do whatever you need to do. Keep it as above board as you can, if not above the belt."

"We're hanging up," Sean said, Cam's counterpart in faultless but nonetheless shameless eavesdropping.

"Don't be crude. No one has cabin fever. I'm a month-long researcher. And editor. And babysitter." *Of De Carli's kid.* Guy slumped back on the couch's blankets.

"You're a tourist," Huw said. "And Campbell's no babe in the woods."

"No, he's probably immortal," Guy mumbled.

Huw spoke over the top of him. "Not with all the sex in that draft."

"What sex?"

"We cut it; it was off the wall."

"Then he *is* a—"

Cam wandered into Guy's cluttered view to stand in front of the hearth, and Guy could no longer finish his sentence with the word "child."

Cam used the towel he carried to dry his hair, which he squeezed into two ropes to either side of his neck. The only garments he wore were socks to guard against the icy wooden floorboards, *because the ground would sully a specter.* Or else Cam needed the fluffy barrier to keep up the ruse he wasn't floating an inch off the floor.

Forget a bath. Guy felt he'd been splashed with cold water instead.

Cam's bones were plainly visible beneath packed, wiry muscle. He was a Florentine statue carved to perfection except for his un-Renaissance but arguably Italian-heritage large dick. Guy was appalled to be trapped staring, but Cam's pubic hair was so black it drew the eye inescapably, like a missing space. It formed a perfect diamond, tapering up the curve of his abs and threading like a single finger's caress to his navel. His nipples, small and a puckered peach pink, were the same color as his lips—

"You're your own legal rep with Fairbanks, right?" Guy snapped his attention to Cam's face. He liked an analytical challenge, but he liked boundaries more and he knew his rights in Canada. Or Neverland. "Where's a pen? I'm suing you for harassment."

Cam's jaw dropped along with the towel.

Guy stalked to the dining table and plucked a pen from a mug full of stationery. An acrid odor filled the air, and he turned back to see Cam still gaping at him, yet to notice the billowing black smoke swirling at his socks and dangerously near the stacks of books. The towel on the floor was in flames.

The phone and pen clattered on the table as Guy dove to grab an unburned part of a stick from the fire, and stabbed the remaining fabric into the hearth. Its glow dulled for a moment, then blazed with the new fuel.

Not only did Cam not react to the danger that had shot Guy through with adrenaline, Cam now used his toes, protected in his flame-retardant woolen socks, to poke a corner of the towel farther into the fire, apparently immune to its heat as well as to modesty. Guy pressed one of the couch's blankets to Cam's chest. He benignly wrapped it around his shoulders like a cloak, looking even more like an elf priest, if elf priests were masters of seduction.

"*Get dressed*, Cameron."

"I didn't think you'd care." Cam had the audacity to frown. "Since you're on the phone to your other half so late."

"Fairbanks's director," Guy growled.

"Oh, Huw Jones? He's a man. I was right. You're gay," Cam congratulated himself.

"He's single," Huw's voice came tinnily from the phone on the table.

"Are *you* gay?" Guy asked point-blank.

"Nah. By which I mean—" Cam hastily continued, as Guy swelled with anger, "I'm nothing." The smile vanished from his eyes, but remained plastered upon his face.

"You're not nothing. You're valuable, and there are terms on spectrums to cover everything."

"Yeah, but I don't know what I am. Probably bi. I don't care."

Guy ground his teeth. "Am I supposed to help you figure it out?"

"Do you want to?"

Guy shook his head more at his predicament than Cam. Cam wasn't going to help him figure *Cam* out.

"It doesn't matter what I am," Cam said.

"Then why does it matter what *I* am?"

"Oh, that's a good line. Can I steal it?"

Guy's stomach dropped at Huw saying through the phone, "Hey, put Campbell on."

He snatched it up. "I'm not going to put him on."

"Put me on what?" Cam appeared behind Guy with the grace of a shadow. He leaned against the back of couch, thigh parting the cloak slit up to his barely concealed groin.

"Pills," Guy said.

"At least we're even now," Cam said, as though his indecent exposure canceled out stripping Guy. Without his glasses and with his hair slicked back off his forehead, he was more naked than ever as he obliviously gushed, "Choice! That's why it matters what you are!"

"Being gay is not a choice," Guy hissed.

"I know *that*. I'm a scientist. And a human being."

His last statement cut Guy. Had he intuited Guy saw him as...he wasn't sure anymore which mythical beast, but he was leaning toward *siren*.

"*You* chose to come out naked. If you're a human being, put on some clothes," Guy said. "Or should I just leave?"

"No," the phone chimed in. Unfortunately for Huw, now Guy was assured of cell reception, he could order a helicopter to pick him up and bill it to Fairbanks. He could ask them to bring pizza. Unfortunately for Guy, however, Cam knew the hollowness of his threat to venture outside.

"I don't have to help with anything, or stay," Guy pointed out.

"Do you want *Distant* done sooner?" A smile curved sensually on his lips. His chin, raised in defiance, was contrarily inviting. His swollen pupils, irresistible black holes, were all Guy could make out as Cam swayed forward to breathe, "Do you want to leave?"

The things Guy wanted to do... Possibilities paraded themselves in his head as clearly as Cam offered himself up a foot away, but all he could ethically do was to turn Cam down without further isolating him. That was easier thought than done while Guy's brain was held hostage by the scent of Cam's scrubbed skin, and sight of his eyes. They weren't the brackish brown of the ones featured in book jackets Guy had at home.

Up close, Cam's blue eyes were those images' negative—*only* the color was different. Cam was definitely De Carli's heir. Come to think of it, De Carli was notoriously...*competent*. Reclusive; possibly unstable.

Guy loved analyzing people as much as books, but usually from afar, without pressuring anyone into revealing more than they wished of themselves. It was disconcerting to now be analyzed himself, and apparently judged to be *not* judgmental. Or deemed someone to play around with. But though Guy could understand if Cam was only interested in screwing a stranger who happened to be present, he didn't know why Cam's stare was stripping him rawer than if he was himself naked. He seemed to be trying to gauge something about Guy, he even seemed vulnerable, and Guy had no idea what answer he sought.

His gaze fell to a small tattoo on Cam's naturally near-hairless chest, guarding his heart. Its subtle white ink resembled scar tissue, unnoticeable unless someone was looking for it or Cam's skin was as flushed as it was now. It gave Guy *his* answer, snapping the tension coiling inside him in time with a crack from the fireplace. He traced with his thumb the two thin letters written there in shaky handwriting—*No*— and wished his face didn't always mix up a serious expression with a menacing one as he explained.

"Cameron, you don't know the first thing about me. So don't toy with me. And if you want my help with anything, you have to *talk* to me."

Cam blinked as though coming to, roused from his own spell. When he fixed on Guy, far from being bitter or at a loss, he seemed to be concentrating, engaged in an inaccessible monologue that soon concluded with a melancholic laugh. "Ha! Okay, then. Forget it."

All traces of sexuality left him as he disengaged from Guy's grip and from the conversation, pulled the blanket tightly around his shoulders, and briskly brushed past Guy.

"Rabbit season kicks off at five-fifteen. See you in two hours," Cam called as he padded up the hallway. "Fully dressed."

Guy didn't know if *fully dressed* was an instruction or a promise. He let out a long breath, unsure whether Cam had only been on the hunt for a casual encounter, or was messing with him. Maybe Cam couldn't help making such a damsel-in-distress, searching expression, just like Guy couldn't help looking blank. *Ugh.* Maybe Guy's inscrutability had been what confused Cam into coming onto him in the first place.

Wait. Two hours? Guy's wristwatch showed it was now seven o'clock. *Still* seven o'clock, and he still didn't know if that meant it was the morning or nighttime. He held it to his ear. Nothing. It had seized up in the cold earlier. *Time-slipping hellscape.*

The mantelpiece alarm clock read three-twenty. Guy cringed as he retrieved his phone to beg for salvation as much as forgiveness. Its clock also read the correct early morning time.

"Huw, I am so sorry."

"Don't be. Campbell sounds mad as a hatter." As long as Cam wasn't a clear criminal—scratch that, a clear plagiarist—Huw could hold out for a happy ending to Fairbanks's fiscal year. "And you seem to have lain some groundwork for tomorrow, if nothing else."

"Give me a break." Guy dropped his voice. "He isn't intimidated by me at all. It's freaking me out."

"If he actually goes outside in that nonsense, he probably stares down death and bears all day, every day. You should be scared of *him*."

Should I? Guy wondered. Why be scared of the ephemera whose coral-red lips had been parted so exquisitely just inches away from Guy's... Why had he said no again?

"I'll tell everyone you're out of town," Huw said.

"Tell them he's off the market," Sean piped up.

Huw shushed him. "Make sure you get him off the hook, Guy."

Guy hung up, settled back into the couch, and let his sight blur on the ashes of the towel in the fireplace. Filaments gusted up the narrow flue while snow fell outside the windows. He was stuck in a whirling snow globe, half expecting the stalactites of books on the floor to crumble and rise like the towel. And he was here for a whole month, when in less than half a day Cam had stowed Guy naked in a father-bear bed in a scene ripped from *Misery*, only the mad captor was the exiled author.

Fine. He wasn't *not* looking forward to seeing what the stir-crazy kid would do next. But he was more looking forward to vicariously getting to know De Carli better and protecting the author's legacy, whether that was the son De Carli was responsible for bringing into and keeping from the world, or saving De Carli's book from Cam.

Chapter Four

HE STAYED THERE, surfing the conspicuously available net on his phone until its battery died. The ambient buzz of Cam's hibernating laptop alerted him to its charging from a multi-adaptor extending from a wall socket, letting him charge his phone too. The electricity generator, which he guessed powered the hut, was probably solar or placed far away outside, as no distant rattling permeated the otherwise still and smoky air of the living room.

Photos and tattered postcards papered its walls. None of the New York mementos obviously belonged to Cam. Some of the things hikers had left bore a second glance, especially an old laptop and collection of dated USB sticks with paltry memory space. On plugging in the laptop and trying them, Guy found none of them were password protected, but nothing contained any document resembling Cam's book draft, so he returned them all to their respective crannies in a cramped storage cupboard.

Softcover notebooks bore no fruit, either, and all of the hardcover notebooks lying around were trail logbooks, each page of which bore a litany of names, scribbled flags, and foreign languages. Some hikers chronicled stories, leaving chapters at each hut on the trail. One man claimed to be on the run from law enforcement. One volume contained a marriage proposal, and an acceptance scrawled in massive letters, *YES*, trailing off as the pen scoured the page.

They showed Cam had had a lot of visitors for a hermit. It seemed when the trail was open, the hut was often so crowded that many hikers continued on to camp on the trail, and Cam as well, apparently. One entry told the sad tale of the resident *hot guy* retreating to the hills when a group of teen girls showed up. It was written as a letter to him, lamenting their loss and undersigned in rows like a petition, names dotted with hearts. Another visitor griped about the muddy trail ruining his new boots. Guy would *love* some boots. He'd packed nice clothes in anticipation of meeting De Carli's son, who for all he knew was permanently decked out in safari silks and a lofty aura of *competence*. Retrieving his still-damp and now smoked brogues from the mantelpiece, Guy cursed his vanity. He figured it was punishment enough to shrug back into the ugly Christmas sweater and his thankfully dry coat.

When the silent alarm clock showed 5:15—so Cam had set it to 3:00 a.m., not the time he woke up, but to remind him to go to bed and catch a nap before hitting the trail? At least he shared the trait of being a terrible sleeper with other writers on Fairbanks's list—the rustling of polyester clothes broke the silence and Guy stood to greet...a stranger.

Gone was the flirty, irate key master Cam. In his place wasn't a scientist, a writer, nor a bubbly con artist. It was a void. A husk. Cam's bloodshot eyes stared glassily stared out from his slack face. Though he brushed past Guy, he didn't look at him nor through him. He just didn't look like he could see at all as he shuffled out of his house sneakers and into the boots propped against the back of the couch, fumbling to tie their laces.

"Cameron?"

In eight layers of clothes, Guy was a human marshmallow, but Cam gangled even in his puffy coat as he walked to the door and piled a massive pack onto his shoulders with a grunt. The buckles he clicked to secure the pack's straps across his chest scritched as they slid over his ribs with every breath.

"Are you okay?" Cam was more unreachable now than when he'd seemed mythical, and Guy's chest beat with the same urgency as before. *Let me in.* "Hey, Cameron."

Cam appeared to muster the strength to glance at Guy's clothes with empty eyes, not lifting his gaze to Guy's face.

"At least give me some of what's in your pack." Guy had retrieved the pack from the rafters for himself, and was ready to share Cam's load. He'd stashed a thermos of coffee inside to act as a hot water bottle—Cam hadn't grabbed any such thing. "Aren't you going to have breakfast first?"

Without acknowledging Guy, Cam rustled past him to open a metal locker storing miscellany like moth-eaten scarves. Scanning its contents, Cam shut it with a quiet click and paused. He closed his eyes again, slipping into reserve power as if detouring the four steps to the locker had overexerted him.

It dawned on Guy he was woefully underdressed. He was already wearing the spare sweater placed in his room and all the warm clothes he'd packed. Cam was too small in stature to share his, and probably had no surplus anyway. No coat, no boots, no service.

"You can't come," Cam addressed the space before him flatly, tightening the Velcro glove straps encircling his wrists. His gaze skimmed the floor as he cut his way through its labyrinth of books. The momentum caused by walking back to the door with his hefty pack meant he nearly hit it, and couldn't turn to face Guy as he mumbled, "We'll...go to town later."

Unzipping a long, thin polyester bag Guy had assumed held tent poles, Cam poured a .30 caliber rifle out of its mouth far enough to check the lever action, before mechanically dropping it back into its bag which he then slung around his neck.

"That's not a great holder for that, you know." Guy stepped toward him but was stayed by Cam with gloved fingertips lightly touched to his chest. There was no hesitancy in Cam's motion, nor demand, merely an instruction flashed impassively as a computer executing code—*Stop*.

"I may be some time." Cam tonelessly addressed the door, pulling his goggles on and nuzzling into his woolen scarf. He flicked up his coat hood, and a draft knocked the wind out of Guy, sending him into a coughing fit as he gasped to recover his breath. When he looked up, the door was closed and no movement shook the shadows outside the frosted glass. Cam had vanished into thin subarctic air.

THERE WAS NO point in feeling guilty for not following Cam out on his whimsical quest to spot a white rabbit in an apocalyptic winter, so Guy fretted instead, very rationally appalled at having witnessed flat affect in practice. He'd seen people with blunted expressiveness before, but never absent. *Town later* had been delivered in such a monotone that Guy wasn't sure if it was, in fact, hostile and Cam wanted to be rid of him already. Forget that. As well as assessing Cam's criminal aptitude and intent, he now had a duty of care to stay until he knew Cam was psychologically sound, especially considering his past.

Off the cuff, Guy listed the usual suspects that could explain Cam's behavior, only to raise a fleet of further questions. PTSD. Drug dependency. Any one of a dozen dementia profiles. Jet lag after falling from heaven. Guy might be able to analyze Cam's mental state if he had a handwriting sample—draft manuscript notes, a shopping list, *anything*—but there were no Post-its stuck to the fridge, no crosswords in magazines Guy could know for certain Cam had filled out. No "Cameron" had signed any of the past year's logbook.

Guy sipped coffee from the thermos taken from his pack as he stood at Cam's open bedroom door, steeling himself to invade his privacy. The far wall was covered, but for its small, high window, with logs and tinder stacked to the ceiling. *They're insulation*, Guy realized. Meaning the book towers in the other room were probably heat islands, strategically spaced to soak up and retain warmth, not just set in a strange formation to invoke some fantastic spell. So Cam's intellect was intact.

A folding army cot bore a thin mattress beside another cast-iron pot filled with black charcoal. The bed's hospital corners were folded so tightly it didn't look slept in or on. Several hand-sized hardcover notebooks were stacked on a chair serving as a nightstand, and Guy memorized their position and order so he could replace them unnoticed later. He returned to the couch with his spoils and coffee in hand, promptly almost giving the game away by spitting black brew all over the first book.

"What the fuck *is* this?" Sean, Huw's husband, echoed Guy's internal shout of seconds earlier. Distant stomping and clattering sounded through Guy's phone after he sent Huw a photo of Cam's writing.

"The fuck is *that*?" Huw repeated. "Elvish? Moon runes?"

Probably. "Or paranoia." The lengths to which a paranoid novelist went to hide—scientific data? *The Book of the Dead*? A transcript of bird chatter? "I need a linguist or a priest, Huw."

An immediate dial tone despite full reception bars let him know Huw was less accommodating of Guy's vicissitude at this hour, so Guy flicked through each book, his hopes dashed that any would be legible. All of their first pages bore the same inscription in ink-blotted, block-print: *Return to Cameron Campbell*, followed by the ecology department's address at Cornell University. Every other page was filled with triangles, squiggles, and curls that belonged in a vision-testing exam. Sure, a lot of hikers stayed at the hut during the summer, but Cam was blasé about exposing his body, so why make his writing obtuse? Or was he so lazy he wouldn't write entire letters, same as he couldn't speak earlier? Was he so into forgery that he invented a language?

"Is it a hoax? Is everything a hoax—the book, the rabbit, Cam being De Carli's son?" Guy demanded when Huw called back minutes later. "Although he looks like him."

"*Cam* now, is he? All right, one Google image search later, you slack bastard," Huw emphasized, awake enough to default to his real morning self. "It looks like Inuktitut. You probably woke me up *again* just for field notes."

"Inuktitut?" Guy's phone pinged beside his ear as a picture from Huw arrived. The image showed a typed script of triangles, squiggles, and curls far neater than Cam's. It looked similar enough that Guy embarrassedly blustered, "Okay, but is it Inuktitut shorthand? It barely looks like that sample."

"I've seen worse prescriptions from physicians," Huw said. "*Your* handwriting's a car crash."

Some pages were spotted with dirt flecks and water damage, and many pages had numbers and tables drawn on them. "It could just be his research about the rabbit, then."

"Ask him."

"Can't. I took it from his bedside."

"You *do* work fast." Huw yawned. "Good, transmit that work ethic by any and all means."

Guy rolled his eyes. "I took it because he seemed really...off earlier."

"How? Why? What did you do?"

"Nothing. He just looked really, *really* blank."

"Wait, what?" Huw laughed. "Is the doctor giving you a dose of your own medicine, then?"

"He was a lot worse than I am."

Huw laughed harder.

"And I might be being sent home already," Guy continued.

That snapped Huw to attention. "The hell you are."

"He's taking me to town later. I'm not equipped for hunting."

"Take the chance to get a notebook translated. Then wine and dine him on me," Huw said.

"I don't think he drinks." There was only one empty wine bottle in a nook of the kitchen Guy had explored by flashlight while longing for sunrise, which was still an hour away.

"*That's* not writerly. So do me a favor, get him drunk, and both of you press ahead. Get it? Press ahead? Publishing? Ah, it's too early. I'll think of a better pun and email you."

"Huw, I have a bad feeling."

Immediately, Huw's demeanor darkened. "*Do not* tell me he stole the book."

"Too early to tell." It was also too early to tell Huw Cam was severely damaged without further evidence. Riffling through cupboards, Guy uncovered only blankets and clothes in Cam's room, food and utensils in the kitchen, and camping gear elsewhere. Of the small reserve of generic painkillers in the locker's first aid kit, only one silver sheet was half-popped. "I have a bad feeling about Cam being messed up."

"If he's weird, *that's* writerly." Confidence returned to Huw. "If he's messed up just the right amount, he'll be good for sequels. Look on the bright side."

"Is there a local equivalent for peyote here?"

"Google it," Huw ordered, "or ask around in town while you're there, and discreetly ask someone if that notebook holds a shiny new book for me or a signed confession. Be *visibly* nice to people, including Cameron."

"I am nice," Guy protested.

"I mean it, Guy. Do whatever and give the kid whatever he needs." A master of subtlety, he coughed, "*Whatever.*"

"I'm not sleeping with him."

"Your words, not mine, and you're going to owe me a Coke." Huw closed with the upper hand, his usual farewell.

"Do you own any Lawrence Oates?" Guy cut him off. "Is he a designer?"

Huw relayed the question to Sean, and came back with, "Oh yeah, the Antarctic guy. Sacrificed himself to save his party. His last words were 'I may be some time.'"

Goose bumps trickled down Guy's back. "Cam said that to me when he left."

"Oh. Hey, Guy." Huw turned serious. "If he is actually suicidal again or having some kind of breakdown, then honestly I want to say 'Forget the book. We'll put it on ice,' but there's a lot of money riding on it."

"I know," Guy said. Fairbanks needed Cam to complete the book and be its author.

"In any case, I leave it to you to drag him back into check or back here if he needs it. What's your professional opinion?"

"I don't have one yet," Guy admitted.

"Well, you know why he was locked up."

"Yeah. Not why he was let out."

"But do you know how they stay warm in Canada?" Huw's grin sounded down the line. He trusted Cam was sane and innocent, then. That made Guy feel better about his instinct to wrap the little wraith in a bear hug until they both warmed up—if he didn't get frostbite from Cam first.

Chapter Five

GUY HAD STUMBLED past Cam's truck the day before and thought it a snow-covered bush in the dusk shadows. In the daylight, the beat-up tank was impossible to miss on the barren, flat valley by the highway, upon which twiggy conifers were scattered like candles atop a white cake. Each of its chained tires looked as heavy as the single cab perched high on suspension rods from its custom axle.

Cam had Guy start the engine to heat the car's interior while Cam cleared snowbanks from its chained wheels with a shovel. When he was done, he hung the shovel back on a spindly pine branch, which Guy supposed was too frozen to snap with the weight of metal and snow.

A draft whipped through the cab when Cam slammed the driver door behind him. He immediately shed two sweaters as the purring engine warmed the cab. The coat he'd loaned Guy for the mile hike to the car had fit okay, having been regularly stretched over many layers, but Guy's shoes got wet again. Cam nudged the socks Guy pressed to the roaring heater vents to retrieve a spray cleaning bottle and rag from the glove compartment.

"You didn't lug your bag here while I was away. Good." Cam leaned against dashboard, wiping down the windows of their building fog. "Thanks for not sticking me with a body to explain to the ranger."

Guy gnashed his teeth until his jaw unstuck enough for him to respond. "If you answered your emails, you'd have saved me walking in unprepared. You can't just ignore editing indefinitely."

"Ha. My father would have sued you for what you call 'advice.' He was *such* a lawyer," Cam scoffed, as though the term was a pejorative. Perhaps De Carli had seen it as such, having retired from his original career shortly after his writing debut.

Guy had been on tenterhooks awaiting Cam's return to the hut, and it completely threw Guy to see him arrive in a bubbly mood, chattering while bundling Guy into all the clothes he could before bustling them both out the door. Cam was so lively that he hadn't given Guy an opening to raise his earlier near-catatonia. He could rule out anhedonia as a cause of Cam's earlier 404. The imp was, again, a shimmering orb of emotion.

Well, if Cam wanted to ramble on about De Carli, Guy could easily oblige him. "I've read all of his books," Guy started. It was no mean feat, considering how prolific De Carli had been over the decade in which he'd been published.

"Really?" Cam said. "I've forgotten most of them, but I know how they end."

"Maybe you can explain the last one to me." De Carli's final book, hurriedly published six months after his death, had a sad ending rather than the usual ambiguous one. It was Guy's favorite, heralding a new direction, and had it been confirmed as finished, it would have been his best work. That it would never be known De Carli intended to keep the ending was, to Guy, the real tragedy.

"Nah. That's third date talk."

"I wasn't fond of *Distant*'s ending," Guy confessed, "when I skimmed your draft."

"You skimmed it? You didn't read it?" Cam gaped.

"Sci-fi's not my thing."

"Me neither."

Clearly.

"Anyway, it was a warm-up," Cam continued. "The one I wrote after it took half the time."

"Yeah, right. *Close to Home*, was it? Which you submitted to Ames." If it were anything like *Distant*, De Carli's publishers wouldn't go near it...unless they too were only interested in Cam's name alone. Guy hoped Fairbanks's competitor wouldn't let Cam rest on nepotistic laurels. It would be an insult to De Carli.

"Mm," Cam murmured. "That's still a maybe. I wouldn't have bothered with them if Fairbanks hadn't pissed me off. And now you say you haven't even read *Distant*, so I guess you're not my main editor? Or even a sub?"

"No, I'm not."

"Are you, like, their problem-solver editor? The bounty hunter Fairbanks calls in when bad authors misbehave?"

"Kind of."

"Then maybe I don't have any beef with you—" Cam grinned "—yet. What's your name?"

"What do you mean?"

"What's your name, guy?"

"Sutton." Guy was almost certain he'd introduced himself the day before, and knew for sure he had in unanswered emails.

Cam's eyes swam behind his glasses. "Oh. Are we on a surname basis?"

"Do you want to be?" Guy, too, was disappointed, though he imagined he hid it better.

"Nah." Cam regarded him curiously. "I never met a Sutton before. Let me guess, mother's maiden name? Mine thought double-barrel names were pretentious too, so my sister got my father's surname and I got my mother's, and Serena got an Italian first name, and I got Scottish. Which I'd appreciate if my name didn't literally mean 'crooked nose, crooked teeth.'"

They were way off. Since Cam's face was perfect. *Crooked understanding* might have been more apt, as he realized Cam was corrupted by Canadian speech patterns. "My name is Guy. As in, what you've been calling me. As in, my *name* is Guy Sutton."

"*Oh.* Did your folks lack imagination?" Cam asked innocently.

I know at least one of yours didn't. "Why choose Cameron Stewart as your pen name?"

"Stewart was my mom's father's name." Cam's chest puffed a little with unabashed pride.

So he has a thing for carrying on legacies. That's a strike against the authenticity of his manuscript, Guy thought ruefully as he stretched to untuck another of his sweater layers, the Christmas sweater, and withdrew from under it the thermos he refreshed before Cam returned from his morning work. He filled its lid and offered it to Cam, whose eyes darkened as a potent aroma filled the cab. *Payback for last night's elixir.*

Leaning back into his seat, Guy wriggled so the corners of the notebook he'd stashed in the back of his jeans didn't stick into his back. He'd chosen the most water-damaged one of the lot to take for examination, rationalizing it was already beaten up, but still prayed the sweat beading on his back wouldn't bleed through his layers of shirts into its cover.

"I could kiss you," Cam said quietly, then swooned as he sipped, eyes closed for a long moment. Despite the flirtatious comment, his chaste calmness in comparison to the previous night was maddening, especially when followed by that damn smile and shy gratitude as he passed the cup back to Guy. "Is this the last of the coffee?"

"Yeah." Remnants of a ground coffee packet were scattered in the fireplace, and Guy feared his arrival had exhausted Cam's supply as his cupboard raid uncovered only jars of stale instant.

"To be honest, I needed to go to town, anyway, to pick up some more."

To be honest. Whether bubbly or a zombie, flirting or not, Cam really did seem honest again today. Whether he was a writer or not was going to be impossible to determine without hard evidence.

"But I was trying to hold off." Cam cleared his throat, twice. "You have money, right? It's just, gas will gouge a kidney here. And this is really an unplanned trip for me. I didn't budget for it..."

"You better believe Fairbanks will cover it." *Huw* had better believe it.

"Excellent. Caribou burgers on you, then." Cam tumbled over himself as he twisted and slid into position in his seat, cranking the manual gearbox into first. "All right! It's ten degrees in here. Let's blow this popsicle."

"It feels warmer than that."

"Ha! Celsius." Cam rocked the wheels out of their bog and the truck crawled onto the road.

"The imp doesn't use imperial," Guy mumbled to himself, earning a peal of laughter that surprised Cam as much as Guy. It was clear as a bell, unlike any he'd evinced so far, tainted by melancholy. This laugh was true. *But then, they all have been, haven't they?*

"After a month here, you'll swear by metric," Cam promised. "I got used to it overseas, and it's the best way to measure evergreens and calculate distance in the Taiga. Which is what this region south of the Arctic is called. Only it has icicle teeth, not bone, ha. And see, over there..."

Spindly pines rushed by Guy's window in a blur of whites and blacks, resembling the static flowing through his mind after being blindsided by Cam's laugh, and a new compulsion. *How do I make him laugh like that again?*

THE FLIRTY LAUGH Cam deployed against the pretty, young general store clerk was charming, too, but one Guy could have done without seeing was aimed at her.

She smirked at Cam in return. "You know it's the second Wednesday of the month today, Cameron, not the first, right?"

"Kind of. I feel slightly older. Wiser." He glanced up at Guy. "And shorter."

Guy felt vindicated at hearing she addressed Cam as Cameron. But then, he was calling Cam the same thing.

"Tourist?" the girl asked Guy in a flatter tone. Guy understood. Only a fool would come to the town in early spring.

"Nah, he's working with me. So we need a lot of clothes. He refuses to share mine," Cam joked as Guy peeled off two layers of sweaters by the steamed-up door.

"Wow. What's with the attitude?" she muttered.

Guy cocked his head, surprised. Cam had been friendly— *Oh.* She was talking about him. As usual, his neutral expression had managed to offend.

"What's with yours?" Cam jibed back at her.

"Guy Sutton," Guy introduced himself. His outstretched hand was ignored.

"He doesn't mean it," Cam interpreted to diffuse the tension.

"Mean what?" Guy asked. He didn't look *that* cold, did he? Weren't Canadians supposed to be easygoing? Wait, maybe that was precisely why he appeared particularly rude.

"Some Silver Sands guys cleared us out of medium-sized gear last week." The girl ignored Guy, shaking her head on mentioning the gold mining company eighty miles north of Ipasila. Guy cheered up at realizing their reception at the store was probably as chilly inside as outside, too. All outsiders were given the cold shoulder.

"Well, I'm not driving all the way to Arviat," Cam said. "I don't need Tim Hortons that badly as long as my mail arrives..." The town "post office" was a collection of wicker baskets behind the general store's counter, one of which bore a label reading "Campbell" in black marker, and which the girl placed on the counter for Cam to retrieve a large US Post envelope. "Coffee," he sighed happily.

Sizing Guy up over his shoulder, the girl said tentatively, "Your man looks like he'd fit large sizes."

Guy doubted that. When not next to Cam, he considered himself slender.

"Doesn't he just," Cam said.

In any event, large-sized clothes in the store's paltry selection were a US extra-large. Cam would swim in the small-sized clothing on the racks.

"Not khakis." Guy shook his head at cargo trousers Cam pointed out. He didn't want to pay a marked-up price on wares that didn't fit and which he wouldn't wear if they did.

"But the jeans here are..." Cam lowered his voice theatrically as he called, spilling an armful of tinned food on the counter beside the girl, "very country-style."

"City boy," she taunted him, then called to Guy. "Hey, settle a bet. Is he some famous writer's son or not? One of the college girls in summer thought he was. Is he rich?" She might as well have asked *Is he single?*

"I don't know," Guy said, continuing internally *if he's rich.* "That's not my problem. I'm just here volunteering."

"Ha. My discount stands." Cam's willowy form bowed with relief as he tugged some crumpled canvas bags from his pocket.

"You're lucky my ma believes there's a rabbit out there," the clerk muttered.

"I won't stop looking until I've found it and your summer trade's skyrocketed with hot guys all turned out for bunnies," Cam proclaimed.

"Gee, thanks. Just tell them a smile goes a long way." She pushed Cam's shopping to one side of the counter and returned to pretending to be too engrossed in her magazine to eavesdrop.

"We're trying the pants on." Cam dragged Guy behind a thick curtain sectioning off a changing booth. A soft wolf whistle chimed over the scraping of its metal rungs. "What's wrong?"

"I'm not a khakis person," Guy said.

"What's a khakis person?" Almost immediately, Cam's confusion dissolved into a frown. "Anything will be bulky if you're wearing stockings beneath two pairs of pants, then layering waterproof gaiters over everything. Oh, is it because they're unfashionable? It's not like it matters out here."

Guy was about to concede when the sweater Cam revealed upon shedding *his* layers fit like water. On close inspection, stitches in it appeared to have been picked and mended above Cam's heart, presumably to remove its exclusive branding, but with undeniable care. Heat prickled at Guy's nape on imagining Cam's tattoo a few inches below the small patch of distressed wool.

"You say that, but you're wearing cashmere. Are you trying to impress her or something?"

A glare silenced him. "*No.* She's, like, barely eighteen."

"You're barely twenty-three."

"Besides, I've already had her brother," Cam grumbled.

"Really?"

"Well, nearly. I would have if wearing a dress on the first date wasn't a step too far. That's what happens when you wait to get to know people." Cam whipped the curtain back and plucked two bulky black sweaters indiscriminately off a shelf, adding them to the counter stash of groceries and gas canisters. Well, at least the color was right. And they weren't unseasonably Christmassy, like the sweater Guy could now peel off and stuff into the bottom of a paper bag where it belonged.

But whatever Cam identified as, then, he liked overtly masculine guys. Not neutral-looking—scratch that, apparently bitter-looking Guys. Not Guys who refused to jump into bed right away. Guy sighed as he thumbed the racks, unable to tell women's from men's apparel. He grabbed some long, loose denim jeans with ludicrously shallow pockets and almost felt as sorry for Huw as he did for himself when the register flashed their total owing.

Laden with bags, Cam and Guy slipped through a service door behind the counter into a corridor connecting Main Street stores: Cam pointed out the general store and gas station, a hotel, small school, and civic office as Guy straggled behind him. They exited another supply door into a bar as though stepping out of one set in a play onto a different stage. *Like Narnia.* Guy was still in awe of fairy-tale scenarios made mundane around Cam.

"Shall we get the burgers to go? The drive back will be a lot slower in the dark, and I can wolf mine down at the wheel," Cam said.

"If you want." Guy bit the tags off his new-yet-musky down coat, and shrugged into it. He was as layered as an onion, but thankfully less likely therefore to cry at the castrating cold outside. He glanced over the chalkboard menu set behind the bar. Seal, whale, caribou, poutine, and some meals Guy didn't recognize were offered in English, French, and what he knew now was the Inuktitut alphabet.

Christ, he'd almost forgotten. Hoping their shopping could be left safely alone for a minute, he ducked into the men's bathroom and was glad to see a bearded Inuk man washing his hands in the basin.

"Excuse me."

The guy ignored Guy's first try, and cocked his head in surprise upon realizing Guy was indeed addressing him. His shoulders immediately arced up. "Are you looking for a fight?"

Guy took a step back, his new puffy coat hitting the back of the restroom door. "Not at all."

"You're with the little biologist, aren't you? Cameron...Stewart?" The man spoke haltingly as he recalled the name, but fiercely when affirming, "I haven't touched him."

"What do you mean? Who has?"

Confusion must have reigned over Guy's features, because the man relaxed enough to reach for paper towels to wipe his hands, though he still faced Guy with a glower. "I don't know. What do you want?"

"Can you translate this for me?" Handing him the sweat-dampened notebook he fished from the back of his jeans, Guy settled on a brusque demeanor rather than brave a smile that would no doubt come off sharkish. "Any page will do. Just give me a quick idea of what it is."

Thankfully, the guy flicked to a center page instead of the title page bearing Cam's name. "December 10... It's about the weather. And there's a list of animals and numbers." He peered closely. "There's some words I can't make out. Looks like spelling mistakes."

"Like, American versus Canadian spelling mistakes?" Guy asked. He didn't remember seeing many, or any, in Cam's manuscript, but then that would have gone through spellcheck.

The man clapped Guy on the shoulder, slapping the closed book into Guy's chest with his other hand as he passed him by. "You mean American spelling mistakes."

Guy took the chance to use the empty restroom before returning to find his and Cam's piles of shopping untouched. Slipping the fieldwork notebook into one of his bags of clothing, he glanced around. The man he'd spoken to was gone.

Like a lot of people in the bar, his gaze was drawn to Cam, who was ordering for them by the register. He'd been mistaken about the nature of Cam's cheerfulness that afternoon. Again, it wasn't like he was faking it, but though it was nothing compared to that morning he was definitely a little disengaged. Quick words and smiles flowed from him to townsfolk left and right, but he flitted from greeting to greeting like a butterfly in a field. Yet his interactions only looked shallow because he also appeared too deeply mired in his own thoughts to notice the brazen stares he drew from men and women. He wasn't totally blind to the ripples he generated, though, shaking his head at a subtle offer of a drink from a woman at the bar. Instead, he juggled a chocolate milkshake, a sealed bottle of red wine, and two large coffees, setting them down on a booth's tabletop beside Guy, who struggled to scrape the countless bangles of bag handles off his padded arms to help Cam carry them.

"Undress," Cam said. "Moose are blocking the road south, so we're eating in."

"Last time you told me to strip and drink, I woke up naked."

"But you woke up," Cam pointed out.

Guy tugged off his new beanie, unzipping his coat as he slid into the booth seat opposite Cam.

"Hey, no one's ever given you a hard time here, have they? Threatened you or worse?"

"Ha!" Cam said. "Did Hamish size you up in the bathroom? Don't worry, he's a gentleman. Probably looking out for me." Cam winked. "Or like Caitlyn in the store earlier. She couldn't tell about you, either."

"Tell what about me? That I'm gay?" If Cam had abandoned a date with her brother, she might have been taking offense at his showing up with a new guy...but then, if she'd been flirting with Cam like Guy thought, she might have been jealous. Or annoyed the latest new gay guy in town was too "cold," so another wrong match for her brother. "If it's just that I look mean, don't worry about it. I get it all the time."

"*Mean*? No, no. She just couldn't tell that you're not actually hiding."

"Hiding what?"

"Nothing."

Guy resisted the urge to sigh at Cam's cryptic speech.

"That, see?" Cam said. "What comes after the watching look. She thought you were waiting for her to fuck up so you could leap down her throat. But the worst you've got is like, a *whatever* attitude. You're no-nonsense, but you have no ax to fall."

"I think 'harmless' is the nicest thing anyone's ever said about me."

"Well, I didn't say that." Cam scribbled with his straw on the surface of his drink.

It was true, Guy realized. He preferred to observe and redefine his impressions constantly after much analysis. It was why Huw trusted him to judge Cam. But the fact that Guy didn't validate others soon and frequently frustrated Nick. It frustrated a lot of people. A regretful smile surfaced on Guy's face. *Is that why my first career choice didn't pan out and sent me to books?*

"That's a shame," Cam murmured, loudly draining the dregs of his shake through the collapsed straw.

"What?" In spite of himself, Guy's heart fell at the prospect of further insightful criticism.

"Never mind. I'll get a real one later."

The shake? "Something wrong with the chocolate syrup?"

"Nah. I'm not after real chocolate tonight, anyway." Cam sucked his shake from its sweating glass through a straw as sensually as a smoker dragging on a craved cigarette. Midway through it, he rose and bought from the counter a handful of chocolate bars he tossed on the table next to the wine bottle lying on its side, inertly fixed on Guy in a game of spin the bottle.

"What vintage is that?" Guy asked.

"The Snickers?" Cam ironically snickered, turning the candy over to see its expiry date. "'Bout a June, I'd guess."

"The wine."

"Dunno. Doesn't matter." Cam gnawed his straw, nibbling at it, crunching it to hear the plastic crack and snap back and forth. "It's cheap, for cooking with."

Right. He was Italian, after all. "You don't drink?"

"Not often."

Not writerly, Guy remembered Huw saying. "Why do you go by your pen name in town?" To Hamish and Caitlyn, at least.

"No one needs to know my real name." Cam watched massive moose wandering past the window, but moved to clear space on their table even as a waitress approached from behind him with plates. Guy hadn't noticed her reflection in the glass.

"Do you have a problem with being—" Guy paused until she'd gone. "—De Carli's son?"

Cam's gaze sharpened on returning to Guy. "It doesn't matter. Fairbanks has my real name, so does Cornell. I use it when I'm legally bound to."

Guy cleared his throat and moved on to a potentially worse topic. He was already in deep enough he might as well keep going. "Look, about when you woke up. Do you want to talk…"

"Not really." Returning his gaze to the moose, Cam tore a chunk off his burger with his teeth and munched. "But I will. When you said I don't know you the first thing about you, so don't toy with you…"

Guy stopped chewing for a moment as the subject Cam referred to sunk in. The memory of Cam, naked and tempting, was jarringly different to the thoughtful Cam seated opposite. Though his attention wandered between his food and the sight of the beasts outside, he seemed steady. Not bouncy, not skimming. *He's properly engaged*, Guy realized, which made Cam strikingly different from how he'd been that morning, too.

"You were right." Cam illustrated the difference perfectly by fixing Guy with piercing eyes. "Sorry if I offended you. I sum people up fast. If you look nice, you're nice."

"No one's ever summed me up as looking nice," Guy said. Not even after knowing him—or being around him for a while but never really knowing him. *Like Nick.*

"The devil wears Prada," Cam said. "Anyway, assuming the best of people and situations doesn't make for a good science career, that's for sure, but when it comes to bridging plot gaps, I'm your man." He sighed dramatically. "I suppose I can take a look at those edits again."

"Good. Thanks. And leaps of faith aren't always bad for science. Who else would go looking for a white rabbit in the snow?"

A smile quirked at Cam's lips. "Right? And who else would come all the way out here just to chase up some stupid book?"

"I never said it was stupid. And that's not what I meant. I mean do you want to tell me why you were so…out of it at five in the morning?"

"*Oh.*" The smile vanished as Cam sucked in a breath. "Five-fifteen. No, not really." No elaboration followed.

"All right. Well, I'm here if you need me. Volunteering and all." Provided Cam wasn't in danger, Guy could wait. He had a month. He leaned across the table to better watch the moose lumber down Main Street, indifferent to the vehicles in their territory, and received a light poke in the ribs from Cam's little finger, the only one not greasy with burger fat.

"So you are." Cam's sincere smile crept back in place. "Very far from home."

"If only there was a book I could relate to about that." Guy dodged a more forceful jab, glad at the unusual twinge of a smile cracking his frozen face. Its pull disappeared as Cam lapsed into a mild frown. He kept up conversation about research projects he'd done, relating anecdotes that instructed Guy as to how they'd go about the next day's fieldwork, but his enthusiasm had waned.

Neat freak, zombie, oblivious flirt, sincere chatterbox, sweet tooth. Pouter. Guy had acquired an inventory of Cam's moods, each as genuine as the last, as well as a set of clothes he could burn for warmth before going home, and Cam had agreed to tackle his book. As they rose to leave, Guy fished his phone from his pocket to message Huw that it had been a productive day but found that, unlike at the hut, he had only a weak signal.

"Reception's intermittent, isn't it?" A cocky grin returned to Cam.

"Did you wire up the house somehow?" Guy recalled wondering at the purpose of the antenna he'd seen on the hut's roof as they'd left it earlier.

"A little, but it helped more to put a makeshift receiver on a mountain nearby it. I'd die without the internet."

"So you *did* see my emails."

"I would have if I'd opened them."

"Huw would say that's writerly," Guy said, reserving judgment.

"You guys don't know the half of it," Cam replied.

Chapter Six

CRUNCHING OVER THE icy tundra was surprisingly easy in Guy's new boots, particularly as Cam moved so slowly it took an hour for Guy to realize he was deliberately dallying for Guy's benefit. It was impossible to tell when he'd stopped sleepwalking. The previous night, he talked at length until Guy excused himself to sleep, and that morning, was again as unseeing as a ghost until they'd walked for miles, checking traps along the way. Perhaps lack of sleep was his downfall. *Night owl,* Guy added to his list.

The traps were large, humane mousetraps. One type was a wire cage about two and half feet by one by one, and the other was a small tin box about the size of a sub sandwich. One of each was snuggled into snowbanks beneath undergrowth decorated with numbered neon ribbons. Cam dropped his toolbox in the snow and kneeled to inspect them all, his pack threatening to topple him. All were empty, but to some, Cam added peanut butter ball baits from his toolbox, which also contained calipers, measuring tape, mammal identification books, canvas and plastic bags, and a handful of .30 Carbine cartridges for Cam's rifle. And a small hardcover notebook identical to the one Guy had slipped back into the pile beside Cam's bed while Cam had filled the bath late the previous night, hoping its noise would hide his actions.

At 8:00 a.m. on the dot, Cam shrugged out of his backpack by setting it on a hip-height stump. Sunlight breached the mountaintops, so he turned off his head torch and downed a gallon canteen of water, hissing at the frigid air stinging his teeth as he panted afterward.

Tongue loosened at last, he whispered, "Drink."

"Good morning," Guy repeated for the third time. "What am I doing here exactly?"

"You have to drink," Cam rasped. Speaking left him breathless. "Even if you're not thirsty."

Guy withdrew a canteen from his own pack, hollow but for his GPS and a thermos, and gulped it down. "Give me some of what you're carrying."

Cam shook his head, rebuckled his pack's straps across his chest and waist, and stepped away from his supporting stump.

By 9:00, the sky had finally turned crisp blue. They'd checked fifty traps and not found a single animal.

"Can we eat soon?" Guy tried not to whine.

"Sure," Cam chirped, his voice sparkling clear, his consciousness restored. He was *fine*. His strength was present and accounted for, too, Guy gathered as Cam firmly clasped Guy's arm to help him ascend a ravine he had wafted up like the sprite he was.

Furious at being cuckolded into concern, Guy let his pack thump in the snow by the one Cam shrugged off onto a feted log, worn clear of moss in one spot. Cam handed him a frozen granola bar from the toolbox to gnaw, but as Guy drew himself up to complain about Cam's earlier silence, his head spun and he reeled.

Cam's hand was on his arm, supporting him, before he knew it. "Heavy packs pull your shoulders back. The position stresses your heart, like, people who were crucified died of heart failure before dehydration. So remember to stretch. And *drink*. You're sweating, right?"

Now that he mentioned it, Guy felt a prickling dampness across his back. Thank Christ the stockings he wore beneath his two layers of snow pants still only itched and didn't chafe.

"You have to drink before you're thirsty out here. See the horizon? Is it fuzzy?" Cam scraped the ice that formed on his lip in the brief time it took to polish off a second canteen. Sure enough, the sparse canopy stretched beneath them rippled in the distance like a monochrome mirage. Guy drank another canteen, watching Cam blow smoke rings with the fog clouding from his breath.

"How did you get into ecology?" he asked when they set off again.

"It's easier to build worlds if you know how this one is built," Cam explained.

Oh, good. They were back to the topic Guy knew well. "So you've always wanted to write, like your dad?"

"I write way better than my father. And who doesn't love fluffy mammals?"

Guy opened his mouth to argue with the first point, but Cam held his hand up, appealing for silence before striding twenty yards to another neon tag. His muffled footfalls were silent next to Guy's creeping crunching, and he gently set his pack down and motioned for Guy to watch over his shoulder.

Cam wedged a starched linen pouch over the mouth of the large trap and a tuft of brown fur waddled into the bag with a rustle, barely wriggling as Cam whipped the bag up, drew its string tight, and weighed its bundle from a hook on a handheld hanging scale.

Cam kept its small pointed head buried in a corner of cloth while he rapidly measured it, and executed a number of other observations, scribbling numbers and symbols in a table drawn in his notebook.

"Pygmy shrew, *Sorex hyori*," he said quietly. "I've caught this one before, but I don't Trovan. Electronically tag," he clarified quietly to Guy, who kneeled beside him. "I make biodegradable ankle bands. This is made of wax and keratin."

He freed the animal directly into scrub brush. It vanished from the bag invisibly with no trace other than a departing rustle in the undergrowth, and Cam's volume returned to normal as he wiped the trap with a rag and pink sanitizer, then replaced its spoiled bedding with a fistful of twigs and cotton buds.

"That was fast," Guy said.

"I hate handling them more than absolutely necessary. Some researchers I worked with talk loudly and show off wild animals. They're not toys. They've been trapped in a freezing cold cage all night and now they're being confronted with a huge predator." His scarf puffed away from his mouth as his voice rose. "Leave them alone as much as possible and free them as soon as you can."

"Roger," Guy said. It was how he had planned to investigate Cam before becoming embroiled in *helping*, which he wasn't, much. With his white waterproof jacket in lieu of a lab coat, Cam appeared a consummate independent scientist. Guy had thought him all eyes and pale soft skin, yet out there he was in his element. At least his doctorate wasn't fake, then.

"For the next one—" Cam tossed him his notebook and pencil while repacking his toolbox. "—you scribe, okay?"

Guy had been so worried about inspecting Cam's notebooks the previous day uninvited, only to now be given them with no fanfare... And Cam had passed the book straight to his left hand. "You remembered I'm left-handed?"

"Well." Cam's eyes dulled. "I've got a good memory."

"You want me to write in Inuktitut?" Guy asked doubtfully.

Cam recovered from his momentary fugue with a smile. "I picked it up in order to read local texts, see if there was tell of a rabbit living here in the past. There wasn't, really. Then I found it easier to read back than my actual handwriting. It's all phonetic, but in there, it's mixed with biology symbols and terms, like the Cyrillic *Pe*—the square lowercase-looking N—means *pes*, foot size. But you go right ahead and use English. And use metric, not imperial, please. Just write down the numbers I say."

"I've been told my handwriting's not perfect," Guy said.

"Good for you. Makes it harder to forge." Cam grinned.

Everything he said provided more proof Cam wasn't unhinged. Yet as rational and present as Cam now was, Guy couldn't shake off a dreamlike élan while following this graceful fawn on its whimsical traipse through a land of eternal winter, each new glen more fantastical than the last.

Cam's intuitive reactions didn't help dispel the feeling. Minutes later, Cam stopped talking yards before they reached a trap, and he went through the motions of measuring a juvenile stoat while Guy recorded data, trying not to be distracted by how smooth the few slivers of Cam's exposed skin were. The care Cam took in juggling the animal for Guy to see made Guy's appreciation of his wide cheekbones, clean swirling hair, and lashes longer than they looked thanks to their blond tips, seem crassly objectifying, but he couldn't help it.

However, when the stoat was freed into brush and Cam tugged down his scarf to reveal a grin, Guy decided he'd sacrifice a lot more dignity to see that look. For a start, Guy's frozen face felt strangely like it was splitting. He was smiling.

"Look at you! Are you kidding me?" Cam beamed. "And all it took was a stoat. Next, I'll show you how to handle them."

"I want to see your rabbit."

"Me, too." Cam rebuckled his pack as he straightened. "Coming up is the most important stop."

"Where you saw the rabbit?"

"Don't be greedy, rookie," Cam said.

They soon pulled up by a broad stream where Cam dropped his pack on a scribble of tree roots webbing the snow, and withdrew from it large, empty plastic bottles. After strolling on stepping stones past the river's iced edges to its central column of running water, he crouched over the clear eddy.

"Drink," Cam ordered Guy, effortlessly lobbing him the first one he filled.

The icy taste was aromatic enough to cut through its stinging Guy's teeth, and he thirstily sipped as much as he could, stopping shy of an ice cream headache. It tasted nothing like water in New York, nor anywhere else.

"This is for drinking and cooking. Bathwater comes from the kitchen tank, but don't drink it because it has antifreeze to protect the metal... I probably should have said that before. Oh, well. You're still here."

So that's *why the coffee's taste killed me. Maybe.* He was willing to believe that magic remained a secret ingredient in it because, here, Cam was more ethereal than ever. The stream's clearing was like a cathedral, its mossy stones and bark pillars lit in shades that only highlighted how miraculously *white* Cam gleamed as its centerpiece, as if his coat were its source of light. Guy could see the appeal of the hostile land at last, but only insofar as it welcomed Cam as an intrinsic part of it.

"It's so serene," he slurred, sucking on his numbed tongue.

"It's idyllic," Cam agreed, "but it's not ideal, guy." A chuckle escaped him as he corrected himself. "Guy."

Which character is he in De Carli's stories? Guy wondered. *A lot of them*, came the answer, *and a lot unwritten.* It was impossible to contain all of Cam's facets in something as short as a lifetime's work.

"Hey. What was it like being homeschooled by De Carli?"

Cam's smile tightened as he refilled his heavy pack with bottles. "Well, he never taught creative writing."

No shit. But the urge Cam had to write books, if not the talent to do so well, was inherited. "Well, his books have adult themes. You were, what, ten when he started getting famous? Makes sense he wouldn't exactly teach his tastes. Or his style."

"Ha! Be a little more disappointed, Guy!" Cam saw through him. "He taught me all he knew about humanities subjects. But I got into science, and he wasn't interested. More fun to go drink."

Guy digested that. "Is that why you don't drink often?"

"Sort of. Sorry to pop your bubble."

"I'd rather you be honest," Guy said.

The wry smile returned to Cam. "Would you, now?"

"And give me some of those bottles to carry."

"Nah, this is only twenty-eight kilos. I could withstand forty-two at the moment if necessary, for a whole day."

"However much that is, I can't allow it. Not on my watch." *First, do no harm.*

Cam opened his pack for Guy. "Don't strain yourself. Lugging your body will be a lot heavier than some water."

"Thanks."

"Don't mention it."

Once his own reassuringly heavy pack was secure on his back, Guy helped Cam put on his pack. The weight of it reminded him of having awoken in the hut's second bedroom after passing out at the front door.

"You've lugged me before. Did you carry me the other night?"

"Seventy-two kilos inside a house isn't a challenge," Cam boasted. "*You* can't scare me."

"I'll have you know I scare everyone." Guy tugged a strap on the back of Cam's pack harder than necessary to check his balance, and caught Cam as he stumbled back, apparently off-balance under his lightened load. Cam slipped from Guy's hands like a feather in the breeze, giggling as he dodged another grab.

"You're so transparent that everyone probably second-guesses themselves. Fairbanks's writer psychologist should do an in-house seminar on how not to flash *all* your cards at once."

"The pop-psych guy?"

"He's the only half-decent author you've got besides me. Who's his editor in charge? Can I get them?"

"I'll tell Huw. He'll appreciate that."

"Good. Make sure you ham it up, because earnestness can only take you so far, guy."

"Lucky for me, you leave prints," Guy replied, bending to heft his pack farther up on his back, then ruing missing the sight of Cam laughing loudly.

Chapter Seven

"Usually I get a fox or two, and more voles. Sorry it was calm today." Cam's pack thudded loudly on the frozen porch boards. "Tomorrow we might see a bear or a wolf. See them first, hopefully."

"Don't jinx us." Following Cam's lead, Guy shed his coat, beanie, and a sweater before entering the hut. Perspiration in his scarf instantly crystallized into razors against his throat.

"Don't push yourself," Cam argued as Guy lifted the back end of Cam's pack to help drag it across the threshold, but let him assist. Guy kicked the door closed behind them as Cam set down his toolbox lightly by the locker, and the long bag containing his rifle even lighter. "And take off two more layers right now."

Guy raised an eyebrow at being miscast as delicate because of *one* well-warranted fainting spell, but did as he was told. Cam poked a log into the fireplace, stirring the light that tinged the room gold. He flexed his fingers over flames before retrieving his pack and lugging it to the kitchen.

"The water I understand, but why carry all the survival gear only not to use it?" Guy asked.

"Dumb luck." Cam stacked the bottles on the kitchen counter, their contents frozen to slush. Alongside them, he unpacked and repacked fire blankets, a fuel stove, first aid kit, food, and EPIRB, then flicked his glasses open and slipped them into the groove on his nose left by his snow goggles. Without a trace of fear, he said, "I'd live for a week if I broke my leg out there and a blizzard barred chopper access. Or if hikers come and I want to leave the hut. There's this one cave I found in summer that's always nice, as long as there're no bears."

"That doesn't sound good at all, Cameron."

"Nah, they suck at travel Scrabble." Cam tugged a shirt over his head, leaving his glasses askew as he unbuttoned the one below.

"Do not strip, please," Guy interrupted him. "Remember you have a guest."

Cam peered down absently, then squinted up at Guy and cocked his head to the side. "Okay... Lunch?"

"Fine." Guy released him from his stare. "I'll make coffee. Or would you like hot chocolate?"

A burst of laughter escaped Cam, chased by surprise on his face that matched Guy's. He clumsily tugged a discarded shirt back on, burying his face in a cupboard. "Black coffee, please. No sugar."

THE MOMENT GUY creaked open his room's door, book he'd been reading in hand, the diminished roar of Cam's headphones hit him. More eerie than the yawn that seemed to nearly dislocate his jaw was his turning where he sat at the table to greet Guy, having sensed his entrance regardless of the din booming into his ears.

He was draped in soft grays and whites, invitingly earthy but also fuzzy in focus. Thermals clung to his chest like bedsheets, seemingly silky and comfortable, but tension in his neck cracked as he stretched his arms over his head.

Each time, seeing his eyes was like witnessing a phenomenon for the first time. He was striking, clothes or not. *Not as in no clothes*, Guy thought wearily, sympathizing with Cam's obvious malaise. He made Guy want to go straight back to bed, and not alone, and he wouldn't let himself linger in the path of that freight train of thought.

"You okay?" Guy asked, nodding at the open first aid kit, spools of thread, and bandages on the table as he sat on one of its bench seats across from Cam.

Cam slipped his headphones down around his neck, gesturing toward a pile of folded clothes on the couch—those Guy had bought the day before. Riffling through them, Guy gauged their fit was tighter than the shapeless clothes he was wearing. The jeans he held up had been adjusted, and were better tailored than anything he owned.

"One hundred eighty-one centimeters, eighty-three centimeter inseam, sixty-four centimeter waist, sixteen centimeters shoulder to collar, shoulders forty-five, sleeve and total length the same, sixty-nine." Cam rambled like a savant, scratching his neck beneath his headphones as he tapped at his laptop to silence the music.

"Did you measure me when I was passed out the other day?" Guy asked, ill with guilt at the trouble Cam had gone to sewing, and at having been violated.

"Look, I know the size and quantity of everything in this house." Cam took a box of matches from the cup filled with pens and miscellany by his elbow. He tossed it across the table. "Go ahead. That packet contains thirty-eight."

Guy spilled and counted them on the tabletop. Cam's jaw tightened as he stole back the matches Guy pushed aside, making a house picture from them, having realized his error before Guy said, "Thirty-seven."

"Doesn't matter so long as there's two point three milliliters of fluid remaining in this lighter." Cam grumbled toward a cigarette lighter mixed in with the pens.

Guy remembered he'd struck a match to light the gas canister stove the other day, before finding the long trigger lighter in the pantry.

"Your inseam's right, though. I measure animals all day. And the steps from tree to tree, and milliliters of water. I know what everything in my pack weighs, and how different that weight feels depending on the environment and how tired I am. A hundred grams can be the difference between breaking my ankle or my back on any given angle and substrate."

Guy bet Cam could calculate the distance in kilometers from the second star to the right back to the hut, too. He probably practiced sewing by mending his own shadow when it came loose.

"You'd make a great drug dealer."

At last, Cam laughed past his tiredness with the same intensity Guy had managed to conjure up in the car the day before.

Christ, that's a nice sound. Suddenly, Guy's brow furrowed. "Cameron, can I ask what your pronouns are?"

"Why? Because I'm sewing?"

"Because you're wearing a skirt."

Cam groaned. "Nobody appreciates good vintage fashion."

Guy shook his head at himself. "So it was *you* who wore a dress on a date with the clerk's brother."

"It was a *gorgeous* dress," Cam insisted. "It's not my fault this backwater is backward, too. And it's not my fault the default for androgyny is pants, but I'll go change if you're going to be weird."

"Don't. You look good." *Fine.* He should have said *fine*, since Cam frowned at the compliment.

"I know," he grumbled, his pixie ears tinging pink. "But so what? That's not why I dress how I do."

Guy's face heated up too, and he blustered, "Fairbanks needs to know how to refer to you."

Cam sighed hard. "God, here we go. All right. Well, I get the kind of crap men get—told I'm not masculine and stuff, which is annoying, and not like what women or genderfluid people deal with. So I guess out of respect for the people I suffer like—and the people I *don't* suffer like—I go with he, not she or they, but I'd rather be called nothing."

"You're not nothing."

"It's not a bad thing. But you're like, I'm gay, right? And you can check the box that says *M* next to it and not think twice? I can't. It's as dumb as asking if I like red or blue. They're both good, which doesn't mean I can check *Other* as if I like purple the most, or white, it means I don't care because they're just colors. Where's the *I-don't-care* box? Claiming anything else feels like a lie. It's pointless, so it's annoying on a good day, infuriating on a bad one. And," he continued, "I know the science and politics of gender identification better than you, probably."

"You probably do, but I'm not totally ignorant on the subject," Guy said.

"Oh, yeah. Because your writer psych guy wrote about it in his book. Did you edit that? Was he hard to edit, too?" Cam asked, tone rising with excitement.

"No," Guy replied.

Disappointment met his denial. "Huh. Well, anyway, I'm well aware of how and why I might feel disconnected from my assigned gender, and I've already fought to answer and re-answer every challenge anyone can ever throw down about it by questioning myself. I don't want to think about it, so don't talk to me about gender."

"Okay. Sorry."

"I mean, *you* can talk to me," Cam said. "It's just that all I can say is 'I don't care' and that sounds rude. Same for orientation. I *know* gender's not orientation. I *know* both can be a matter of life and death, and I'm not ignoring what a big deal it is to say 'I'm a man and gay.' I get and I respect other people having identities, but *I* can't pick a title. And that—me not being able to say—is not a choice. To me. What's my gender? And am I pan? Bi? I don't *care*," he concluded, rubbing at a smudge of ash on the table with his sleeve.

"Cameron?"

"Yeah?"

"No, sorry. I mean should I tell Huw to only use 'Cameron' when referring to you?"

"That's unwieldy for people to read over and over."

"That's not your problem," Guy said. People would adjust.

"He and him is fine."

"If you ever want to be known publicly as nonbinary or neutrois or anything else, tell Fairbanks, if not me. And I am sorry for making you uncomfortable."

A thin smile broke Cam's frustration. "Thanks, but I'm not sorry if you're uncomfortable with me wearing anything."

"I'm not." Guy was glad Cam was wearing *something*. "You can talk to me about anything like that. You don't have to, of course."

"All right. Thanks."

"Do you want to talk about how or why you disconnect in the mornings? Have you thought about that, too?"

"Oh." Cam stretched an arm behind him to a stack of books, trailing his fingers down their spines and prizing out a dog-eared paperback, which he flicked open like a Chinese fan and buried his nose in. "Nope. Don't want to."

Dammit. Guy realized too late he couldn't tell which question Cam equivocally answered, and his review session was terminated. Considering himself dismissed, he turned away too, to browse the room's books. He coughed softly. "Thank you for fixing the jeans, but you should be writing."

"No need. My editor's on holiday."

"He wishes." Huw's emails about manuscript revisions had been hammering Guy's in-box. "Can you show me anything you've written in the past? So I can get a flavor of how your writing's developed, and see what you need to work on."

Cam snickered, slipped on his headphones, and clicked his music back on, nearly drowning out his "Later, okay?"

Well. The guy had worked and sewed all day while Guy at least rested in the afternoon. Guy gave them both a break, and snuggled into the couch's bed of blankets with a new book in hand.

"Your reading is as expressive as your face," Cam said, pausing his music when he removed his headphones.

Guy couldn't help smiling at Cam's nerve. "That bad?"

"You mean, like, too expressive?"

"No one's ever called me that in my life. My ex said the exact opposite."

"Then he couldn't see the trees for his wood," Cam said. "You can't hold a single expression for a full second. Bored, nervous, horny. 'Insert coffee.'"

Guy shook his head, taken aback.

"Wonder, surprise, fear, even your order is weird," Cam continued. "It's scary how many ways you judge people every minute. I'd rather be ignored, but it's fascinating to watch. Like a flip book. And yet, no ax falling at the end. I *am* going to steal it for my next thing. The character trait, I mean."

Guy hoped Cam's *next thing* was a book, not a con job. He replied obtusely enough to discourage further armchair analysis. *He* was the investigator here. "Flattering me won't get you off the hook. Go edit."

Cam laughed. "Look at you, so proud you can't contain it."

What did Guy have to be proud about? That someone observing him was, for once, *pleasantly* surprised by Guy? Proud he appealed to a stranger he barely knew but was glad, even relieved that Cam existed in the world, even if unfortunately he was at the edge of the world? Before, what he was most proud of was his luck at finding Cam's father's works, and taste, for being able to appreciate them before De Carli was gone. Guy wondered how Cam fared with his grief—

At proving Guy's transparency, Cam huffed a small laugh, propping his headphones on just as Guy opened his mouth to ask.

"If you think I read well, then you should trust Fairbanks's edits and fix your manuscript," Guy said.

Cam was far more obvious than he argued Guy was. His face clouded as he cued a game on his laptop, soon surrounding himself with a buzzing field of sound effects and background music.

An hour later, Guy was roused from the De Carli paperback he'd found buried in a book stack by Cam slamming a mug on the log coffee table hard enough for a flying drop to hit its wood. Cam wiped it immediately, scrubbing hard.

"Dinner will be ready in a half hour," Cam said, glowering at the table. "The water heater's boiled for a bath if you want to go first."

Huh. Apparently cabin fever had filled the fragrantly smoky air alongside computerized dragon roars while Guy was immersed in fantasy.

"Thanks," he said, taking the mug, book, and hint, and leaving Cam to the kitchen alone. A long sigh followed him up the hall and haunted the steamy room into which he retreated to wash, and he wondered if Cam would have been less pissed to know Guy had zoned out thinking about him, too, not just his father's books...and not just thinking about whether or not Cam had stolen his dad's work, because that wasn't looking great at all.

But Cam in a skirt, with those legs... Guy really hoped the sylph only twenty feet away couldn't read *all* he thought about.

Chapter Eight

GUY GREW USED to rising when his cell alarm sounded ridiculously early, but not to the oddity of never hearing Cam's alarm once he'd warned Cam not to leave the 3:00 a.m. go-to-bed one set. There were never any sounds from Cam's room either whilst Guy himself stumbled about making coffee and enough noise to wake the dead. When Sunday came, he figured they had an excuse to take it easy—or easier, with a shared coffee before setting out—and repeating that excuse to himself, knocked and opened the door to Cam's room at 5:15 on the dot, a mug in each hand. It ought to snap Cam out of his regular morning funk—

Surprise twitched his wrist, sloshing his sleeve with burning liquid, which made him jump again while swearing under his breath. Cam's room was as empty as Guy had seen it days before, spartan bare but for folded clothes on the chair serving as a bedside table. The bed was empty, securely made up with hospital corners, without a single wrinkle in its taut blankets.

Guy stomped back to the kitchen, as helplessly angry as the first morning Cam had ditched him. He couldn't let Cam carry all the water bottles he'd him put in his pack the night before, but he still didn't know the circuit of traps well enough to be able to find him out there. *I'm not useless.* He fumed, only to jump when Cam walked into the living room, dressed and ready to go.

Guy was too stunned to greet him with *Good morning*, which Cam would ignore anyway. He looked like a zombie elf, as usual, but neither elves nor zombies could simply disappear from a room, *Christ.* Had he been hidden behind his bedroom's door?

"Where were you?" Guy demanded. Cam wasn't the only one for whom it was too early in the day to deal with enigmas harder than fumbling on gloves.

Ten long seconds passed. "Bed."

"No, you weren't."

"I was." Cam swayed on his feet at the front door, not yet having shouldered his pack, but collapsed all the same. Guy could almost see Cam's gears grinding as he searched his dimmed memory banks, shuffling endless reams of syntax to greet Guy.

"Come here."

Immediately, Cam stumbled to the kitchen counter and leaned heavily into it, eyes closed, his head lain on its surface. Moving must have been easier than thinking to refuse. The pungent aroma of the mug Guy pushed toward him drove Cam to lift his head until his mouth was level with the lip of the mug. He chewed the porcelain before slurping a sip, chin cradled in a drooping elbow on the counter.

Each sip infused intelligence into him, evident first as surprise, then joy at being treated kindly. By the time the mug was half downed, his gratitude was tempered with defensiveness and his eyes hooded more sulkily.

"I don't like how you are in the mornings, Cameron."

A quiet reply came slowly. "I know. I'm not here."

"No. It's like *I'm* not." Guy was sick of being treated as invisible, especially when Cam lacked the decency to be visible in his own bedroom.

Cam grimaced as he rubbed sleep from his eyes, then steadied himself to stare at Guy, concentrating. Guy was ready to receive a rebuttal, a denial, anything but the purest of small smiles with which Cam disarmed him.

"Sorry."

"Accepted," Guy croaked. "Now, come on. We're late."

Still he slouched. Guy moved around the counter and rubbed Cam's back, alarmed at his corrugated ribs, but reassured at the solidity of Cam's waist as he slipped his arm around him and tugged him onto his feet. Cam leaned back into him, letting himself be waltzed to the door. He didn't say a word about his heavy pack's lightness, since Guy had transferred some of its contents to his pack. Guy suspected it was only because he wasn't coherent enough to argue.

"DON'T STEAL MY stuff, Guy." From transcribing the day's notes into his computer, Cam looked up so suddenly he had to blink to adjust to the new perspective.

Guy sighed. "Did you just remember that?"

"I knew right away. I didn't want to fight then." Cam removed his glasses and rubbed his eyes, the flickering fire and computer-screen glow rendering them opalescent from Guy's angle. "If you get in trouble on the trap circuit, it'll be with me, so you don't need to carry anything. You *shouldn't* carry anything. Don't mess with my inventory."

"Don't expect me to ignore you breaking your back. Share some control. Starting with your pack, and ending with listening to your editor." Cam still hadn't touched his manuscript in Guy's presence.

"Ah, shit. I don't want to fight that much." Cam groaned loudly, rubbing his fingers over his laptop's keys without pressing. It was annoyingly sensual.

"Too bad," Guy said. He'd been listless since receiving an email from Huw that *Distant* had secured European and Asian releases through a distribution partnership Fairbanks held with a UK firm, Rival Publishing. *It'll come together with good editing!* Huw had assured Guy, *so you absolutely have to prove it's all ours!*

"I sent it fixed to Huw yesterday. He already slammed it back with more notes. You know, having papers peer-reviewed for nature journals was simpler than Fairbanks's editing system. Even Ames doesn't care what anyone turns in."

Guy hadn't seen him editing it once, and again, Cam was namedropping De Carli's publisher. Well, if he wanted to change the subject, Guy could do that. "Why do you suddenly want to be famous, anyway?"

"I don't."

"You will be, even calling yourself Cameron Stewart." It was unavoidable once his connection to his late father came out, which it had to for Fairbanks and now *another* publisher to sell any copies of his book. "For glory? Posterity?" To succeed his father? Or surpass him? *Ha.*

"Ha." Cam stole his derision. "Nah. It's just that fieldwork is fun, but the reports are boring and I can't *not* write fiction. I'm a writer."

"What does that mean?" Guy asked.

"You should know. You're gay."

"*Cameron.*"

"I was born this way. Showed undeniable hints as a kid."

"*Stop it.*"

"Then don't make me come out and say it! So what if you don't think I can write? What would you know, anyway? You can read, fine, but what have you written?" His voice rose. "Who have *you* blown in your packed lifetime?"

Guy shook his head. Cam's veering the conversation to sex was a new diversion tactic that bore none of the luster it held the night Guy had arrived, now Guy knew not to take it personally. "Seriously, Cameron, what other topics have you got? I'd rather talk rabbits." *If not De Carli.*

Cam reddened. "Food and sleep."

"You don't sleep."

"R-reading." At revealing his stammer, Cam's hand flew to his mouth but stopped short of clapping over it. He nervously nibbled his thumbnail, frowning. "Movies. If you want to talk tokusatsu, I'm your—"

"*What?* Takotsubo?" Guy asked. *The heart attack caused by an adrenaline rush?*

"Why do you know that word? Are you okay?" Cam cried, genuinely worried, and Guy remembered De Carli had died of a heart attack.

"No. What did you say? Taco..."

"Tokusatsu. Cheesy superheroes and monster movies, like Mothra. The worse the better, but good ones, too. I like animals. Especially mutants."

"Is that why you did science? Because of sci-fi movies?" *Hence the trope-filled book.* It was so...*fantastic* a reason to cast himself to the ends of the earth, and definitely not worth the danger of a subarctic winter. If it was only rabbits he loved, Guy would buy him the fluffiest damn bunny ever to grace a New York pet shelter. If snowscapes, he'd personally paint Cam's apartment walls the starkest white— *No.* Cam had probably seen enough white walls when he was locked up in hospital.

Cam's ears were currently not their usual snow white at all, having lit up pink in embarrassment. "So what? What's it to you?"

"I'm not criticizing. I'm trying to get a handle on your imagination."

"*Ha!*" Cam slapped his laptop shut, crawled over the back of the couch to nestle in the blankets beside Guy, and drew his knees to his chin. "You read my father's books, didn't you? What did you like about them?"

Finally he'd raised the topic himself. The thought of De Carli's last story, so sophisticated despite being unfinished, made Guy break into a smile. Cam quailed a tiny grin at his enthusiasm.

"The romance," Guy began.

"What romance? Everyone dies at the end."

"No, they don't." What stung the most was that it was *Cam* who was wrong, clever Cam, who was biased by his relationship with De Carli. Of all people, De Carli's son didn't understand his books. If he didn't like them, he'd never understand Guy. *Wait.* Why was Guy eager to be understood by Cam? He was here to understand Cam instead. "What do you mean?"

Cam scratched his hair roughly. "Why do you think none of them had sequels? Because once they were finished, they were done. The end."

The books were discrete stories, Guy admitted, but they weren't isolated. Their worlds and themes overlapped... "But the characters live," he insisted, his confidence shaken. Was this how De Carli himself described them?

"No, they're left behind. Their stories are over. Forget them and move on. That's a good thing." Cam defended the idea against Guy's frown. "Writing's ecological. Past books are fertilizer for new ideas, same as species evolve with every new generation. It's only fun to focus on fresh stuff."

Nice try. "*Distant* didn't establish context confidently," Guy declared. "It had no backstory, no universe building. Not enough to feel real, accomplished, or even fresh."

"Bullshit." The jarring violence in Cam's tone made Guy draw back, and Cam quickly reined himself in, hissing, "You *cut. It. All. Out.*"

"You know the real problem?"

"You mean *your* problem." His bravado fell short behind a wavering voice.

"Every single word matters, in their place. You catch and release them after measuring them letter by letter." Surely, Cam could understand it if he explained it in those terms. "Your word choices were careless. And the characters were unreal. Dishonest. Boring. You need to get *raw* to relate, to craft a shared experience with a reader. Because they're alone in bed at 2:00 a.m., or on a crowded train, or at an office desk, but they're part of something, sharing the open letter you give them. It's a communion, Cameron, so you have to be honest."

"My father"—Cam kneaded his knuckles—"just vomited out shit so he could sleep."

"Not meeting readers or giving interviews doesn't mean he wasn't part of their lives." Guy stretched out his hand to touch Cam's shoulder but, seeing Cam tense up at his approach, let it hover and drop. "Your book is your chance to be heard, Cam." *To literally come in from the cold.*

"I just want to sleep," Cam muttered. "So basically you're saying I should pretty up the language, and restore some anecdotes but make them more relatable? Why didn't Fairbanks just say that in the first place?"

"Not just relatable. Raw."

"But it's fantasy," Cam decried. "It's meant to entertain. And it's an escape from real life."

"No. It's where you go to find yourself when these—" Guy cast his hand over the book stacks surrounding them. "—and that—" He pointed to the outside world. "—don't show you. Like, when you want to see representation and...purity..." he trailed off, unsure how to explain.

"Are you saying, like, reading is cathartic, the same as writing is? I get that. You could show people any random words and they'll create meaning by relating it to themselves. But I never saw myself in any of these." Cam gestured to the book stacks.

"It doesn't happen often. But with the right words, which *aren't* random, you aren't just inferring things based on memories and experiences. It's more like they're universal truths."

Cam clicked his tongue dismissively. "No such thing."

Guy scanned the clean, cramped room to find the De Carli paperback he'd noticed amongst the book stacks, a third-edition Ames issue of De Carli's debut. Guy didn't need it to quote the line he'd absorbed into his core during college, but wanted Cam to trust him. "No is more powerful than yes."

"Yes agrees. Yes accepts. No doesn't need a reason." Cam continued the rebel hero's speech. "Yes swears, it promises. No screams. 'I will' is already triumphant. 'I will not' fights, anyway."

"You know that one," Guy observed. "I thought you didn't read his books. Or you'd forgotten them."

Cam rapidly blinked as his eyes brimmed with tears. *His tattoo*, Guy remembered, shutting the volume with an accidental thud. Eyes cleared again, Cam tilted his head to face Guy squarely.

"Are you okay, Guy?" he asked softly.

"I'm fine," Guy reassured him. He could be moved by De Carli's darkness without being dark himself.

"But that line. It's about resisting when you've got no reason to. It's about how you keep getting up and fighting when you know you're going to lose."

"It's about hope, isn't it? Love."

"Is it?" Cam cried, honestly asking.

Guy flushed. Just because he'd never shared love with anyone didn't leave him unqualified to speculate. "That's my kind of love, anyway. Wanting to do and be everything for someone while asking nothing in return. Having friends you're prepared to die and kill for."

"And live for," Cam said. "That gets forgotten. Just existing, even when everything's no. That's important."

"So say that." Guy wondered if he should give Cam more credit for dragging himself out of bed at all. *If* he slept in a bed, at all. "But say something. You *need* to write for me, Cameron."

After a long pause, Cam remarked, "You got animated for a bit there. More than usual."

"Did I?"

"Mm. Very passionate."

Very unprofessional, Guy, he chastised himself, but answered his mind back with *It worked, though.* "I guess talking about De Carli—your father—makes even me look not so indifferent anymore."

"You're never indifferent," Cam challenged him.

Guy wondered what Nick would make of overcoming his alleged disinterest in everything. Nick, and all Guy's exes for that matter, were never fond of De Carli's works, so he'd never sought to impress his ideas on them. That was probably where Guy had gone wrong trying to relate to them, whereas with Cam, talking deeply, fast, was almost suspiciously too easy. The discussion had sent a surge of warmth through his limbs, and now it was over, they prickled with cold, making his muscles burn beneath the raised hairs of his goose bumps. He set the paperback down and briskly rubbed his arms.

"I think I just had a breakthrough."

"That my book's okay?"

"Ha!" Guy unwittingly imitated Cam. Fantasy books *were* removed from real life, but Guy loved their layers, at the bottom of which were portrayals of pure emotion. So why did he always date realists who considered fantasy books a waste of time? *Am I that lonely?* "My ex said I was the most distant person he'd ever met."

"Ha!" Cam copied Guy as guilelessly. "Was he a shut-in, blind, or did he have amnesia?"

"He was normal," Guy defended him.

"Sounds boring," Cam said. His dimples deepened, bracketing a grin that spread when Guy didn't defend that charge against Nick. "You're better off with books."

"You walked right into that one," Guy pointed out, watching Cam's face fall as he realized he'd set himself up for another order to edit or write.

"All right, I'll try again." Cam pulled at a loose thread on his sock, snapping it off. "But I'm tired. So do you...do you want to see my butterfly collection?"

For all that Cam claimed to be inspired, then, he was still dodging the issue of his manuscript. Guy sighed, argued out. "Sure."

Cam grabbed his laptop as Guy resettled on the couch by him.

He laughed aloud as Cam started a Godzilla movie. *Mothra.* "How is that a butterfly collection? There's only one and it's a moth."

"In my stomach." Cam shifted back on the couch, laying his head close to Guy's shoulder. Cam held his breath when Guy placed his hand on Cam's forehead, smoothing back his hair, so Guy removed it and resolved to keep to himself, comforting himself with the thought that Cam didn't have a fever. Unfortunately, that meant every iota of angst he'd just shown.

It took hours to watch the film, as Cam kept pausing it to explain lore and characters, cultural contexts, and social impacts of the franchise in various countries. It evolved into a conversation lasting long past dinner, where Cam listened intently to what Guy added, adapting his opinions, appreciating them. By midnight, they'd watched one more.

"We gotta watch more tomorrow," Cam promised. "There's, like, more than thirty Godzillas alone. It'll be like a film festival. I haven't been to a film festival in, like, *two years*."

"All right, educate me," Guy demurred. Cam relaxing and getting into a sci-fi mindset would surely spark some creativity in him soon. The fact that he laughed throughout every movie, and laughed harder with glee at Guy's joining in with his giggling at the movie, was just a bonus for Guy to enjoy.

It wasn't until Guy lay in bed that it occurred to him Cam's kaleidoscopic talk was reminiscent of his father's writing. It had influenced Cam, or De Carli himself had. He melded science, novels, biology, and bad movies into an impressionistic wonderland. He counted and weighed up the world around him seemingly effortlessly, with passion borne of fascination, and engaged in it only on his terms. Cam was a compressed ball of light, a tiny universe of wildly different elements that swirled and never conflicted. He was infinitely entertaining.

If only he could write to the world's satisfaction as well as he did his own.

Chapter Nine

THE STACK OF clothes on the chair. The undisturbed bed. Like the day before, Cam's room was empty but for a beat pulsing in the air. The same tinny blur of noise that once confused Guy when he first heard it days before while lying in his bedroom, reading. He'd guessed it was construction nearby until he remembered there was no road nearby...and saw its source when he entered the living room. Now, the sound leaked from the cupboard next to Cam's door.

He was only surprised that Cam still managed to shock him. *It's too damn early for this.*

He knocked on the cupboard door with his boot, pounding more aggressively than intended as he leaned to place the steaming mugs he carried on a corner of the bedside chair to avoid staining the wooden floor. Thinking better of it in case heat rings stained the chair and upset Cam, he set them down instead on a sweater he tugged from the chair to the floor. Finally, he kneeled and opened the sliding door, exposing Cam's den.

The music booming in Cam's ears through his headphones became clearly audible. Cam's thin arms weren't goose-bumped as he pulled them under a fur blanket, curling up like a bug disturbed by the draft.

At least he's warm in there, but...he really doesn't care about nudity. It's possible he wasn't even trying to seduce me the first night. He certainly hasn't looked twice at me since then anyway. Like he wasn't looking at the moment. His eyes stared at nothing. Their pupils shrunk in the dim light, however. He was conscious.

"Get up," Guy growled, his voice thick with morning.

Cam's face turned somehow paler, making the shadows ringing his bloodshot eyes darker. He pulled the blanket up to cover his face, leaving exposed his calves where they dipped into his woolen socks.

Guy may as well have inadvertently kicked a puppy. "Are you sick?"

"No," hoarsely escaped the lump. "I'll do it myself today. You don't have to. And another ten minutes won't matter."

"What about the animals?" Guy asked.

Cam tried to kick the sliding door shut.

Guy wrestled against it, nearly catching his fingers where the panels met. "Trapped in a cold cage all night, then confronted with a huge predator? Free them as soon as you can, that's what you told me yourself." The parallel dawned on him. "All right, I'll do it all today. I know how by now. You can stay here."

"*Don't.*"

"A trained rhesus monkey could go reset your traps." *And a thousand could write your book.* The music tapered off, then a new song filled the stale air. Guy tugged the blanket down, Cam's headphones dragging with it. Fast as a whip, Cam pulled his head down beneath the blanket. "Cameron, *get up.*"

"I *will,*" came a rumble from the blanket.

The form was so still, Guy wasn't sure how long Cam had been holding his breath by the time he noticed it was too still. He grew more pissed as he started to get scared. He waited thirty seconds, feeling more wretched with each passing one.

"Fine." He grabbed one of the mugs and left.

HAVING HIS MOODS disregarded by someone who actually recognized they existed—and someone who *willfully* repressed his own communicative ability every morning—was more irritating than being called emotionless. Guy had gritted his stinging teeth to stop them chattering when he first stepped into the cold, and after breaking a sweat still found them clenched an hour later as the sky turned from black to lilac.

I shouldn't even be here. I'm supposed to just get notes and leave. If there's something seriously wrong with Cam, besides him stealing his dad's work, he needs proper treatment, not pep talks and help finding a stupid rabbit. For that, Guy would have to come clean, but now he wasn't sure how Cam would take the news he was being investigated. A confession would result in *Distant* being stalled. *You have a duty of care,* Guy railed with every trap he inspected alone.

Cam caught up to Guy at their first rest spot, his small white form electric with hostility, which was so much better than the usual nothingness that Guy grinned with relief while steeling himself for a thump as Cam stomped toward him.

"There was a stoat in the third trap," he said as Cam slipped out of his pack and dropped it. "I got its hind foot length. Its tail was tricky but don't worry, I got that, too, and a photo of fresh tracks that might be the rabbit's—" Guy stopped in surprise when instead of shoving him, Cam stepped into him.

"Too...dangerous," Cam whispered, his goggles a hard pressure on Guy's chest, though not sharp enough to hurt through Guy's many layers. The ache that welled inside him, Guy understood, came from within.

Too...close. Guy wrapped his arms around Cam's shoulders as if by reflex and pulled him yet closer. His gloves felt suddenly too thick as his fingers curled into claws embedded in Cam's coat.

"Gun," Cam elaborated, the word muffled in Guy's jacket. "Bears."

"I know how to use it." Guy slipped the rifle bag over his head and lowered it over Cam's hood, transferring it to him. "You're the one who shouldn't have come outside without it."

"GPS?"

"In my pocket," Guy confirmed. He'd carried the one he'd brought from New York every day on the trap circuit, though he recognized enough landmarks now that he didn't need to refer to it.

"Good," was all Cam managed, in a distant murmur that sounded like a moan.

Guy was still hardly able to feel his shape for all the padding dividing them, but he welcomed Cam's weight, and its lingering, until within a minute, Cam's breathing had slowed so much from its initial pant he was probably...

"Cameron. Are you falling asleep?"

"No." Cam yawned.

The ice formed on their coats crinkled as Guy released him, holding Cam's shoulders at arm's length until he'd stopped swaying and blinked his eyes open behind his thick goggles.

"Drink," Guy ordered, cracking open two canteens and handing one to Cam, who finished the whole canteen as mechanically as if he were sleepwalking.

Until Cam could talk, Guy would. He shared with Cam his accomplishment of handling a wriggling stoat without injuring it or himself. He spoke about his apartment, cafés, theatre he'd seen this year, anything to keep him from thinking about things he shouldn't consider, let alone dwell on.

Like the way, once he was awake, Cam twirled a pencil in his thinly gloved fingers. How he spun calipers on his palm like a baton, tossing them up to turn them over not for show, but for efficiency. Cam's lashes brushing the inside of his goggles as he tended to a possum's foot, injured in a trap door, apologizing to it in a low murmur. The white tattoo beneath his clothes, beneath his blanket in the cupboard. How the curve of his neck would fit into Guy's palm.

How he hid in a cupboard and didn't want Guy to join him. "So what happened this morning? You weren't up at five-fifteen."

Cam's rewrapped his scarf tighter around his mouth and said a muffled, "Yesterday's talk about books...well, really the *no* quote threw me a bit."

"Did you stay up editing?" Guy asked eagerly.

"Ah. No. I just remembered some stuff. Made it hard to..."

"Sleep?"

"No, to wake up."

"I enjoyed the conversation." Guy had thought he was getting somewhere at last.

"Good," Cam mumbled.

Shit. Fanboying was out of place when it impacted a grieving kid who'd been hospitalized after his dad had passed away, but Guy still wanted to know how Cam's mind worked so he could work out why it kept shutting down daily. A sheen of sweat turned to needling ice beneath the gloves' Velcro straps. He clasped his wrists to melt it. "About the cupboard. Is it because the small space traps heat more than the bed?"

"Yeah, that's the short answer."

"What's the long answer?"

Cam took his notebook from Guy, flicked to a bare page, and scribbled a complicated algebraic equation and diagram. "This is how heat's lost from that room's window."

"What I don't get is why you sleep naked when it's freezing."

Cam snapped the book shut on the pencil, then handed it back. "One large piece of cloth creates an insulation field better than small pieces. Like it's proven two people naked in a sleeping bag treats hypothermia. I should have slept with you the first night."

Guy's heart flipped. "I don't think we could have both squeezed in the cupboard."

"Ha. You would have overheated at that time. And I learned my lesson." Cam's rational reply bore an undertone of melancholy. "Charcoal bowls suffice."

"Why don't you just sleep next to the fire?"

"I did," Cam said, dropping his voice as they approached a trap Guy could now tell at a glance held a marmot. "I caught fire."

GUY ASSUMED THE house scrubbed itself whenever Cam donned a wizard hat while Guy wasn't looking. He learned Cam in fact secured his hair with bobby pins, not a hat, as the reason for the midafternoon's brisk scraping noises coming from Cam's room became clear when he moved to Guy's room, bucket in hand. He ignored Guy's protestations that he would clean his own room and mopped around him.

Since he couldn't be beaten, Guy joined him, dusting the living room, in turn ignoring Cam's "You don't have to do that."

Guy held his tongue when Cam took all the clean pans out of the cupboard and rewashed them, scrubbing hard, but when he mopped over the same floor Guy had seen him clean once already, he couldn't hold back.

"Stop procrastinating."

"I'm not. It's been a week since this place was cleaned properly." Cam wiped his forehead with his sleeve and muttered, "Gross."

So sweeping the hut every day in a Cinderella-esque flurry didn't count. That day he was Snow White, Guy thought, noting Cam's inky hair glued to an alabaster complexion, cheeks turned rosy by exertion. The only reason birds and chipmunks weren't pitching in to help clean was the elfin prince must have given them the season off.

Guy stirred heated milk on the stove and added to it melted chocolate guiltily procured from Cam's stash, rationalizing Cam was due a sugar rush. "I've never once seen you edit."

"Because you sleep so much."

"Because I don't stay up after the *third* monster movie every night?" Pouring hot chocolate for Cam and black coffee for himself on the counter, Guy watched Cam roll his shoulders and sigh. "Hey, Cameron. Sit down."

Cam returned his mop to its bucket at once, peeled off and tossed his dripping plastic gloves on its handle, and sat on the couch. Wincing, he removed the bobby pins from his fine bangs and placed them in a neat row atop a book stack. Guy sat above him on the couch's backrest, knees clamping Cam's shoulders.

"Take off your shirts." They were close enough to the fire that Cam shouldn't have been cold, but his skin nevertheless prickled with goose bumps when Guy squeezed the back of his neck and instructed, "Deep breaths." Time to find that crack of hostility, and release the emotion behind it.

Cam's soft skin made touching him like kneading his fingers in silk sheets stretched over iron planks. Guy drove his fingers over their flats of his back, its ridges and valleys, as Cam flushed, the fire's warmth seeping into them both.

"Trapping really does take a lot of time and energy," Guy began.

"Yeah."

"Why don't you just hunt the rabbit only?" Guy couldn't help second-guessing the joy Cam showed outdoors, considering the fatigue it caused. "For less hours each day?"

"No one's surveyed this area in winter."

"No one else is as unhinged as you."

Cam was silent.

Shit. Again, Guy had unwittingly alluded to Cam's time institutionalized, which Huw forbade him from raising—and which he didn't want to raise uninvited. Still, it was something he wanted to know more about. Especially since Cam's back was peppered with tiny indents. Unlike the pale freckles made visible on his face when he flushed, these resembled old needle marks.

Guy cleared his throat with a hum. "Have you ever self-harmed?"

"Nah. The tattoo's the only way I defaced this canvas." He let silence linger long enough Guy ascertained clarification wouldn't come soon.

"It's a good tattoo."

"Really?"

"Have you had acupuncture?" Guy slid off the back of the couch onto its seat, behind Cam, his legs stretched either side of him, feet flat next to Cam's on the floor. *Amateur acupuncture?*

"Yeah. When I helped look for a frog in Cambodia." Cam's biceps flexed as Guy dug his thumbs between Cam's shoulder blades. "But I've never had massages."

While Guy contemplated whether they could afford to sacrifice the kitchen's olive oil for massage oil, Cam's muscles began to melt on their own, turned tender beneath Guy's palms.

"This is actually...huh." At last, a positive reaction. Cam yawned deeply, and lay his head against Guy's shoulder. As Guy massaged knots in his lower back, Cam raised a hand and stroked the back of Guy's neck and head, repaying him in kind.

"You don't have to do that." Guy teased him with his own catchphrase.

"Mm." Closing his eyes, Cam's stony face melted as he nuzzled into Guy's collar, finally relaxed. His fingers turned gentle, tracing loose circles that burned the nape of Guy's neck, sending a fiery spark down his spine. "I thought this was off the table?"

"What is?"

"You know. But that...that feels really good."

"Here?"

Instead of the satisfied groan Guy expected to elicit, Cam gasped quietly. His expression turned so vulnerably open that Guy was at once distracted from the scent of his sweat by the knowledge in his bones that there was *no way* Cam was lying, not about *anything. Forget the book. Forget everything. I would eat you alive. I'd tear you apart, I'd adore you so much.*

The violence of his desire froze Guy. After a beat, he rubbed Cam more roughly to stop his fingers shaking.

Wake up, Guy. He *couldn't* touch Cam. He couldn't just rely on instinct and trust Cam didn't steal De Carli's book, not when his instinct was stupid enough to be howling at him to hurry up and kiss Cam. *Christ*, when Cam leaned farther back, eyes closed, and his warm, open lips falteringly brushed Guy's jaw—

Guy jumped, knocking a tower of books by the couch arm with his elbow. He leaned to gather them up, but Cam took his hand and put it back on his own neck.

"Don't worry about it. I'll fix them later."

Of course, he would, to *his* specifications. Guy paused. Unlike Guy, Cam wasn't flustered. He didn't care what atmosphere this massage was churning up. It was almost as if he was obliviously goading Guy, like the first night. After a fortnight, they still weren't on the same page, which was what, anyway? Not books, not sex, not science... More than wanting to prove Cam innocent, Guy would settle for having him *present*, then, in the mornings, and always, able to register what was in front of him...or, right at the moment, behind him.

"Sorry. I like clutter." Cam pushed his glasses up his nose, fingers lingering to press the crease between his brows. "It feels like a home."

Guy couldn't picture De Carli working in a tiny chaotic library where nothing was in disarray but everything was a mess. He imagined him typing in a cinematic study on a huge oak desk, a lamp at one elbow, and an interrupting kid tugging on the other—Cam, even smaller, his massive eyes inspiring tales of otherworldly beings. If they could replicate those conditions, Cam might focus.

"What conditions did your father work in?"

It was like he'd snapped his fingers to call back every ounce of tension to Cam. "We're back to him *again?* I can't believe you have a crush on my father. Jesus. Of all the pointless—" Cam stopped himself, unwilling to speak ill of the dead. Of his father.

Of Guy's favorite author. It was enough of a slap to Guy's intellect to rouse him and remind him he shouldn't be this close to Cam in the first place. Cam's innocence was up in the air, his mental health was questionable, and most of all, if they couldn't see eye to eye on De Carli, then it didn't matter if Cam could read Guy's moods. He'd just turn out to be another Nick if they got involved.

"I admire his work."

"Sure you do." Cam shrugged out of Guy's grip. "Anyway, now I do you? I give a mean back rub."

His posture was worse than when Guy had begun massaging him. *Christ, what does he need* now? *Space? What will it take to wake him up to the responsibilities...I can't let him know are urgent?*

"No, thanks."

"Foot rub?"

Guy clenched his jaw. "No."

Cam frowned quizzically, but then the insult of being rejected landed. For a moment, he looked taken aback. "Or do you want to plait my hair while we watch a—"

"I need to see what you've edited so far."

"Look, I've still got today's data entry to do. You know, I can just email the thing to Huw. He's given me enough notes to work with, and I *am* getting through them on time, so you can leave whenever you want. You're not a hostage."

"Neither are you."

"Ha!"

Guy flexed his fingers, made listless by the massage, and tapped Cam's shoulder. "You can get up."

Cam bounded into the kitchen, picked up the coffee mug instead of the by-now-cold hot chocolate, and avoided Guy's glare while slurping and smearing a damp dishcloth over the kitchen window.

Guy counted to twenty. At twenty-one, he took tools from the locker by the front door and strode into Cam's room, where he unscrewed the single bed frame and stacked its pieces against a wall in his own bedroom. He then dragged his mattress to push it together with the unused one on the floor of Cam's room. The two cast-iron charcoal pans he placed at the foot of the *double bed*, hopefully far enough from the firewood covering the far wall. When blanket after blanket were piled high, Guy lay down and read until the sunlight gave out.

The aroma of rich Italian food drew him out. It had been a welcome surprise to learn Cam could actually cook, considering how poorly the pantry was stocked on Guy's arrival, but he'd almost come to expect Cam proving himself infinitely, peculiarly adept at just about anything. He was elbowed away from the gas stove when Cam stomped back into the kitchen after inspecting Guy's modifications to his—now their— bedroom.

"I am not living with someone who sleeps in a closet," Guy said evenly.

Cam clattered two plates of pasta onto magazines serving as mats. Guy's battered tin bowl was as polished as silver, and the meal upon it almost antagonistically sumptuous. The bottle of wine that Cam had added to dishes for days on end finally lay spent on its side on the counter.

It was clear that while Guy had been occupied, Cam had been busy too with more than cooking. Cam's pack leaned against the door fit to burst beside Guy's, which was crumpled, empty.

"I'm not living with someone who takes what isn't theirs," Cam said.

Guy accidentally bit his fork. "I *am* going to help you tomorrow, Cameron. Outside and with *Distant*."

"Please yourself. Just don't touch my backpack," Cam said, looking far from pleased at whatever he was reading in Guy's expression. For the first time ever, Guy wished he could hide his disappointment better.

Chapter Ten

SHARING COCOONING BLANKETS made it warm enough that Cam, always nude but for socks, would kick off the thinner sheets during the night and Guy would wake with them tangling his feet, overheated himself and needing to strip off. His temperature wasn't helped by the hypnotic rise and fall of Cam's ribs in the morning's moonlight long after the glow from the charcoal bowls had died and Cam lay curled up in his pill-bug position, head pressed tight against Guy's body.

While Guy fell asleep around midnight, Cam always came to bed hours later, then rolled around making chicken scratches in a notebook he kept under his pillow, lit up by the coals—but even when he didn't write in Inuktitut or scientific Latin or whatever else, Guy still couldn't read what he wrote. It took a coffee by Cam's nose to lure him out of his torpor at 5:15 a.m. and another in the kitchen to wrench him far enough from his fortress of solitude that his eyes focused behind his goggles.

Once, Guy was rewarded with a strangled "Thanks" as they laced up their boots.

The first night, Cam had jerked so hard in the limbo between wakefulness and unconsciousness that he'd kicked Guy and woken them both. Too sleep-addled to cope with the fallout, Guy pulled him close and hooked his chin over Cam's head, forcing him to calm his breathing to match Guy's.

"I could break your jaw," Cam worried.

"I assume the risk," Guy murmured, eyes closed. "I waive the occupational health and...safety rights...to volunteer."

"You can't consent to grievous bodily harm," Cam spouted the legal maxim.

"Your dad was such a lawyer." Guy yawned before falling asleep. He turned out to sorely need it, as in the days that followed, there were so many animals in the traps they didn't wrap up until 3:00 p.m.

"Because of the full moon," Cam explained while entering the day's data into his laptop on the couch after dinner. He was chatty once more, but Guy was sick of the cold, bored of trapping, and missing his apartment's bathroom—and Huw was growing as impatient in his emails as Guy was to prove Cam's innocence.

"Book." Guy leaned over the dining table he sat at to tap an arm of Cam's glasses behind his elfin ears. "Show me. The first draft, the latest draft, anything."

"Why? Not enough overtime already today? I'll work you harder tomorrow." Cam straightened his glasses and stretched his arms above his head, then brought his hands crashing down to slam his laptop shut.

"I bet your password's something to do with Godzilla," Guy guessed.

"Yours is probably some fucking De Carli quote," Cam muttered under his breath. The whir of his hibernating laptop reverberated in the echo chamber of the hut, providing a steady bass to the crackling fire's percussion. Cam turned, jaw clenched in defiance that turned to worry on clocking Guy's concern. "All right, you go to bed then. I need privacy to write."

"It's been two and a half weeks. You've been looking for the rabbit for what, nine months now? But you have a deadline with Fairbanks. I'm not here just to help you with that and you know it."

"You said you'd assist me."

"And I didn't lie." *About that.* "What else do you want? I'm the volunteer, so coffee? Chocolate? You still haven't touched all that you bought in town."

"*N-no.* Thanks." Cam's voice climbed but failed to drown out the tremor of fear tainting his words.

"Coffee it is." Guy pushed off his seat and flicked on the gas stove, inwardly swearing. Cam only stammered when he was exceptionally tired or pushed too far. Guy lay his forehead against the cool steel of the water tank above the sink as he waited for the kettle to boil, and closed his eyes...only to feel the warmth of an invisible presence behind him. It was made tangible by a pressure square between his shoulder blades—Cam's head—and hands resting on the counter either side of Guy's hips.

Already light-headed with fatigue, thanks to the draining morning, Guy was drunk on Cam's by-now hauntingly familiar scent. He moved his hand back until it gently rested on Cam's thigh, light as a feather, so Cam wouldn't notice the pressure until he had to second-guess his own sense of touch. As gently, Guy trailed his fingers in and up, stopping high upon Cam's thigh. Cam's hands froze in front of him.

"This is beneath you, Cameron." Guy couldn't tell if the throbbing at his fingertips came from his fingers themselves or from Cam's thigh, giving away his anger. He couldn't tell if his own pounding heart was flooding his worn system with adrenaline and amplifying his senses, or if Cam was just drowning him in pheromones through light breaths aimed below Guy's nape, where his hair no doubt stood to attention. "I said no when I arrived."

No answer. Since Guy's voice had fallen so low he wondered if Cam had heard him properly, but remembered there was no risk of him not. He *always* noticed when Guy entered a room. Guy frowned hard, squeezing his eyes shut and risking losing himself in the darkness, falling backward—one small step backward would do. He'd press against Cam, and the heat he'd feel would erode the last of Guy's reservations, so he could finally give in, turn, take Cam's face in his hands, and kiss him...

The pressure on his back eased as Cam lifted his head and took back his hands. Guy let his fall from Cam's thigh and pivoted to face him.

"I just thought...a massage again, or whatever," Cam mumbled, downcast eyes wet with frustration.

SHIT. Guy lay a hand on his shoulder, and he writhed out of reach, dancing away and clomping down on the couch. He reopened his laptop and hammered his password in.

"Forget it," Cam said when Guy crept behind him, as if he expected a massage. He straightened, swiping a lock of hair behind his reddening ear when all Guy did was set coffee on the log table.

"I'll give you privacy. Just don't stay up all night."

"Don't tempt me," Cam muttered, stabbing his laptop's mousepad to open a series of documents Guy avoided glancing at.

"I owe you a massage tomorrow," Guy said, wincing as it hit him that promising *tomorrow* was Cam's line.

"Ha."

"I honestly just want what's best for you, Cameron." And to accomplish that as painlessly as possible, because ever since Cam's name had started to hum on his tongue like sherbet, Guy *knew* Cam wasn't a plagiarist.

"Thank you," Cam said with sincerity that made Guy's chest ache.

He paused for a moment, then closed Cam's laptop and pulled him up by the wrist. "And *you* forget it. Bed, now. You're too tired to think."

"So are you," Cam weakly protested, letting Guy drag him to brush his teeth, then climb into bed all the same. He obviously didn't fall asleep before Guy—since no jerking limbs jolted Guy awake—but he at least caught a few hours' nap, Guy hoped, when he woke at midnight to find himself alone on a half-cold mattress. Dim white light spilling in the open door from the other room, listening to the nearby tick-tock of steady typing and the buzz of tinny music.

PALE LIGHT FILLED the air like a puff of powder, scattered by lacy ice on the window pane. The waning moon's glow painted white the rafters overhanging the bed. It was close to the hour they needed to arise. Cam would be able to spout the precise time, temperature, and moon rise stats, but he was snoring like a kitten. He'd joined Guy around two, Guy guessed, dimly recalling that he'd appreciated the softness of Cam's hair as he snuggled in beside him. As usual, Guy had woken before him without reason. *Without good reason*, his stirring brain warned.

Cam's warm arms loosely encircled Guy's waist, his head resting on Guy's stomach, legs curled beneath him, socks dangling off the mattress's edge. His fingertips twitched lightly on Guy's waist.

Guy took in the rise and fall of Cam's lithe back. His solidity was deceptive when his skin was soft as milk, especially around his mouth. Guy had learned Cam always shaved before coming to bed to save doing it in the morning when he struggled to get a grip on reality, let alone a razor.

He brushed a fallen strand of hair from where it collected in Cam's long lashes. Running his fingers through the light dappling his dark hair, he found its long tendrils to be as soft as shadows and dipped his hand more deeply into Cam's beauty, caressing his neck.

Guy grew conscious of Cam's warm, moist breath on the lowest part of his stomach. If he concentrated, he could feel it reaching his cock...and then he could feel nothing else but that. It shook him awake, how rapidly he plunged into crimson lust, as if he'd sunk into a hot bath. His heart pounded and his hand trembled in Cam's hair, which was too soft against his palm. He wanted to grab it, pull it, and scratch the skin between his fingers with it.

Don't, he pleaded with himself, *you'll disturb him.* His motive was selfish too. He wanted to look at him like this, in this light, that wisp of hair laced across his eyebrow, for as long as possible.

Shifting so his erection wouldn't touch Cam's face, he ended up burying its tip in Cam's hair. It felt so good his whole body was poisoned with longing, his skin stinging in the cold air as it tightened around his growing cock. He sighed raggedly, trying to calm down, but automatically kneaded the tresses of hair he clutched tighter.

Cam stirred in his grasp, rubbing his forehead against the trail of downy hair on Guy's stomach before hazily blinking, registering that this wasn't the usual cloth. He squinted a yawn as he stretched his arms, brushing cold fingertips up Guy's sides. He brought them back down lightly over Guy's chest and slid them to resume their position underneath Guy's waist, returning to the warmth, refilling the space they'd left, now gripping.

As Cam nuzzled the goose-bumped curve of Guy's stomach, his nose nudged Guy's erection, which throbbed harder at his brief touch and traitorously twitched toward Cam. Guy felt Cam's lips curve into a smile, heard the soft crackle as his newly woken lips parted. So lightly Guy could hardly follow the sensation except by sight alone, Cam trailed his lips along his cock, planting a kiss on its tip. He lingered there, breath hot.

"Stop," Guy whispered, his voice thick with sleep.

"Uh-uh," Cam sighed out. "Please? You won't owe me."

"But..." *I want to.* At least Cam was speaking, however. He *was* awake, and sharp enough to suddenly squeeze Guy's ass in a sneak attack, lifting him an inch into a draft as his back arched. The sheets he fell back on felt coarse now, their former warmth turned hot. Guy slid behind his head so he could see Cam's pale back, his calves, his socked toes curled into the mattress's edge as if clinging to the edge of the world.

Guy shifted to push his balls harder into Cam's cradling palm, but Cam released them to wrap his hand around Guy's cock. Guy's arms locked beneath his pillow, one fist clenched around his other wrist while Cam licked between his fingers from the base of Guy's shaft to his tip. The friction of his tongue increased as he lost saliva, sending a charge ripping through Guy as he pushed his pointed tongue shallowly into the slit of Guy's cock.

Cam pumped him loosely while teasingly lapping at the head of his cock in time with Guy's hips jerking up, in. Cam then sucked hard, not looking the slightest bit absent. He was focused as if hunting, expertly. Guy was pinned by his gaze.

"Thirty-eight degrees Celsius," Cam's silken voice hummed. "You're too hot, Guy."

"Whose fault is that?" Guy gasped.

Cam smiled as he drew himself up on the foot of the bed, prizing Guy's thighs apart with his knees. His own cock was erect and pink, and he stroked precum from its tip. Cam eased his wet finger into Guy's clenched ass, then returned Guy's cock to his mouth, deep-throating him, hard, fast, sorely, while tormenting his prostate.

Forked lightning stabbed his heart, frying his mind. He thrust his floating hips up into the smooth contours of Cam's throat, aware he was cutting off Cam's air, and had to finish. He struggled to care about anything but the imagined sight of Cam, shivering at how deep Guy's cock was buried in his ass, whispering to Guy he needed him.

He pictured Cam's delicate muscles shining with sweat, suspended above him, and imagined Cam's chipped and broken exhalations raining upon him. Glancing down, however, he found Cam gazing up, his huge eyes clear. Detached.

Don't. That's not what I want. For him... Guy closed his eyes to see searing blue flames instead, open and welcoming, begging Guy, not to hurry up and come already, but for more. "Cameron—"

An answering moan ricocheted through his hips, up his spine, and coiled around his heart like a whip. He came in a single hot jet that wouldn't stop, filling Cam's throat and feeling it contract around him as Cam gulped, milking the last of Guy's strength.

Guy's pained frown smoothed as he came to his senses and the realization that Cam hadn't come up beside him as he'd hoped. He glimpsed a smile prick at the corners of Cam's swollen lips before he rubbed his middle finger inside Guy on withdrawing, while rolling his palm against his balls. A hailstorm of sparks lit up Guy like fireworks in an empty sky, shaking him out of his stupor as he soared from zero to half-erect again in the blink of a watery eye.

Cam only released him and, turning toward the window, twisted his long hair into a rope. Guy sat up and nuzzled it, scooping cool and dry Cam to his dewy chest.

"What did I do to deserve that?" Guy murmured, the salt in Cam's hair like thinned blood on his lips. His morning voice was graveled, but not as coarse as Cam's.

"Be you." Cam's breath steamed in the dim light, but Guy froze at the sobering reminder he still hadn't come clean with Cam.

"It's five-ten." Cam spilled off the bed and pulled on the folded briefs placed atop the bedside chair. He wasn't hard.

With each layer of clothing Cam added, Guy counted a new doubt. *He's not into men. Or me. He knows why I'm here and he's getting revenge. I disappointed him. He only wants to manipulate Fairbanks through me. He's gathering writing material.* If he were using Guy, was that forgivable? It was horribly lonely here, or it would be for Guy if Cam weren't around.

"I'll do the traps alone. You can…sleep." Cam slumped under the weight of his final sweater, becoming the usual morning ghost who stared through Guy before shuffling out the door.

Shit. Shit. Shit. Stop. Guy's protest caught in his throat. He was struck by a turbulent sensation of falling—it was too early to think, but he suspected he was about to regret a lot at once, and it was best if he dealt with that alone. Fists balled on his thighs, he toppled with a thud back onto the mattress the moment the front door closed and pulled the blanket over his head to black out the gray dawn.

Alessandro De Carli's son, Cameron Campbell—no, Cam, gorgeous, clever, fun, interesting Cam—Cam just made a real move for once. But in which direction?

Chapter Eleven

GUY STRIPPED THE bedsheets and laundered them by hand in the bathroom. He stared in bewilderment at clumpy rice balls set on the counter for breakfast, no doubt fumbled together by Cam late the night before while Guy was asleep. He threw another block of wood on the fire and lost himself staring at the flames, until his vision blurred into the memory of Cam's hazy, hooded eyes and slurred grin as he nuzzled Guy's stomach. Worse even than the guilt filling his chest with cement was Guy's recollection of, after the smile, the familiar sight of Cam's vacant expression giving him nothing.

Huw had emailed Guy again, having gotten confirmation at last from a contact at Ames that there was no whisper of Cam having a book in the works with them under a pen name or otherwise. *Please, let him have an excuse for lying*, Guy prayed, knowing if he asked Cam properly he might get a straight answer. Only if he caught him in a good mood, though. Perhaps if Guy tidied up, swept, mopped, that would do....

The patchily bare floor was sparkling when a knock at the door told him Cam had finished early. *We're knocking now?* Guy braced himself and opened the door. He drew back in shock at the sight of an Inuk...cop?

"Is Cam okay?" Guy blurted out.

"You tell me!" The man barged past him and closed the door amid swirling snow. "What are you doing here? You'd better not be hiking. Are you mad?"

Guy scratched his hair into a semblance of tidiness as he shoved a mop and bucket behind him with his foot, out of the guy's way.

The man looked him up and down and took in the bedsheets stretched out to dry by the fire. A leer spread across his face and he called out, "Oi, Alice? You up?"

Guy narrowed his eyes. "If you mean Cameron, he's doing the traps."

"Still? What a moron." The man hung his coat on a hook and looked around, hands in pockets.

"The moon's full this week, so there's been a lot of animals to measure and release," Guy said.

"Oh, wait, I think I heard about you. No one believed a volunteer would be crazy enough to come in winter. You're still here?"

"I'm with his publisher. Guy Sutton." He shook the man's hand as hard as the guy squeezed back.

"Brendan Bourgeois." Closer inspection of his uniform jacket showed he represented a local land council authority. *A ranger?*

"Are you here to evict him?"

"Shit, no," Brendan said. "Do you know what he's saving us on cleaning up this place in spring?"

So Cam's occupation of the hut *was* legal after all.

"Just checking he's alive and up for the usual monthly. Ah, taking each other's pulses, if you get me. I'd been looking forward to this, too. Kind of a shame...or do you want to join us? Rumor is he'll take more than one at a time."

"*What?*" Guy spluttered.

"Hey, no one's judging his routine. He's already had everyone in town who was game enough to approach him, and God knows it's boring out here. You'd know, right? I mean, the kid wears a dress, can you believe that? And with that hair? Can't blame anyone for trying to test his limits, hence the usual... But he got published? Good for him."

"He—Not yet. We're working on it."

Brendan laughed. "Like pulling teeth, eh, trying to get him to slow down?"

"Kind of." Guy's heart raced. "If he'd shut up and work, it wouldn't be so—"

"He's *talking*? You managed to get him to stop scribbling and sucking you off for five minutes?"

WHAT? "He writes at night, probably."

"Just at night? What's that, doctor's orders?" Brendan made himself at home, taking an apple from the fruit bowl on the kitchen counter and crunching into it. "*And* he's eating fresh shit?"

"Sometimes sleeping, too," Guy said sarcastically.

"You fucking with me?" Brendan asked. He raised a hand at Guy's indignation. "Hey, easy."

Brendan's recognizing Guy was annoyed shocked him into silence. No one *ever* saw how Guy felt.

"Everyone's heard stories, and I know the kid. Know him, if you get me, which you do. Won't say better than most, am I right? Takes a rabbit to know one. Or imagine one. Fancy one, boom boom." His mouth twisted in a smirk as he polished off the apple in four bites, followed by the core. "So he's writing. Huh. Guess as long as he's got a carrot to chase, he's happy enough, eh?"

"I don't...know what you mean," Guy said, wishing he didn't, praying he was wrong.

"Hey, do me a favor and don't crack the whip too hard. We have writer workshops in town in spring so I've met a few authors, yeah? I know the kid's a no-name, but from what I've seen, he works his loony arse off. Hell, you need to be mental to stay out here, and God knows he needs a hobby. It's not like he's going to find a rabbit even if there was one. Anything too little or dumb to migrate—winter kills everything that matters."

"Not everything," Guy said.

Brendan wiped the juice from his mouth, and the sweat beading on his brow with his forearm as he tugged his gloves back on. "All right, all right. I figured he'd be alone, but all right. I'll leave you to the love shack. Word of advice, though, guy. Best not get too attached to Alice or his—" A leering grin spread across Brendan's face. "—book. What's it about, anyway? Rumor has it his dad was a writer, too. Wrote about wizards or something."

"It's sci-fi."

"Oh. Wizards in space."

"*No.* It has a complicated story. It's good for a first try." It pained Guy to defend the book, but it was worse to let criticism slide. Cam had *tried* to write well. Probably.

"It better be good; a lot of people in town will probably read it." Pulling his hood up, Brendan opened the door to another flurry of snow.

The fire had gone out with the draft. Whether the first or second, Guy didn't know. He relit it with steady hands he flexed hard to relax out of fists.

Ten matches left. Guy rattled the box. He wondered if it was crazy of him to notice, like Cam would do, that there was also—finally—one less chocolate bar in Cam's stash in the kitchen, and he was almost certain Brendan hadn't taken it.

PRESUMABLY INFUSED WITH the extra sugar, Cam was his reassuring motormouth self over lunch, and had recounted all the animals and sights Guy missed that morning while avoiding the topic of why he'd ordered Guy to stay at the hut.

Stacking an array of sci-fi books on the table, Cam burbled, "I think I just need inspiration at this point. For the last push. All I have to do now is skim *Distant* and it's good to go."

Christ, don't compound the plagiarism charge by copying more *books.*

"You know what? After it, maybe I'll start a whole new book for Fairbanks. I started working on something else recently, which I think—"

"Did you know he was coming?" Guy asked.

"Who?"

"The ranger. Or Mountie or something. I don't know what term they use here."

"Oh, which one?" Cam said airily. "The short guy?"

So he didn't care to remember "the usual monthly." It was entitled to expect Cam cared romantically about Guy, then, but he had to have some motivation for blowing him, or else why bother?

"Cameron, what was this morning to you?" *Besides a gift. A compliment.*

Cam blanched. "That was my fault."

"How dare you," spilled from Guy before he cupped his hand over his mouth. How dare Cam minimize what happened to something worth an apology? But it really *wasn't* his fault; it was Guy's. There was something wrong with Cam, which Guy had willfully overlooked.

That much was apparent by the stunned confusion now on his face. "Oh, no. Did I take advantage of you? I didn't ask. I should have asked." He fretted to himself, "Did I hurt Vincenzo or Vance or whoever? Or the guy in the citadel? Or that guy's name at the...and on that boat...Rebecca whatshername."

"What about Brendan?"

"Who?"

Guy rubbed his temples. "Cameron, what's my name?"

Cam's eyes widened in horror. Guy could practically hear gears in his head screeching as he tried to think, but soon gave up on the impossibility of blustering his way through a lie. "It's either Guy something or something Guy."

At least he possessed the grace to let his voice falter. "*Best not get too attached.*"

"Wait. Sutton. Isn't it?" Cam said. "Guy Sutton. I'm sorry. I'm *sorry*, Guy."

Guy's formerly good impressions were proving as insubstantial as Cam's shadow in the firelight. According to Brendan, Cam was a callous workaholic who townfolk thought was crazy. Cam didn't seem manipulative, but if he could present so differently to different people, and forget people at will, it proved he could compartmentalize honesty. Meaning he could hide other traits and actions in plain sight, like writing...and *not* writing.

"I never *actually* slept with half of them," Cam said strongly. "That's not my thing."

"Then what is? Who?" Such an understated phrase, *slept with*. What did it even mean? Anything besides penetration didn't count as sex? Guy tried to make a tactless question more tactful and failed miserably. "How many people have you...dated?"

Cam's blush caught up to his indiscreet disclosure. "*That* is not your problem."

Wrong.

"Why? How many hearts have you broken?" Cam asked. That was all that mattered to him, apparently. Casual encounters didn't count for anything. Not the first night Guy arrived, not today.

"None that I know of." Guy might have left a few people cracked, but not for want of trying to requite their emotions. Not having things in common, not being expressive—if that failing saved him from the angst Cam was now causing him, he missed it.

"Yeah, right. Well, I don't fake anything. You shouldn't," Cam ordered as though he had a right to give romantic advice. "It's not nice. There's torture and then there's a broken heart."

"*I* don't fake anything."

"I know," Cam sulked. "Which is why I bet you wrecked Nick with a clear conscience."

"Nick is an ex for a reason, and *he* dumped *me*."

"Exactly."

Cam probably hypocritically had a hundred, yet somehow recalled the name of Guy's ex after overhearing him say it once to Huw on the phone the night he'd arrived. "How can you remember Nick's name and not know mine?"

Cam gnawed his thumbnail for a minute in which the silence grew more oppressive. He broke it with a casual lilt. "I wasn't kidding. I finished editing the last chapter last night."

"Great. Fantastic. What do you want from me? Hand it over and I'll be on my way."

"But it's not perfect yet. Or you won't think so." Picking at the hangnail he'd torn, Cam asked carefully, "So...do you want to cue a movie while I make dinner, and tomorrow—" Guy's incredulous glare cut him off, and his hand crashed upon his thigh with a thump. "Don't look at me like that. I'll do it, just it's easier when I'm alone. And r-relaxed."

"Cameron, I only stayed here in the first place so you *could* relax all afternoon."

"Ha! I thought you came to tell me how to write. Like I don't know how already."

"I'm here because I care about you *and* the book. Huw's paying up overtime because *he* cares, and he works damn hard to take care of Fairbanks' writers. I personally—" Guy closed his mouth. "Forget it. Work however's best for you. Screw whoever you want, just not me. Not now."

An interminable pause dragged. Soft cracks of the fire accompanied Cam's audibly grinding his teeth. "You can see what I've done so far, but I can't promise you'll like it at the moment."

"Maybe Brendan or someone else would. You know what? Don't trouble yourself. What I think of quality doesn't even matter at this point, and I can't face dealing with driving to the airport tomorrow, anyway. I'll deal with it all at once when you've finished. You've got ten more days." Now who was stalling? It wasn't a helpful response or one worthy of an editor, but Guy didn't realize it was also insulting until Cam chewed his lower lip so forcefully Guy feared its skin would split.

"It's not a crime to like attention sometimes," Cam muttered. "And shallow's...nice and easy to deal with."

Because you're here! Guy remembered Cam saying the night he'd arrived. If that was the only reason Cam had bothered coming on to him—frankly, if he wasn't nursing some kind of psychological complex or caught up in a strategy to hide his plagiarism, Guy would be pissed.

Raising an arm to shield his wincing, Cam ripped a blade of his hair free from his glasses' hinge and pushed it behind an elfin ear. "Thank you for not calling me Alice."

"Thank you for managing to call me Guy, even if it's by accident," Guy responded, earning an hour's stony silence.

GUY AWOKE SHIVERING. His phone told him it was after two. Usually Cam was beside him by now, against him, around him. Although Guy had resolved not to get naked in his presence again, he'd habitually stripped off after climbing into bed, ridding his tightened chest of constricting thermals. Now he was freezing.

Let him regret what happened in bed, just please don't let Cam be avoiding me out of guilt over the manuscript, he implored the shadows as he tugged on freezing jeans and socks, followed by his thickest sweater. The house was empty, but the fire still burned in the hearth. Guy shook his head in despair. Did he have to check all the crannies and cupboards for monsters again to find the one he wanted?

An unnatural glow from the front porch caught his attention, and he slipped on boots and stepped into the stinging night air. Cam sat cross-legged in a wooden chair, a frozen blanket covering his legs beneath his whirring laptop.

Immediately, he minimized a document so Guy saw only his screen background—a moth with a thorax as fluffy as the scarf obscuring Cam's face but not his goggles from the snowy vista spread out before him. He looked like a masked superhero standing guard, hands quivering in thin gloves that apparently let Cam type as well as dexterously handle animals in the mornings. But when they walked in the mornings, he kept them regularly shoved in his pockets. Now, they hovered above his keyboard, trembling as Cam stared ahead at the sky's low sea of milky clouds.

"It's really annoying that I've been here three weeks and not seen any northern lights," Guy chattered.

"Wrong time of year, and night," Cam said. "And it depends on solar flares and things. It's not that predictable."

Like someone else Guy knew. "Come inside, Cameron."

"You said to leave you alone."

Leaning against a pillar too frozen to creak was like pressing against an ice block, so he stood straight again on shaking knees. "What if a bear comes?"

"One already has."

"Ha," Guy retorted. "I'm lanky, you're just miniature."

"Don't weigh yourself when you get home to some scales, Guy. You won't like it unless you were looking to gain muscle from fieldwork. And the two-hundred-kilo grizzly left that way." Cam nodded toward a thicket.

"*Christ*, Cameron—"

"Two nights ago. Earlier tonight was just a wolverine, maybe. Something small," Cam said, and Guy relaxed a little, shuffling closer.

"You could ch-chill out bears reading s-stories to them." His melodious voice would pacify anything.

"Read 'em to sleep?" Cam tugged down his scarf and pushed his goggles onto his forehead. His lips were blue and downturned, beleaguered with self-doubt. He pressed his back into the seat of his chair, allowing Guy a view of the rifle propped against his left leg, its icy metal barrel doubtless scouring his blanketed thighs. "If the stories are bad enough, I won't need this."

"Cameron." Guy folded his arms. He should have disillusioned him more gently. Hell, the fact the book was terrible was good, because it made it less likely to be De Carli's—unless Cameron had mutilated it to distinguish it. "Your book's not that bad." *Your book.*

Polyester rustled as Cam scratched at his face. "Sorry I forgot your name. I forget my own sometimes."

"Is that because you find it gendered?"

"No. The past few weeks you've said my name more times than I've heard it in my life. We don't use names in my family except to refer to someone who's not there. If you want something, you face who you're talking to and speak."

Guy loathed hearing about De Carli now he blamed him at least in part for screwing Cam up, but he still wanted to uncover more of Cam's background to help plot damage control. "What if they're in another room? How do you call them?"

Cam peered at Guy curiously. "You knock."

Guy understood names often sounded unfamiliar to their owner, but it hadn't occurred to him that Cam might consider stating *any* name aloud disrespectful. To Guy, names were inextricably linked with the emotions they stirred. Just thinking Cam's name evoked a sensation in him like he was reading a strongly written word, like the *Yes* firmly carved into that logbook inside, answering a stranger's proposal. The imminent inevitability of not saying Cameron's name as often, and soon not being able to say it to Cam, hurt. *I can keep saying your name until it sinks in*, Guy wished rather than thought.

"Names are language, and you're a writer. They must mean something to you."

"All right, yes. Names don't matter, but a legacy does, for my mom. I'm happy with just having Stewart on books," Cam mumbled, "as long as there's a *Lepus campbelli*. The rabbit. That Campbell's going to be for my mom. *Campbellini* would suit her better because in photos you can see she was tiny, and so is the rabbit, but she'd yell at me for adding flourishes. Like you guys."

Mom. He'd used a colloquialism, an endearment he never granted De Carli. Cam had been a toddler when she'd died, but Guy didn't put it past him to remember her clearly.

"Are you...trying to protect your dad's legacy? By being a writer?" *Like I want to protect it?*

"Nope." Cam's computer screen turned black as the screen hibernated, and Guy's attention turned to the brighter landscape ahead where the waxing moon's glow permeated the clouds. Ridged snowbanks on the trail stretched like a fallen giant's ivory spine, pocked with shadows. It was a good atmosphere for a fantasy writer.

Less so for a half-frozen human. "Why are you writing out here?"

"You tell me." Cam's breath billowed before him, obscuring his face. "Why do you read again?"

Not for escapism. To confront. To work things out. Guy went to war with a good book. He fell in love. Sleep and comfort had no place when passion took hold.

"You know how art's cheaper than therapy?" Cam ran his fingers over his keyboard, not pressing. The screen stayed a black mirror. "I wonder what exorcisms cost."

"G-Google it, rich kid."

Cam paused. "I spent Fairbanks's advance on traps and food. I can't even pay you back for last month's gas."

Guy's eyes widened only to sting at exposure to the frigid air, so he squinted at the horizon. Summits of craggy teeth, canines overlapping molar plateaus, were all washed white by starlight. Cam was out here for a rabbit, not to elude money trouble...the rabbit only he said existed. Guy sighed a plume of mist. Well, De Carli's estate would be released when Cam was proved innocent. *If.* Could he hold on until then?

"But I don't want to sell that book anymore," Cam muttered.

"You already did. You have a contract."

"Not *Distant*, the other one. And I can still cancel *Distant* with you guys. Or you can," he sulked. "You won't get your advance back, though."

Jesus Christ. If he was contracted to provide another stolen De Carli to Ames, Guy couldn't protect him like he might be able to against Huw, and Fairbanks couldn't keep ties with Cam after his reputation was tarnished. Guy rested a hand lightly on Cam's shoulder, pressing to feel contact through the cushioning. He made out shoulder bones, and squeezed until Cam's reassuring pulse ricocheted up his arm.

"Forget about Ames. Can I read *Distant*?"

Cam swiveled to blankly meet Guy's stare. His vagueness when lost in thought wasn't empty as in the mornings. He wore the same lost expression when asleep, his face clouded with untouchable tempests he at least saw. Guy had never known anyone so in need of a hug, nor as prickly beneath his armor of a half-dozen layers of clothes. "I... I need another day."

"You need to come to b-bed." If Guy were the hugging type, this would be easier. *Warmer, too.*

"You know, I used to think I was Lord Byron or Percy Shelley."

Guy released him and cupped his gloves over his own mouth. The makeshift mask warmed him enough to speak a muffled "If you're going to have literary heroes, you could do worse than the romantics."

"Not because of that," Cam said quietly.

"Because they were in exile?"

"You don't... You're so *good*. You don't get it. What happens inside stays inside, all right?"

"Inside what? A hut? A book? Your family? You?"

A distant howl sung in the air. Cam slid his hand over his rifle again.

Guy realized he couldn't coerce him off the porch ledge by pushing, and creakily stood, hand outstretched. "Get up."

Cam's gaze swept up Guy's sleeve to meet his eyes. His own were pleading from miles away. "I can't."

Guy shoved open the swollen door with his shoulder and staggered to the fire to defrost his hands. In minutes, he shuffled back out onto the porch to see Cam staring into space. Steam poured off the coffee cup Guy passed him like liquid nitrogen, fogging his goggles. His white coat was so immaculate, he frayed into the moon-blanched snow beyond the porch, a ghost who flinched when Guy placed a numb hand on his hood. Guy gulped down his already tepid brew and slipped away inside.

He stood a while in the living room, staring into the fire and listening to the clicks of Cam's resumed typing. He wanted Cam to come in and be warm. He wanted to have him over to his apartment for dinner. To take him out to an amazing restaurant, to the Bronx Zoo, to meet Guy's parents. He wanted to be the reason for Cam's determined looks, his chattering, his laugh. And he wanted...he wanted Cam's smooth neck to turn as he looked at him, to have Cam in his arms, to taste the flavor of Cam's sweat on his dry lips, crisp and salty, the scent of Cam's skin at night. Guy wanted to turn Cam on until he melted into insanity; he wanted to pay Cam back for years of joy, and show him how loved he was and should have been and would be from now on.

But he couldn't do any of those things without first figuring out whether he was innocent, and regardless of whether he was or not, coming clean about who he was and why he was at the hut in the first place. A strong shiver rocked through him despite the nearby fire, and his circuitous, tired thoughts dissolved. He went to bed.

Cam crawled beneath their blankets soon after, sealing himself under their covers. Guy found Cam's hands in the dark and held them against his chest while Cam's pressed his socked toes to Guy's feet, recreating their usual circuit of warmth in which Cam's pulse slowed to echo Guy's steady heartbeat. That ethereal Cam even had hot blood to flow, and so strongly, stirred in Guy a melancholy, and he squeezed Cam's hands. Cam drew them back, and Guy suffered their withdrawal like the removal of a thorn that had plugged a wound. The loss endured as Guy forced his breathing to flatten, to lead Cam into the lonely darkness of sleep.

Chapter Twelve

CAM HAD STOPPED typing some time before. Stopped scrolling and sighed in exasperation. He glared at the screen before him on the dining table, but he snuck furtive glances at the couch where Guy was seated, reading. His headphones boomed with a song Guy had heard playing on repeat for a while. Guy waved to get his full attention and motioned for Cam to remove them. *They'll hurt you.*

Cam snatched them off and threw them blindly at the coffee table log, sending them spinning as they clattered, nearly bouncing into the fire.

In an instant, Cam was on his knees on the ground before the couch, pulling apart Guy's thighs and unzipping his fly. "Please let me do this."

Guy recoiled in shock. Had he invited this somehow? Okay, so he admitted he adored Cam, but Cam couldn't know that. He grabbed his hair only for Cam to force his head harder into Guy's palm.

"Get up," Guy gasped.

Cam mistook it as acquiescence and rose to straddle Guy's thigh, knee buried in his crotch, grinding. He was half-hard.

"Cameron, get *off*." Guy stood, spilling him onto the ground and towering over him. Aghast, he stretched out a hand Cam didn't take.

"But I—" A hundred emotions flickered over Cam at once as he second-guessed himself.

"What? You finished a chapter, so you earned it? You're bored? You're stuck? You want to distract me?" Guy had established through Cam's distance ever since the other morning that he wasn't interested in Guy the way Guy was in him.

"*No.*" Cam appeared to have settled on fury.

"Then why?"

"Because *look at you*," he yelled.

"What do you think sex is? A favor? A bribe? Distraction? What do you take me for?"

Cam leaped to his feet and tried to step into him, but stumbled in his haste, collapsing several towers of books.

"What do you take *me* for, Guy?" He didn't wince at the wave of heavy, sharp spines that crashed over his socks. "It's all I've *got*."

"No, it's not," Guy argued. "I'm already on your side, even if—"

"But you could hardly stand to skim that stupid trash book," Cam shouted, batting away Guy's outstretched hand. "What kind of *communion* is that, then?"

"You *know* how bad it is!" *That didn't come out right.*

"I know you don't like anything I have or do or am. It's always all over your face. So what *do* you want from me?"

"I want you to *write!*"

"I did!" Cam's voice cracked as he yelled, "How can you like my father's old books and not mine? You're better than that, Guy."

"You're not," Guy growled. It didn't matter if the prince lacked his father's talent. *Everyone* did. If Cam wanted to be a writer, Fairbanks could help him. Guy would help him. Hell, he was already resigned to helping him should Cam be sued by Fairbanks and whoever else. "But you'll get there one day, Cameron."

"I *am* there. I'm *only* books and sex, and you don't—"

"You're also r-rabbits and monster movies," Guy said.

"Fuck you." Cam's eyes shot wide open with dismay. He stopped wringing his hands and snatched his white coat off its hook by the door, slung his scarf around his neck, and stamped his boots on.

"It doesn't matter if you can't write," Guy tried.

"Yeah, it doesn't matter what I am!" Cam struggled into his pack, tossed his glasses on a book stack, and tugged on his goggles, cap, and beanie, then yanked up his hood. "It doesn't matter what I do!"

"*You* matter, Cameron, all of you," Guy yelled. "And what you do!"

"Then I'm *sorry*," Cam shouted, then wrenched open and shut the door behind him.

Guy knocked over a pile of books as he made it to the door in two steps and threw it open. He closed it behind him and shook where he hunched on the porch, every cell in his folded arms instantly stinging as blood fled them to warm his core.

"Get back inside," Cam cried.

"Did you even wr-write it?" Fury had Guy spitting the words through a jaw immediately locked by the cold.

"What?"

"The book! *Distant*! D-Did you write it?" Guy shouted to be sure to get the words out. They dissipated immediately in the open air, but their effect on Cam was profound.

Emotions appeared to flood him, anger, indignation, but relief, too. He raised an arm to point at Guy's chest. "Did you even *read* it?"

"*What?*"

Whirling around, Cam stalked away down the powdery spur trail, his colossal backpack bouncing with his practiced strides.

Guy slammed the door and stomped to the coffee table log to silence the song blaring through Cam's headphones. There was no off switch on the headset itself; he had to turn off the program running on Cam's half-shut laptop, which was perched precariously on tousled blankets on the couch. Guy opened it and closed the music program, leaving visible two documents open onscreen, *Distant_edit9CC* and *notes_9*. The bar at the bottom of the screen was littered with further minimized documents, each labeled with various draft numbers.

He's trying. Cam *was* writing something, so he hadn't stolen a De Carli, right? If he just had enough time and less pressure, maybe he'd be able to craft something decent... Guy's finger hovered above the mouse touchpad, itching to scroll back up from the bottom of both documents, which were scrolled to their maximum and showed simply *The End* side by side. He balled his hand into a fist, retracting it, not wanting to compound his misery with yet more disappointment.

Guy snatched his phone from its charging cord by the wall and dialed. "Why did you have to sell the foreign rights on to Rival?" Guy demanded as soon as Huw answered. "Do they know Cam's keeping his pen name? He doesn't want to be connected to De Carli, Huw. You can't just go around telling everyone he's De Carli's son to drum up interest."

"I didn't tell just anyone. I didn't tell anyone, in fact," Huw denied. "I sold it on the strength of a recent edit he turned in."

"But you told me last week that you contracted with them."

"Yeah, on the strength of that last edit. I forwarded Nancy Evans—remember her from NYU? I know you met her at one of Chris's parties—"

"Get to the point."

"She's working in London now. I only sent a sample chapter to brag, 'Hey, look what I've got,' and she wanted to agree overseas terms right away. You haven't told Cameron yet, have you? Thought you could hit him with it as an extra celebration when he's ready to give me his final edit. He still isn't happy. Guess you put the fear of God into him."

Suspicion swamped Guy and he retrieved his tablet from the table, scrambling to call up his own copy of *Distant.* It bore the initials MH in its name and header, not CC as all Cam's copies did. Those of another editor?

"Then you don't think it's a De Carli? At all?"

"I like it way more than any De Carli I read. I have no more notes for him," Huw said. "Hey, Guy, do me a favor. Put your hand on your forehead."

"Why?" Guy snapped.

"You aren't getting a cold, are you? You sound lively," Huw drifted into a singsong tone. "You sound like Guy the drunk freshman who tried to pick me up in our room by talking books. Is there something in the water up there?"

"Shut up and send me the last thing Cam sent you."

"Already done," Huw sang, hanging up at the same moment Guy's tablet chimed with a received message.

Guy pushed Cam's laptop away, sat on the couch, and began to read. After the first few pages, he rose with a strong urge to pace, but he couldn't peel his eyes from the screen to be mindful of the book stacks entrapping him, so sat down again, legs crossed to still them. His foot started to bounce.

The metaphors. Sentence length. Characterization. Setting. Dialogue. The cadence, sonority, alliteration. The caliber. The familiar feeling it stirred in his chest was accompanied by nausea welling in his stomach. By the time he'd skimmed three chapters then jumped to the end, he was nauseous.

Temporarily released from his stupor, Guy traced a zigzagging path through the living room maze to retrieve his phone from the table, and punched its screen with trembling fingertips.

"Guy?" Sean answered. "Sorry, Huw will be a second."

"Can you ask him to hurry? And hi, Sean." Guy clenched his teeth. "Hey, for the hell of it, can you please ask Huw what number draft I read in New York?"

There was a rustle as Sean momentarily covered the mouthpiece. "Uh, you got one that went through Michel...maybe Huw, too, after the first structural edit. Why? Does that affect your analysis much? Oh, wait. Here you go."

"Guy!" Huw's voice pealed down the line. "So phone reception's still good there?"

"Fucking Welsh bastard can't even spell your own name right, let alone edit an original De Carli," Guy shouted.

"Guy?" Huw asked, wonder eclipsing worry. "This is Guy, right?"

"No shit it's me, and you should be ashamed!"

"Does this mean he stole it?"

"No, it means Cam *is* Alessandro De Carli. *HE'S DE CARLI."* Guy gripped the phone so hard in his fist its casing creaked. "This thing he's pulled together after your butchering is *more* De Carli than any De Carli I've ever read. His father stole his work since he was ten years old and passed it off as his, but it was Cam writing all along, the goddamn little genius, and I swear to Christ, Huw, if you touch a single comma in his latest manuscript I will *burn* your house down. *SORRY, SEAN, BUT I WILL,"* he shouted louder, though he was probably on speakerphone by now and being recorded to capture his breakdown for comedic posterity. "I hope he *does* sell his next book to Ames. *Fuck you."*

Dead silence broke with a burbling chuckle, which quickly became a torrent of laughter. "Guy, do you know how much money we're going to make off this kid, then?"

Guy hung up, his throat blocked with a lump that hadn't been dislodged by yelling. Scalp tingling, he scratched his hair roughly, as his chest fizzed with pride that erupted as a grin, stretched painfully wide.

GUY DOVE INTO every copy he had, grinning against his knuckles. The charm in Cam's original draft, *which was fine,* was concentrated by Fairbanks's suggested edits so the latest manuscript was flawless. Guy wouldn't admit that to Huw for a while. All he could thank Huw for was the fact that if Guy had seen the original draft while in New York, he'd never have come to Canada. It was undeniably a De Carli, even more polished than his final book, and it had since evolved into the ultimate De Carli.

Its predecessors were famed for their stream-of-consciousness prose, and in hindsight, the idea of them welling from a kid wasn't inconceivable, provided that kid was *fucking Mozart. Distant* flowed, but Cam's recent scientific focus gave it structure and his maturity gave its themes depth. The unlikelihood of it being a debut might fuel conspiracies if Cam let it be known he was De Carli's son, but he'd easily deflect criticism by giving interviews, because the book *was* Cam.

It was the Cam who placed himself in Guy's line of sight and waited, fearing it was rude to get his attention by calling his name aloud. The Cam whose earnest bubbling over wolverines and Godzilla made Guy's heart race, the Cam whose murky surface Guy had barely scratched yet knew there was a universe inside he wanted to be part of. The stubborn Cam who wouldn't come home, and who Guy hadn't thought he could like more.

Guy wasn't done by 1:00 a.m., but his eyes were. He dozed lightly on the couch, ready to leap up should the front door open. At five fifteen, he set off for the traps, but was too cold to stay still at the first one, awaiting Cam, so he wandered along part of the circuit. After finding two checked traps, he realized Cam had already passed by them, so returned to the hut satisfied Cam was definitely still alive, mobile, and not so dissociated or bitter as to ignore his wildlife survey.

At midafternoon, Guy stretched on Cam's bed, restless but exhausted. Mandarin spokes of sunbeams on the ceiling heralded the early evening. Still the house was silent. Guy ducked his head into the blanket, inhaling the scent of Cam's hair. He bet Cam was cold and tired somewhere. He ought to be sleeping there right then, naked but for socks, as always. Cam's face should be right there, mouth opened a crack and sticking in its corners, a thread of drool spilling onto Guy's thumbnail, which he sucked. Guy gripped the corner of the bed, his palm sliding heavily, dragging grooves into the blanket he then balled in his fist. His restless heart pounded.

He bit into his pillow until his jaw ached and his vision flashed black and white, like the text on electronic pages. Words rose in him, things Cam said and wrote, the white shine of his near-invisible tattoo, and Guy realized he'd been absently stroking himself and now firmly filled his hand. His fingers tightened their grip automatically, sending his lust spiking and he gave in to thinking of Cam alone.

Precum beaded on his agonizingly hard cock. It had been too long since he'd been alone. His erection curved down into the sheets, his hips hovering above as he imagined Cam beneath him. The coolness of the blanket against the head of his cock drove him into a haze.

He's alive. Cam's alive, unlike his father who stole from him and put storms in his naturally starred eyes but couldn't dim their fire. I haven't lost him. I haven't lost the writer I loved.

He whispered longingly, "Cam."

"Guy," Cam said in the doorway. That unexpected and longed-for voice, as blunt as a blow—*Guy*.

Guy froze, kneeling on the bed with his throbbing erection in hand, glistening with precum and saliva. He wanted to die of shame, but his lurching stomach had leaped in blessed relief instead of the fear he knew he was due in this position, and instead of wilting, the sight of Cam just a few feet away at last turned him regrettably harder.

Cam didn't lower his piercing gaze from Guy's burning face, fumbling to unzip and shrug out of his white coat. "At first, it was just because you were here. You have a very cool face... It's easy. All you do is look." After he'd tugged over his head the first of the four sweaters Guy knew Cam wore, he blinked, brushing a stray hair from his eyes. "Usually I go with people who want a slice of something, sex, books, science, whatever. But you liked most of those, and honestly, too. So I get the reasoning behind pushing me away before, saying I didn't know you, because now that I like you more, I can see it'd be nicer to hook up. But I like just hanging out with you too. And I think—" His mouth twisted. "—so do you. So if it's just about the book being...not your style..."

Guy rasped, "You still don't know me."

"Oh. Is that why we can't fuck? But you can jerk off? Then can you tell me what I don't know? Because I'm not playing anymore. This isn't fun."

"That—" Guy swallowed hard. "—I can fix." Releasing himself, he stood up on the mattress and surged to the doorway. Grabbing Cam's belt buckle with a sticky hand, he tugged him forward, turned him around as they shuffled two steps, and Cam fell beneath Guy onto the blankets. He was so light, he bounced and settled, resting on his elbows, looking up now with curiosity...not the desperate lust he'd aimed at Guy the day before.

His inscrutable stare drove Guy into a frenzy of worry, and unthinking, he pressed his mouth against Cam's as fast as a viper striking prey. Cam's mouth stayed closed as Guy rained down more gentle kisses around and upon his lips, and cool fingertips wavered against Guy's naked stomach, about to push him away. But Cam's hand hesitantly snaked around his waist, seemingly beckoning, and as Guy slowly lowered his hips, a firm bulge under Cam's pants brushed his own.

Guy peered at Cam through hooded eyes he feared resembled a glare, craving definite permission to proceed. The instant Cam's neck corded as he arched to meet Guy's mouth, Guy bore down upon him ravenously, finding him sweeter than he'd fantasized. His lust spiked, his erection so much harder than it was seconds before.

Guy roughly broke away from the kiss and trailed his hands down Cam's sides as Cam arched into him. He fumbled with his belt buckle and fly, slid his hand into Cam's boxers, and wound his fingers around Cam's hot cock. Its shape was as he remembered, perfectly straight, but it seemed larger than his memory or hope had allowed.

I can make it larger, Cam, until it hurts. He dipped his head and made his tongue slick before running it softly from the base up to the salty top, his palm grabbing hold of the shaft in his wake. Genes were the sole thing Guy could thank Cam's piece-of-shit father for bestowing upon him. His cock was large for his frame, and utterly perfect in shape and form. It was a work of art. Its head was as round as the globes of his perfect ass, which Guy squeezed hard as he swallowed Cam's long length. The sharp cry Cam evinced was worth the momentary pain.

"We don't have to do this, you know," Cam rasped between shallow breaths. "I mean, I'll get you off, no problem, but you don't have to do me."

Guy released him. "Cameron. Do you want me to touch you?"

Cam laid a trembling fist against his eyebrows, which met in anxious consternation. "Yeah, always. It's a problem. But you never do— *Ah.*"

Guy licked up his shaft before flicking the tip of his tongue against the head of Cam's cock. Cam grasped at the undershirt covering his stomach, and Guy slid his hand beneath the material, gently forcing Cam's hand aside and tracing the satin skin of his nipple with cold fingertips, turning it hard.

Cam clumsily thrust out of time when Guy took him in his mouth, and Guy pinned his hips with both hands, returning to licking his shaft. When Cam was set shivering, Guy commenced bobbing his head teasingly, and was gratified as Cam throbbed in his mouth, swelling hotter. He glided the cool surface of his front teeth up Cam's cock, circling his head and, hearing a sharp intake of breath from above, lifted his chin. Cam was looking at the ceiling, stealing occasional glances at Guy. After each, he squeezed his eyes shut and reopened them cast to the rafters. His neck was flushed.

"Are you okay?" Guy asked.

"It's just you're..." Cam swept back his bangs and nervously mumbled, "se-sexy."

Guy chuckled in spite of himself. He'd take sexy for a description.

"But you always are. I mean, you're the best-looking guy I know." Cam grinned at the pun, but his smile rapidly faded into a frustrated frown. "Hey, the traps were pretty empty today. Considering the full moon."

Oh, no. As he'd been after blowing Guy, Cam had suddenly fallen out of emotional range. Cam's resilient independence must have saved him from De Carli, but the barrier it left was horrendous. What was worse, Cam's misery was now ballooning at seeing Guy's discontent. He paused, unsure how to proceed.

"I just meant I won't have much data entry to do. Sorry, I'm not good at talking during this kind of stuff. You can stop. Or go ahead, whatever. Shut me up."

Guy crawled beside him and laid his face on the pillow corner made hot and moist by Cam's erratic breathing. His voice cracked as he said, "*I'm* sorry. For yesterday."

"Don't worry about it. What you said sucked, but I learned from it, so thanks," Cam replied, aloof in discussing the previous day's argument. "I'll fix the draft however you say and you can go home."

His sorrowful pout was intoxicating, and Guy clenched every muscle to keep himself on track. "I'm sorry, Cameron."

A flush spread to Cam's ears and he pushed his face into the pillow.

"Hey, look at me."

Without hesitation, Cam pulled his hands from his eyes and stared at Guy straight on. He brushed stray hair from his line of sight, then returned his hand to rest lightly on Guy's bicep.

The suddenness of his response to the command struck Guy as strange, especially as Cam's expression turned decidedly blanker.

"You can close your eyes." *If you want.*

Cam did so, all tension in his expression melting away. But far from being relaxed, he seemed to be disengaging worse than before.

"If I said...hold your breath, would you?"

Cam didn't inhale deeply as Guy expected; he simply ceased breathing at once. Calmly, he opened his eyes, which reflected Guy's alarmed face while enough adrenaline for both of them coursed through

Guy. The horrible thing was that the fear poisoning Guy made him harder. At least Cam stayed hard, too. If anything, he grew harder at Guy's command, though that might have been because stress tightened Guy's fist.

Guy's heart skipped as he noticed Cam hadn't resumed breathing. "Breathe, Cameron," he said loudly.

Cam inhaled obediently, with no effort to recover his breath. "Three-twenty," he mumbled. "I could hold my breath for three minutes, twenty seconds right now." Misunderstanding Guy's horror to be disappointment, he added defensively, "I can try longer. Will, I mean. Sorry."

Guy had never engaged in S&M, but knew this wasn't it. Because prior communication was paramount, right? "What...what do you want me to do right now?"

"That's..." died on Cam's gnawed lip. *Not your problem.*

Or maybe Cam didn't know. Maybe he didn't want to do anything. He appeared to be thinking hard, maybe perilously close to tuning out. Guy suppressed another flash of panic at the rejection he assumed was forthcoming. "We can stop."

"No," Cam insisted.

"Then...what do you want to do to me?"

Cam wriggled closer into Guy, breath hot on his collarbone, avoiding eye contact. It would be so easy to pin his arms back and steer them both to ecstasy, but Guy couldn't do a thing until he knew how deep Cam's surrender ran.

He nudged Cam with his nose until he looked up and asked again, "What do you want?"

Cam's brow unfurrowed, and caution, eagerness, and wonder battled it out like storm clouds on his face. He inched forward, reading Guy for permission to continue, and slowly pressed closed, quivering lips to Guy's.

A kiss? Guy brushed his lips lightly against Cam's, drawing Cam's pout into the crevice of his own. Tilting his head, they fell into place as Cam's lips parted and Guy advanced to seal them together, Cam's breath moist in his mouth and filling his lungs with dense gravity that pulled him forward. He ran his tongue over Cam's teeth and retreated, kissing him chastely to mark a pause should Cam wish to take it.

Cam's swollen lips dragged over Guy's, inviting, promising to accept a deeper intrusion. The tips of their tongues met where their lips thrummed against one another, and Guy tasted the sides of Cam's tensed tongue while coaxing his mouth open. He ran his tongue behind Cam's teeth and rose up over Cam, his body cresting like a wave as his breath mingled with Cam's syrupy sighs in a shared moan. Cam had returned to the moment.

Cam curled his hands into weak claws that flexed and rested against Guy's chest. Guy took one, which gripped back hard, having finally found something solid to secure them. He slid forward to lodge his cock against Cam's, and arousal overcoming self-control, he growled and was met with a whimper. Swaying to roll the pressure of his cock up Cam's, from their base to his tip, he stroked Cam gently before wrapping his fingers around them both and dragging his knuckles from Cam's navel to the bottom of his stomach, massaging them together, guided by Cam's clipped breaths.

Guy wrapped a thigh over Cam's hip to secure him and squeezed their cocks together in the tight space, feeling both their pulses race. Cam added a shaking hand to his and tried to entice him to jerk hard, but Guy nuzzled him to make him meet his eyes while he set a rhythm Cam mimicked. They fell into thrusting through Guy's fist in unison.

"Shit," Cam gasped. "This is new."

"Too much? Want to stop?" An incredulous glare met Guy's question. Encouraged, he rested his cheek against Cam's, mouth grazing his ear. "Cameron," he murmured heatedly, as he lengthened his strokes in time with the palpitations in his chest. Cam spluttered as though he'd forgotten to swallow, and Guy reminded him, "Breathe."

"I *know*," Cam snapped, yanked free of his immersion again. He breathlessly added, "Sorry."

"Shh." Guy pressed his forehead to Cam's, the long lashes of the eyes in front of him sweeping his own as they rapidly blinked. "You're fine, Cameron. Just stay..."

Cam's glare of frustration shifted to suspicion, which in turn dissolved slowly. His eyes fluttered closed as lust overcame him for a moment before concern once more crossed his face.

"Okay?"

"Perfect." Guy's firm statement was met with a whimper. "Trust me," he commanded, and for a second, Cam melted so utterly with relief that Guy wondered if he was about to come.

It took another five minutes of steady, heated kissing, shifting, and swaying before Guy felt dragged so high he was in danger of coming the second either of them increased the pace...which Cam, though he trembled, showed no indication of doing.

Guy pinched the head of Cam's cock and bore a crash of teeth against his as Cam jerked in response. He drank in a dose of Cam's heady scent while chewing his earlobe, and tongued his ear. Cam's breathing turned ragged and his muscles tensed.

Anticipation doused Guy, and he bit his lip, trying to distract himself but pushing himself closer to coming himself. Denying the flare lit between his hips, he closed his eyes, but Cam's whisper cut through the dark.

"C-can I come, Guy? Please?"

CHRIST. His eyes were blown out black all the way to the navy-blue fray encircling his irises, but he queried without pleading, strong enough to last another ten rounds of delirium if Guy directed.

It was all Guy could do to pant, "Cameron, *I'm* about to."

"Really?" Cam cried. "Just from this?"

"From you."

Cam's whimper was electrifying. The sound of his name being called urgently, the fatal last word that squeezed the trigger—"Guy"—pushed Guy too far, and he lurched forward to chase the overcoming feeling of falling, gushing heat into his palm as Cam too coated his fingers. He refused to open his eyes until his chest stopped heaving, but it was too late. Reality slammed cold into his fevered body as Cam turned away.

Chapter Thirteen

GUY DRANK FROM the canteen of fresh water in the tiny bathroom sink in gulps large enough to drown him. His hands shook as he brushed his teeth, too disgusted to cast anything but brief glares at his frowning reflection in the shard of mirror duct-taped to the wall. Both his eyes were black for lack of sleep, like he'd been punched. *Good.*

The toothbrush bent, near snapping in his fist. Cam said he could hold his breath for *three minutes goddamn twenty seconds*? Those were competitive swimmer times, weren't they? And Guy had no reason to doubt him. So Cam's trance routine cropped up during sex, too? And Guy had just pressed ahead, anyway.

"Cameron, we need to—" *talk.* The word evaporated amid the steam of his breath.

When Guy had first seen the fur cover Cam in the cupboard, he'd mistaken it for a blanket, but now realized it was a woman's coat, worn with age and use. It was spread out on the mattress like a mini-mountain range. A steady beat bled from the pair of headphones, its cord poking out from the coat's upturned collar, while the center of the form expanded and shrank as it breathed, drawing in on itself over and over, a closed bud.

It was a woman's coat. *Not a woman's,* my *coat*, Guy imagined Cam correcting him. It was also old. His mother's, more likely than his sister's, but perhaps Cam's dresses had once belonged to her, too. Serena was a year older than Cam and, unlike him, had gone to boarding school so it was possible she never knew of their father's exploitation. She might have been Cam's only occasional salvation, until she decided to contest his inheritance and lodge the injunction on his manuscript. *She* had been able to tell it was a De Carli. She just didn't know who De Carli was.

"Are you okay?" Guy asked from the doorway, knowing Cam would hear him through the music.

"Yeah, just tired. I spent the night in a cave. Didn't know if you were mad."

"I was worried." He was still worried, hearing Cam admit to having been out in the elements all night.

"You didn't have to be."

Guy lay behind Cam where the mattresses came together. Cam's hands breached the coat's lapels to cup his phone, navigating its playlist. The model was years old; its background a stock photo. *How many numbers are stored in it?* Guy thought sadly. The secrecy surrounding Cam's life had forced him to grow up as isolated as if he'd lived his whole life in this hut. Guy lost count of the number of songs to come and go by the time the phone exhausted its battery with a short series of strident blips.

Guy cleared his throat. "Don't ask me for permission to come, Cameron."

"All right." It was a quiet but clear assent, a standard roger to a direction.

"Or anyone."

"It's just a bodily function, though. It doesn't matter to me like it matters to other people."

"Are you...disconnected from it? Like with your name?" *Like your body?* "Or is it you feel that the act itself is gendered somehow?"

"Nah," Cam said. "That doesn't bother me. All my parts are totally me. That's why they don't matter to me."

Guy could hardly breathe for his hatred of De Carli. He'd stolen Cam's identity and alienated from him any sense of pride, forcing him to seek refuge in his mind where his autonomy could never be touched. He'd reduced Cam's body to compensation, a lure to be reeled out for human contact because, by Cam's reckoning, his personality failed to entice. And De Carli would never pay for it.

Guy reached under the coat and laid his palm flat on taut skin. Cam pulled the coat away, leaving the ribs Guy rubbed exposed and trembling as Cam stretched his arms before him to drop the coat and headphones on the floor.

Nerves mixing with the heady scent of Cam's long hair were a toxic combination. He wanted to apologize with a kiss, but the recollection of launching himself at Cam and mistaking him for responsive before he knew Cam would agree to anything nauseated Guy.

"Cameron, can we talk about what just happened?"

"Ha! Can we not right now?"

"Do you want me to go?"

"No, but what do you want?"

"I want you to feel good. That's all." Guy inched forward and wrapped his arm around Cam's body. His hands were warm from being beneath his head, and Cam didn't twitch when he slipped them beneath Cam's shirts to run his nails across Cam's stomach, its muscles rippling in their wake. "Do you want me to touch you like this?"

"Fine. Yeah."

"'Fine, yeah' isn't consent. I want what you want," Guy said. "Telling me to go now or at any time won't change the fact I like you."

"Okay, then go ahead." When Guy didn't budge, Cam quietly added, "Please."

Goose bumps prickled against his fingertips on Cam's tensed stomach. Very slowly, Guy traced the contours of his abs and chest, growing fascinated by how smooth Cam's nipples were. They were so soft, he needed to apply pressure to even feel them, and was distracted until Cam's breath hitched. He trailed his nails down, running them over his jeans, finding Cam hard as glass.

"Here?" he asked quietly, heartbeat climbing as Cam shuffled forward to press himself into Guy's palm. Guy unbuttoned Cam's fly and slid his hand beneath his briefs, clasping his smooth but humidly hot and damp cock. A whimper escaped Cam and his breathing stayed shallow after Guy returned his hand to rest over Cam's open fly.

"Do you like this?" Guy murmured into his hair.

Cam stifled a chuckle. "What a question. Do I have a choice?"

What a question. "Always." Guy lifted his hand, but Cam put his over it, trapping him as he was and shaking his head, his hair itching Guy's nose.

"This means something to me, Cameron. 'Okay' isn't good enough." But *Tell me you want it* was an impossible order to give, now Guy knew Cam couldn't resist orders.

"O— Go ahead." Cam squeezed Guy's hand. "I do"—he dropped his voice—"want you."

"To do this?"

At last, there was no hesitation in his "Yeah," so Guy stroked his cock gently. Over long minutes, his motions firmed until he had Cam strung high at the end of each stroke, but Guy was aware that this remained a purely physical engagement. He raised himself on one elbow and saw Cam press his pursed lips together over and over, a frown marring his pale complexion.

If he didn't want this, but he couldn't think of another way to encourage Guy to stay at his side, Guy would distract him with conversation. "I read your latest draft."

"You read my shitty story?" Cam's pulse spiked. "Which one?"

"*Distant.*" Guy placated him and Cam relaxed a little, but his jaw twinged as he nibbled his lip, indifferent to sex now, awaiting a critique. He was quick to resign to the expectation it would be harsh, and reached for Guy's forearm presumably to comfort him, tell him it was okay, understandable that he didn't like it.

"Don't touch it," Guy said.

Cam pulled his hand from Guy's arm as though burned.

"No, I mean don't touch the story anymore."

Cam's eye twitched. "You liked it?"

"Yes," Guy said firmly. "It's brilliant."

"Really?" Cam writhed, his cock swelling in Guy's hand. "Because I tried. I did everything you said."

"You should be proud."

"M-more is okay," Cam said breathlessly. "You want to do more?" Licking his lips, he remembered the responsibility Guy vested in him. "Please?"

Warmth shot through Guy's veins. He should have known; Cam's body and mind were more linked than anyone's. He was a zombie when tired, twitchy when awake, and only listened to music if it was loud enough to bruise his ears.

"You have a thing for praise?"

"I...wouldn't know."

"Your paragraphs are great." Guy tried to tease him with an honest compliment, but Cam's gasp and instant tensing reminded him this wasn't a joke. "It's come from practice, hasn't it? From working hard?" His voice turned rough at recalling Cam's stomping out the day before, confounded by Guy's rejection of his body. "I didn't notice how hard you always work."

Cam moaned as he rolled his hips, thrusting into Guy's hand now while rubbing his ass against Guy's growing bulge. Guy was collapsing the distance between Cam's brain and body at last, and all it took were words.

"You fit me," Cam whispered hoarsely. He could probably calculate how many inches—centimeters, millimeters—Guy's cock covered in the cleft of his ass.

Guy tugged Cam's jeans down his thighs but left his briefs up, the heated friction of its cotton rubbing his knuckles raw as he stroked him. "Your eyes, Cameron," Guy continued. Now he'd started to list Cam's wonders, he wasn't sure he could soon stop.

"They're weird." Cam buried his face in the blanket beneath him.

"They're stunning, but I like the way you look at your computer. The way you read. Your hands, your fingers"—that now clenched the blanket, entangled with his hair—"splayed in books."

"But you're the one who's...you *are* sexy, all the time," Cam argued, resuming their earlier disagreement. "And transparent and...*hot*..."

Guy slipped his free arm under Cam's ribs and pulled him so Cam lay on top of him, facing up, his throat arched to breathe better. The air changed as though charged, and Cam's chest heaved deeply.

"Is this okay?"

"Shit, *yes*."

He stroked Cam's cock carefully, pinning his legs against Cam's to surround him with pressure while lightly teasing his chest with mild scratches. He adored concentrating on the fine hair beading with dewy sweat behind his ears, and as Cam began to roll his ass back against Guy's erection, he realized he didn't want to come again, only watch. This time was all about Cam, and Cam was already nearly there.

Hooking his feet between Cam's, he sat and slid Cam forward onto the mattress, kneeling between Cam's thighs and encouraging him to spread them. The promise of penetration alluded to by the angle and exposure of his skin to the cold air made Cam moan. His nape boiled against Guy's lips, his hair cool in comparison.

"JD Salinger talked about how rare it is," Guy rumbled against Cam's ear, "when you finish reading a book, you wish you could call the author up on the phone, like a friend."

"You should have called ten years ago." Cam shivered. "I'd have run away from home in a heartbeat. I'd have stalked the shit out of you. You're *gorgeous*."

So much for not caring about physical appearances. Cam clapped his hand over his mouth, and they both realized what he'd said. It gave Guy an opening. "Why did you let him get away with it? Your dad, calling all your books his own."

It was as if Cam prized his own hand away from his mouth, his fingers lifting one by one. "Because I had everything I needed," he said, making Guy recall the De Carli interview: *My son wants for nothing.* "I didn't know there was more to want."

"But now you want to be published under your own name?"

"No, I just want to write and—ah—for you to like it."

"I loved it. It's perfect, because it's so you."

"What's wrong with you?" Cam moaned.

Cam had asked before if Guy was okay when he said he liked De Carli. Now, his concern threatened to derail his passion again, so Guy clearly replied, "Nothing."

"Then how do you...read me? Not just the books, but— *Oh, this.*"

"Practice," Guy whispered, receiving a shiver in return.

"God, thumb through me," Cam squeaked. Guy twisted his ear but stopped trying to tease when Cam didn't react to the pain. Instead he gulped, his body as tense as trip wire.

"But I don't know what you want to do to me, or with me," Guy said. "I'll do anything. What do you like?"

"I don't know," Cam spilled out, hand flying to his mouth again to chew the backs of his curling fingers. Guy turned him around, marveling at how easily his lithe form was manipulated. Cam straddled Guy and hung hunched over him, knees clipping Guy's waist like pincers. He anchored his hands on Guy's biceps, which bulged as Guy caressed his chest.

"Guy." Cam searched his face through hooded eyes. "Guy," he repeated more urgently.

"What?" Guy asked before understanding there was no request to follow. He smiled gently. "Cameron."

Cam's pupils blew out like drops of blotted ink, and his whisper, broken as the spine of a loved book, repaid the inadvertent blow by causing Guy's heart to lurch. "G-Guy..."

Guy had told him not to ask to come, and he looked tormented for it. He struggled to keep his eyes open, refusing to lose sight of Guy, his breathing a mess.

"Will you come on me?"

"*What*? No. No, I can hold—" Cam's cheeks flushed lurid red as Guy wrapped one finger at a time tighter up his cock's length. He folded forward on Guy's chest, his heart booming against Guy's ribs.

"Please?" Guy rolled Cam's cock against his own stomach, its head buried in Guy's cotton sweater, and jerked hard, stripping him roughly. Cam whimpered against Guy's lips, and Guy barely pressed his lips back before Cam came with a cry, craning his head forward to chase the climax flowing through him.

Panting, Cam tore himself away from Guy. He frowned at the sight of his come on Guy's sweater. "Sorry. I'll clean that." As he peeled Guy's sweater and shirt as far as he could off him, his anguish turned to frustration as he waited for Guy to sit up so he could remove them. Guy stayed still, hands on Cam's thighs, taking in the sight of him. "Guy!"

"Cameron," Guy said, smiling.

Slowly, a small smile curled the edges of Cam's lips. "You really liked my book?"

Guy sat up, sliding Cam down into his lap and against the wilting erection he banished from mind. "I love them all, especially *Distant*. I'm so proud of you."

"All right. Good. Books, check," he replied spacily. "Good to know."

"Cameron." Guy nudged him with his nose, locking Cam's eyes on his. "You are not just sex and books. Not rabbits, not movies, or science or De Carli's son; you're Cameron Campbell, who is wonderful."

"That's...nice of you to say." Cameron wrapped quailing arms around him. "Bit wordy. Needs editing."

"Give me a break. At least I'm well-read." Guy's shoulder, made wet with tears, stayed warmed by Cam's hot sighs in the cold room long after the short day's light faded.

Chapter Fourteen

THE CRACKLING FIRE punctuated their silence while they sat together on the couch. Cam set his book aside on a nearby stack and sighed contentedly through a smile that broadened as Guy tightened his grip on Cam's waist like a slowly wound vise, then trailed his hands up to his hair. Cam twisted to let him taste familiar lips, then the ribbed roof of Cam's palate as Cam's velvet tongue snaked around his, claiming it. Guy's heartbeat sank lower, sending pulsing signals to his hips, which ached with the tension of holding still as he drew Cam closer.

A high-pitched shriek cut the still air, and Guy jumped.

Cam hadn't reacted, but to now giggle. "That's Mothra. If you don't know that sound by now, we need another marathon." He rose and tipped out the cup of pens on the dining table, spilling their contents and finding his phone.

"Hello?" His businesslike demeanor quickly turned casual, his eyes gleaming as they met Guy's. He twisted the phone so it wasn't by his mouth. "Hey, Fairbanks is happy. They want to release *Distant* in three months."

"Is that Huw?"

Cam nodded as Guy took the phone from him. "Ask him to send more coffee. And say hi to Sean, I can hear him in the background."

"Hey—" Guy began, then covered the mouthpiece with his hand. "Wait, you've spoken to him before?"

"Yeah, all the time when I signed. Now, mainly emails. He never mentioned me?"

As if Cam could be forgotten. "Asshole," he snarled into the phone. "You knew there was no chance of plagiarism, didn't you?"

"I'd hoped not, but it didn't hurt to have a professional opinion." Guy heard Huw smile. "A man on the ground. And against the wall."

"Plagiarism? Ha!" Cam said behind Guy.

"Were you trying to set us up?"

"Did it work?" Huw asked. "I waited ages for you and Nick to break up. Campbell flirted over the phone, the minx, so I figured if he were that desperate a hermit to harass me, your dumb ass would stand a chance."

"Oh, no. Reception's breaking up." Guy tossed the phone into the fire.

"Wow." Cam marveled at its screen blackening.

"It was old. I'll get you a new one."

"Give me yours instead." He took Guy's from the kitchen counter and held it aloft like a trophy. "Your number's mine now! So you can't escape."

"You can't call me if you have it," Guy replied, standing and following him to the kitchen.

"Oh, yeah." On cue, it buzzed in Cam's hand, and he laughed when Guy took it back, silenced it, and tossed it into the sea of blankets on the couch. He leaned against the counter, arms folded, as Cam poured two cups of the lukewarm coffee leftover from the brew he'd made alongside dinner.

"So. Celebrate with me? An end of engagement party," Cam joked, but a forlorn smile soon rose to his lips as he clinked the rim of Guy's mug to his. "Or a farewell party, a few days early."

I'm not leaving here alone. A lump in Guy's throat prevented the words spilling out. "Why don't you come, too? You've got more than enough data for a wildlife survey. And you can come back for the rabbit anytime."

"There was a parrot in Australia that wasn't seen again for over a hundred years after it was discovered," Cam stated. "And people spent a lot of that time looking for it."

"But rabbits breed in spring. They'll be easier to find then."

"The Ili pika rabbit was missing for twenty years in Chinese mountains," Cam countered. "This part of the tundra hasn't been used, let alone occupied, until the hiking trail was mapped through it and no one strays off that. Well, not intentionally. There's mention of a strange rabbit in local legends, but it's considered to be either extinct or a description only, relating to spirits. It's not that the topic or the land is off-limits to me, just there's nothing but ancient lore to guide me."

And no one to save you if you *are near-dead.* All possible calamities flooded Guy's veins with ice water. He wanted Cam safe in the city, even if he didn't want to know Guy after he found out...

"Cameron, we have to talk."

Cam cringed. "No, we don't. Talking's just one kind of therapy. It's not as big in non-Western cultures."

"I didn't say anything about therapy. Do you think you need it?" Did he know, more to the point, for his behavior in the mornings? Or for not wanting to return to New York? His dad wasn't there to control or threaten him, so he could talk freely about being plagiarized—"Did your father do more than steal your books? To you?"

Cam set his mug down by the kitchen sink, visibly debating how to respond, maybe pondering technicalities or definitions. He couldn't answer with the usual—"That's not your problem." He chewed his thumbnail and met Guy's gaze in an unmistakable plea. After tearing off a strip of nail, he blew it on the floor before realizing what he'd done, the neat freak breaking his own rules, and glared at it.

The significance of his silence hit Guy like a freezing gust. Cam didn't move, but everything around him fell into place. His disconnected promiscuity, his first resort being to trade sexual favors for a stab at friendship, his conditioned subservience. The self-preserving isolation.

Cam cracked all of his knuckles one by one before speaking so softly Guy strained to hear him. "That." *Crack.* "Is not your pro—"

"If he weren't dead, I'd kill him myself."

Cam stopped pulling at his hands, having wrung them dry of courage. "I'd let you. But he didn't... Look, the truth is... I went to an asylum because I proposed to my sister." Cam said it frankly, but the way the last syllable died off showed he found no relief in divulging it. "Or, you know, because there're laws against it," Cam said slowly, "I said, 'Will you spend the rest of your life with me?'"

That part sounded cathartic. Regretful, but wistful. *If* I *were asked that...* Guy swallowed. Cam had sought protection from the sister he loved by actually proposing to her, and since De Carli's death, she, too, had sold Cam out. Guy wanted to break the kitchen counter in half with rage. More than that, he ached to touch Cam, to embrace him for a month, to hold his hand—but Cam wouldn't look at him.

"I'm not mad at you for not saying anything about *anything* earlier."

"I know, you're not stupid," Cam muttered.

"It's not your fault."

"I know, *I'm* not stupid."

"Do you want to talk about it? About anything?"

"No."

"When you do, I'm here." Guy's throat closed off as Cam's eyebrow flickered up in disagreement. "When I'm not here, you can call me whenever. Anytime of night."

"Ha." Cam rounded the couch, fumbled with his laptop, and put on a monster movie while Guy washed their dishes in the cracked ceramic sink. He was shocked to find when he settled beside him on the couch again that Cam had nodded off. He snored in a gentle purr, but his body was tensed.

It occurred to Guy he'd never seen Cam relaxed, even when asleep. Whenever Cam at last passed out with fatigue, his muscles released their tension in bursts without warning, like an old house settling at night. His shoulders' hypnic jerks were more unnerving that the onscreen explosions.

"You'll hurt your neck at that angle," Guy murmured and drew him into the dent dividing the two halves of the sofa. He removed Cam's glasses and tossed them carefully onto the coffee table log far enough away Cam couldn't accidentally kick them on waking, then returned to stroking Cam's hair. After the credits stopped and the laptop screen dulled, Guy squeezed his shoulder. It was as bony as a sparrow wing. "Cameron. Get up."

Cam stirred and lifted a hand but not his head, waiting to be pulled up. Guy paused, taken aback, and Cam roused enough to see his own outstretched hand and dropped it. He stumbled as Guy led him down the hallway, kneeled on the mattress, and sank into it face-first. Guy sat beside him and rubbed his back, recognizing the tiny moan he rumbled into the sheets before turning his head to face Guy. It meant he was waking up.

His eyes blinked wider with every staggered second, but his body stiffened and it occurred to Guy Cam probably wasn't confident enough to refuse him. He might even be awaiting instructions.

"Sorry." Guy began to rise to retrieve the cast-iron basins from their corners. "I'll go get the charcoal."

"Can I touch you again?" Cam blurted out, pressing his palm on Guy's thigh to stop him from standing. "May I?"

"You don't have to." Guy stole Cam's line, trying to be stern to stress the importance of what he imparted, but his traitorous breath hitched. "Ever. Not with me. Not for anyone."

Determination focused Cam's eyes. "Right. So?"

He's imprinted by the first person to hear him out. Guy choked up at the gentle way Cam explored his thigh. *He's running a personal experiment, or getting material for a book,* he tried to convince himself in spite of the certainty in Cam's eyes as he gripped Guy harder, reflecting his desire. *He's paying me back the only way he knows how.* The phrase *only books and sex* and the memory of Cam storming out with the cry "*It's all I've got*" burned in his mind.

"You don't have to," he repeated. "I already adore you."

"I know, that's why I want to do this properly. You're the one who asked what I wanted to do, and I want to try...feeling it, I guess." Cam shuffled onto his elbows and sat up, cross-legged. "Once more with feeling."

So earlier didn't count? At all? "I want to do this properly. Not tonight. Not until I know more."

"And if I don't tell you?"

"I can wait." Guy would wait as long as it took. He'd never been as personally invested—and accountable—in a relationship before, which made all his past failed ones his fault, he guessed, swearing, *Not with Cam.*

"Can you trust me to know what's best for myself?"

The longer Guy's pause stretched, the more clouded his will not to deny Cam grew until he dropped his gaze, unable to behold Cam's disappointment.

"That's not fair," Cam muttered. He groaned loudly as he flopped back on the mattress.

"But you understand." He shuffled aside and flopped back too, his weight causing Cam to bounce an inch closer. His giggle lifted Guy's spirits. "I'm thirty-three," he began.

"My condolences, but you're not exactly past your use-by date," Cam said, dodging the elbow Guy aimed at his ribs.

"I'm starting, okay? I'm going first."

"By establishing you probably will go first," Cam carried on the joke.

"I was born in Des Moines. My parents owned a hunting and fishing store in a town two hours' drive from there."

"Oh, my God, you hick!"

"I've got three older brothers..." Feeling Cam quiet, he turned to see him staring with full attention at Guy. Recalling his flushed complexion a few hours earlier then and transposing its image onto Cam now, staring innocently wide-eyed as usual, brought butterflies to Guy's stomach and he interrupted his own tale to sit up. "You know, I will go fill the charcoal bowls after all. This will take a while."

"Yeah, thirty-three years is a long time." Cam was on his feet in an instant, bouncing out the door. "I'll make coffee!"

THANKS TO CAM'S enraptured interruptions—which were more like interrogations—they made it only to Guy's mid-teens before he'd bored himself too near sleep to continue and left Cam on the couch to join him in bed later, as per usual. Come morning, Cam was disappointingly dead-eyed once more but not so out of it he'd let Guy carry out his plan to split up so they could divide and conquer the traps in less time.

"One gun," he whispered at the hut's door, then said nothing for hours, long past the time when he'd usually drift out of his stupor. Guy's conscience ran rampant in the silence. Cam didn't seem to be brooding, but nor did he seem happy. He didn't seem to care about anything except processing animals efficiently, as usual.

Guy snapped to attention at hearing a gasp behind his back shortly after ten. "What's wrong? See something?"

"Nah, it's nothing," Cam said at last. Their midmorning snack further broke his seal, and Cam started chattering about romantic poets as if he knew them, which was a lot less odd than Guy would have thought a fortnight before. The snow beneath his boots seemed to crunch oddly, however, but it wasn't until they reached the river and Cam handed bottles to Guy to fill that Guy noticed his limp.

"What's wrong?" he asked, worried. "And don't say nothing."

Cam burst out laughing. "No. I'm fine. Just turned my ankle. I'll fix it when we get home. Or you can kiss it better."

That laugh. The gorgeous laugh. Relief surged through Guy as he filled the bottles. He refused to heed Cam's protests and insisted on carrying Cam's pack as well as his own for the trudge back. The moment their coats hung on hooks, Cam balled his hands in Guy's shirt and pulled him into a numb kiss.

"You took a while to warm up," Guy understated.

"Adrenaline helped." Cam hobbled to the locker and retrieved a blanket and the first aid kit before stepping back out onto the porch.

The kettle had boiled and the fire recovered enough to defrost the windows through which Guy made out Cam seated in his chair on the porch, blanket over his shoulders, knee drawn to his chest as he surveyed the damage to his naked ankle. It was swollen to twice its size.

Guy dashed out into the cold, clutching both his and Cam's coats to drape Cam's over his trembling shoulders. "Christ, Cameron, get inside."

"This won't take long enough," Cam argued, but pulled its hood low over his baseball cap and slipped his arms into its sleeves. "And doing it in the cold stops the swelling."

Guy shrugged into his own coat and kicked away Cam's empty boot to kneel before him. "You should have said something when it happened..." But he'd still been in his typical fugue. "Why do you wake up like you do?"

"This pretty, you mean? Or cool?"

Guy flicked Cam's hood before pulling his own gloves off to wrap a bandage around Cam's ankle, securing it with a safety pin. He wrapped his fingers around Cam's swollen ankle and lightly pinched his Achilles. The muscle twinged, but Cam's expression remained unchanged. Not blank, but still.

Guy rubbed his calf, where light hairs contouring its shinbone like a quill feather's strands, puckered upon goose bumps. *So he reacts to that stimulus.* Small stature, low muscle tone, tripping earlier... Cam had no trouble with coordination but accounting for his stuttering, small stature, low muscle tone, and compulsive cleaning, maybe he really couldn't tune in to his body all the time.

"Have you ever been assessed for dyspraxia?"

"No," Cam replied.

Guy pulled Cam's thick sock down to see if his foot was all right. It was, but relatively—now seeing Cam's lily-white foot bare for the first time, the smallest toe was half-missing, reduced to a mangled stump. Keloid bumps scarred where it had been removed from, the product of poor suturing.

"Did you lose your balance because of this, then?"

A flash of terror whipped across Cam's expression so quickly Guy wondered if he'd imagined it, but the uneasiness it stirred in him lingered. "No. That's old."

Guy narrowed his eyes in suspicion that refused to be quelled by Cam's smile, and held his foot tighter when Cam tried to tug it away.

"Is this what you meant when you said you were like Byron? That you have a deformity here?" Cam shook his head, so he continued, "Did you feel your ankle when it happened? Or were you, I don't know, partly blacked out like you get? And what about after it?" Cam had been as effusive as ever in the woods.

"Of course, I felt it." Cam leaned forward to replace and tie his boot, and Guy reclined, sticking his hands in his pockets to warm them.

"We're not just talking minor neglect, are we?" he asked about Cam's past. "Physical abuse? Sexual?"

"Do I have to talk about it?" Cam retorted wearily.

"I don't know any other way to deal with it," Guy insisted, settling to sit on the porch's iced boards. "You know PTSD physically changes your brain structure? And none of this is your fault, but you can and should get treatment. Counseling."

"I know a lot of things, Guy." Cam left his laces, arched his back, and let his arms fall in his lap before calmly meeting Guy's inquisitive glare. "You know when you wake up, there's a momentary gap before you remember your parents are dead and you have to deal with it?" he began patiently.

Guy's parents were alive and well, but he understood the mechanics of grief and wasn't lacking experience regarding death, so nodded. "It lessens with time."

"True. But I have...had? A lot of memories of that...caliber," Cam proceeded slowly, choosing his words. "Too many. If I deal with them all, I'd never get up. So I don't think. I've done it so much it's automatic now. I do it without thinking, ha."

"What do you mean? You meditate?"

"Not quite. I used to think of song lyrics, or stories to overwrite thoughts, but now I don't have to. I'm just blank. Clean. I know it's only on the surface, but I think because I've ignored some things so hard I've properly forgotten them. Don't want to check, though!" His chuckle this time was genuine. "It's not like I'm unconscious; I still know what's going on around me the whole time. And when I notice I'm thinking again, focusing on being outside, or the animal in my hands, or talking to you, it's a nice day."

"Then when you woke up normally...but switched off after...blowing me?" Guy said, unsure of how to put it delicately.

"It had nothing to do with you."

"Yes, it did! I was worried!"

"I wouldn't hurt you," Cam assured him.

"Worried *for* you," Guy clarified.

"Why? I'm okay. I'm always okay," Cam said. "Nearly always."

He really thinks he is. He actually seemed to be, too, most of the time. Guy conceded he couldn't be in denial if he honestly didn't remember what to deny. And Cam was proud even of his coping strategy, so to undermine it wouldn't do Guy or Cam any favors. He bit back asking *What* do *you remember?*, aware he couldn't broach that, either, and frowned, baffled at the stalemate.

"The morning after we talked about the *No* quote," he proposed.

"Don't know. Don't remember." Cam sighed. "When I was a kid, I tried overthinking things until they lost shock value, but not many. Back then, I knew no one would believe me, especially if I was found out to be a writer."

"That doesn't make you complicit in your father's plagiarism. You were just a kid." Repeated exposure psychotherapy was better than flatly burying trauma, so Guy nodded for Cam to go on.

"You know Fran Lebowitz, or the quote 'I write so slowly I could write in my own blood and not die'? Well, one time I had to paint my room. It took eighty-nine days, and another twenty-two to fix the patches where my blood was a different color."

"What? The whole room? You painted it in *blood?*"

"Just the walls." Weariness returned to Cam's face as his shoulders sunk. "The time it took is all I can remember now, which is frustrating, because I know I was nine, and short. How did I reach the roof? Even standing on a chair on top of the desk? I don't know why I had to, either, not that it matters." He quickly cleared his brow of its furrows on seeing the shock that froze Guy in front of him. "Anyway. Que sera. Forget that."

Guy's first instinct was to disbelieve it; his second, disgust at himself for doubting Cam again—who searched his face carefully, relaxing only when Guy didn't reject the tale. Revulsion at it and his own precarious reaction pitted in Guy's stomach.

"How can anyone forget that?"

"Practice." Cam shrugged. "Ah, really, enough. Let's move on. What do you want for lunch? There's rye bread or rye bread."

"No, thanks, I prefer rye bread," Guy joked as he reeled in place. He supposed the only comfort he could draw was Cam's coping somehow, even if it was with a bad method. Until they sorted that out, Guy would give him all the praise he needed to recover. Maybe he could get through to him better when Cam was receptive while they made out? But how to make Cam trust that Guy was truly harmless, that Cam had control?

Guy withdrew his hands from his pockets and rolled the remaining bandage around his wrist to fold it before returning it to the first aid kit, but had an idea. He wrapped the other side around his opposite wrist and knotted it with his teeth, binding his wrists together.

"Hey, Cameron. What do you think of—"

Cam had pulled his hat off and bunched his long hair at the back of his neck. He casually cut it off with one jagged snip of the first-aid scissors. "What do *you* think? I've been—" He stopped short on seeing Guy's reaction.

Guy's face was on fire. He expected his unblinking eyes were almost as wide as Cam's.

"Don't *you* blush," Cam cried, blushing furiously, too.

I'm the wrong person to ask; you always look good. But Cam looked *so* good. He looked like an otherworldly model all the time, so this upgrade from angel to a god was just too much.

"Why did you do that?"

Cam buried his face in his hands, mumbling a muffled "It got in the way, I don't know."

Christ. "We won't talk about anything bad again." Guy raised his bound hands to prize Cam's gloves from his face, then gripped his kittenish scruff to pull his head back for a kiss.

"I'm sorry." Silken hair veiled Cam, as he brushed strands from his collar. "You don't like it."

"Look at my face." Guy pressed his lips together to hide his grin but gave up when Cam smiled back, his dimples exaggerated by the fall of his newly shortened bangs. "You don't have to change for me. We don't need to rush. Is it a gender expression because I'm gay?"

"I didn't think about that! Aren't you vain?" Cam's embarrassment disappeared with a laugh. "But maybe. Huh. Or maybe you can't call yourself gay anymore if you like me."

"As long as I can call you."

Cam snickered, but his face fell. "Yeah. When you go home."

"I can't leave you like this." Guy nodded at Cam's injured leg as he helped him up from the chair. *Or at all*, he thought as Cam tugged his collar down to his level. The frigid cold numbed their noses and lips to rubber, but the heat generated through the kiss bled into Guy, making it feel the only parts of them that were real were those in contact with one another. *Don't* you *dissociate*, he warned himself.

"This is cute," Cam gasped when he pulled away, holding up Guy's bound wrist. "Can I undo it?"

Guy nodded. Cam unfastened the bandage and dropped it by the chair along with the blanket. Clutching Guy's arm, they both rose to their feet.

"I like your 'choices' kink," Cam said happily. "Hey, would Fairbanks pay me another advance now I finished *Distant*? Or do I have to turn in another book first?"

Guy laughed. "I don't know, your first draft might get rejected. After your first book's out, you can't coast on secondhand fame anymore."

"I need to buy more traps and bait."

"Fair enough," Guy answered. Many had been damaged by animals.

"Besides rye bread, what's your favorite food?" Cam baited him.

"You."

Chapter Fifteen

"IF I'M STILL tracking the rabbit in summer, do you want to come back?" Cam asked, stacking their dinner plates for Guy to clear. "You'll like it here in summer."

"Sure," Guy said, "as long as no hikers show up to stay the night."

"I can cause an avalanche to keep the hut closed," Cam promised.

Guy didn't doubt Cam could, either by using science or asking a mountain to grant his wish. But his new haphazardly chic haircut had Guy picturing him in cafés and bars dressed to kill instead of in his interminable layers. He wanted to show Cam his world, and Cam could show him Cam's New York. By his anecdotes, he, too, knew some places in New York well, that was clear.

Nevertheless, Guy tentatively inquired, "Cameron, do you not like the city? Have you heard of the *Wolfpack*?" The group of brothers raised in a New York apartment who rarely left it, convinced by their parents the world beyond its confines was too violent and corrupt to survive.

"Ha! I love New York, and I could go out anytime I wanted. I was told to. How else was I going to pass home school without the museum or the movies? Besides the internet." Cam's jaw tightened. "I had a good education."

"So you *were* neglected."

"Nah, I got food and clothes and birthday presents," Cam argued. "My father loved me. Just badly."

"Don't cheapen the word," Guy said.

"He did, Guy," Cam pleaded.

Yet he said before he'd let me kill him. "I love you more."

"I should hope so, that wouldn't be hard," Cam replied, following with a scattered, "I mean, you better." His eyes widened as Guy's words sunk in.

"Has anyone ever said they loved you before?"

"I don't read reviews."

"In real life."

"What do you think this is, a fairy tale?" Cam asked, taking the invitation of an outstretched hand as Guy slung his arm around Cam's waist, bearing his weight as he rose from the kitchen table's bench. His gasp as Guy lifted him off the ground entirely was cut off by Cam's own loud laugh of surprise. It sang through Guy's body, amplified by Cam's closeness and the snow drowning out the world beyond the hut.

"Not the couch," Cam said, throwing an arm around Guy's neck as he moved to drop him. "Take me into the other room."

Guy set him down lightly, letting him find his balance on his good foot. *Bad idea. Bad idea.* His heart ached at the way Cam's hair curled under his pixie chin. Cameron licked his lips as he set his glasses down on the log table... Guy wanted to indulge him—*Christ,* he craved Cam—but could he trust him to speak up if things turned too intense?

"If we do this, you have to talk to me, Cameron."

"I'm not going to talk about—"

"I mean talk me through it. Don't drift off and lose focus, or leave me straight afterwards."

Cam pressed his face to Guy's chest, exhaling warmly over his heart as he assented with a single firm nod. His hand found Guy's and led him behind his limping form to the cool bedroom made dark by the closing of its door. They lay in a tangle on the mattress, moving too slowly to fumble as their hands found each other's faces and the warmth of one another's breath. Guy knew the word running through Cam's mind before he said it, because it was all he could think, as if stolen from Cam, on reading him like an open book and finding a dedication to himself inside the cover.

"Finally," Cam mumbled against Guy's mouth.

Guy was steadily overwhelmed by his tender hesitance, his sweet taste, the softness of his tongue, the clumsiness of his teeth scraping Guy's. At last, he admitted what he'd tried to deny for weeks. This wasn't simple admiration, or infatuation, filling his chest and squeezing the life out of his lungs.

His hand traveled lightly over Cam's clothes and settled on his hardening crotch. A rush bled through Guy as he pressed his palm against Cam's gyrating hips. There were many reasons why this wasn't a good idea, but none were more important than giving Cam what he wanted.

"I haven't done this before. I mean, I usually just jerk off or give blow jobs. I don't know much, so you lead. Do whatever you want." Cam's lashes swept downward along with his gaze, fixing on the grooves of Guy's collarbone, which he mapped with his fingertips, enraptured.

"I want what you want." Guy raised Cam's hand to his own throat to show the rapidity of his clamoring pulse.

Cam's lips curved upward before he pressed them to Guy's neck, and he slid his fingers down to rest against Guy's heartbeat to reconcile its beat with the jugular pounding against his lips. Heat soaked Guy below Cam's mouth, and he massaged Cam's nape beneath tendrils of newly cut hair.

Far from obscuring Cam's reactions, the darkness amplified them. It was clear he was different. He no longer numbly caressed Guy's arms, mimicking something he'd seen or parroting Guy. Now he rose to each light touch Guy administered while striving to apply the same pressure. His hands trembled, determinedly fighting their own hesitation. Every one of the tender circles Guy drew in swirling commas down the links of his spine were met with humid sighs.

"Lie down, Cameron." Guy unbuttoned Cam's jeans and stripped them from him while Cam took off his shirts. Guy undressed himself and leaned beside Cam on the mattress, then rubbed his thighs while spreading them to reach beneath one and press his knuckle into the glossy skin behind Cam's balls. After sewing a line of kisses down Cam's stomach, he touched his tongue to the tip of Cam's flushed cock.

Cam struggled to sit up. "You don't have to."

Guy's hand on his small stomach stopped him. "Stay down. Please. Unless you need to move, but if this feels good, just relax."

Cam's back arched as Guy took his cock in his mouth, laving his tongue against its gossamer skin, tasting its rich salt. Cam grasped at Guy's hair. "Really, you don't have to prepare that mu—"

He cut himself off with a moan as Guy sucked hard. Cam's inner thigh, which was trembling against Guy's cheek, was as soft as cream and Guy bit its sweet, smooth surface before pressing his cheek to a cool spot behind Cam's knee, feeling he was burning from the inside out.

Cam tugged his right foot away and buried it in loose sheets, instead pressing the sole of his unblemished foot into Guy's thigh, kneading the thick muscle exercise had cultivated. *He'll tell me about his toe when he's ready.* Guy let it go.

Though Cam was getting hotter, he was covered with goose bumps, so Guy snapped a blanket up from the pile they'd kicked to the foot of the bed and cast it over Cam like a swooping net. It bunched across Cam's stomach, blocking Cam's view of him, so Cam struggled up on his elbows. Guy licked his way up his chest and pulled the blanket over their heads. Kissing in the closed darkness was more intimate, the sounds amplified.

The blanket slid away as Guy shifted over Cam, and Cam's eyes appeared even more strangely proportioned than usual in the low light, his pupils the size of dimes. Guy's aching erection sliding against Cam's inner thigh and leaving a slick trail of precum. He gently ground the base of his shaft down upon Cam's balls and closed his eyes at the sound of Cam's breath catching. Cam placed his open hand over Guy's heart and Guy too traced the tattoo on Cam's chest.

"Lube," Guy muttered, taken aback by the guttural depth of his voice. "Condoms?"

"I ran out." Cam sat up and kissed his chest by way of apology.

Guy paused. In his haste to pack, he hadn't brought any. "I've never not used them." His face tightened at having revealed he'd never been in a relationship secure enough to trust there was no risk, let alone accept his partner's tolerating the possible discomfort. Still, excitement at confessing trilled through him.

Cam smiled. "Me, too, since I was tested, so we're safe."

"It might feel bad afterwards."

"I'll deal."

Okay, fine, or not fine but okay, but what about lube? They'd run out of butter. Olive oil, perhaps? No, too unsanitary.

"Spit," Cam interrupted, scattering his racing thoughts.

"What?"

"Use saliva. I want you in me. Everything of yours, nothing else."

Guy's mouth filled to accommodate the request before he'd processed it. "Did you say that to make me drool?"

Cam raised his eyebrows and leaned up, but Guy pushed him back down. "If you kiss me, you'll waste it." He shook his head, unable to believe he was considering it. "No. It'll hurt too much. This has to be—"

Cam grabbed his shoulder and stretched his neck upward to kiss Guy hard, drinking his breath and saliva alike before pulling away. "First, don't underestimate me. Second, try to make it not hurt, you and all your experience... Third, if it does..." he lifted his hips into Guy's, eliciting a gasp, "good."

"Wait, I have an idea. Hold on." Guy stood and staggered down the firelit hall to the locker by the hut door. He grinned as he tossed up a tube of Vaseline retrieved from the Cam's toolbox and snatched it from the air. Returning to the bedroom, he kissed Cam, sucking his tongue dry. Now confident he could do this properly, he hooked his arm under Cam's thigh and stroked Cam with one hand, the other rubbing lube around Cam's hole before sliding his middle finger inside and scaling Cam's smooth, inner wall.

Guy added a finger, then another, watching blood pool in Cam's cheeks and his abs tighten. He prized both thumbs inside Cam, stretching him wide while caressing his thighs with his palms. Entering slowly, Guy found Cam naturally gave to his pushing much easier than expected. He withdrew over and over, advancing incrementally, each time kissing Cam, sinking his tongue as far as it would be accepted, patching Cam's gasps with steady breaths. Cam's breathing evened out, but he kept twitching with irregular jolts.

"Does it hurt?"

Cam shook his head to the side, trying to bury his frown of concentration in the bedsheet scrunched beneath his hair. "I'm trying to calm down."

Guy lured him into facing up again by meeting Cam's lips and drawing him out with his tongue. "Don't," Guy whispered. "I want you to feel all of this."

He slowly pulled out, and Cam looked confused, then worried he'd done something wrong, until Guy slid back in smoothly, squeezing out his breath. When he pushed Cam's knees up, thrusting still deeper, the moaned cry of relief and breathless Italian curse that met him made his hips buck. For a moment, fear crossed Cam's face and his hand absently strayed to his tattoo. Guy's hand met it and entwined their fingers.

"Okay." Cam shifted his hips, rolling from side to side, concentrating as he puffed. "Is that..." Trying to increase the depth of penetration, he pulled his knees up high, level with Guy's back, and Guy hooked his elbows under them before leaning forward.

"Shit, *there*." Cam bit the crook of his index finger hard. Guy pulled it free from his mouth and kissed his fingers, and Cam closed his eyes. "The...your curve."

"What curve?"

"Yours." Cam licked Guy's pressed lips, murmuring into his mouth, "Fits like... you were made for me."

Guy rolled his hips in a steady cadence. Cam's bangs kept hiding his face, so Guy smoothed them back in order to keep kissing him, conscious of how Cam had wanted him to earlier.

"Do you want me to stop talking?" Cam asked.

Guy hadn't realized he could infer that. "No, talk to me."

"And say what?" Cam asked, then moaned, "Guy."

Christ. "Say my name."

"Fuck, yes. Okay." He bit down on Guy's neck, chewing, sucking, and Guy felt drool run between his goose-bumped shoulder blades, though if it were blood he didn't care. Cam wheezed gasping pants and tightened his grip on Guy's back. His whole body was trembling, buzzing, bubbling over. "G-Guy..."

Cam pulled back, floundering, burning up and tight, too tight. His flushed face was peppered with electric-white freckles. Guy needed to get Cam's head above his body to let the blood drain from it.

"Cameron, get up."

Immediately, Cam struggled to comply, and Guy reminded himself to be more careful with instructions or else Cam would recklessly hurt himself. He hooked both hands between Cam's shoulder blades and drew him up so Cam straddled him, seated in his lap. Cam groaned at the piercing angle, and the blanket slipped from his shoulders.

"D-doesn't hurt," Cam stammered. "It's... *Jesus*, Guy..."

His heart clanged far more rapidly than Guy's throbbed.

"Didn't know it would be this intense." The tendons of Cam's neck were strung tight as high wires, and he convulsed in shudders as though stricken with hiccups. "So d-*different*. Twenty point five centimeters isn't supposed to be like this."

"I don't know how much that is."

"Jesus, you suck at math," Cam whimpered, "but when you're packing twenty, you're allowed, huh."

Guy nibbled Cam's shoulder in a futile attempt to control his grin.

"I can take more than that, but it's like forty-four degrees centigrade, *ah*— L-lust, luxuria, no one told me, I never read..." Cam shivered, trying to pin the words down, confine the flood clearly overcoming him. He was nearly hyperventilating. "I thought having a crush was violent, but this is...it's too much."

If he couldn't breathe, it was cruel to keep him focused. He might save himself by retreating into his usual catatonia, but Guy couldn't help himself selfishly gripping Cam tighter.

"I've got you, Cameron. Don't leave."

"I'm trying." A solitary tear rolled down his face, and Guy licked it, then kissed his cheek.

"I know."

Cam let out a ragged sigh against Guy's neck. "You're huge. Around me and inside...everywhere. It's so weird. You're seventy-seven kilograms, thirty-eight degrees in air temp six, but it feels like more and I...I didn't know I could occupy all my body at once, feel it all. It's so *much*."

Guy raked Cam's hair back, brushing his bangs away to cover Cam's quivering lips in gentle kiss after kiss as he rubbed Cam's back and his chest, smoothing out his heart. He grew heavier as tension left him.

"So this is feeling?"

Cam shook his head. "It's you."

The pause gave Guy a moment to realize he too was on the brink of annihilation. *I didn't think I could love you more.* He laid him down as moonlight broke through the trees outside, scattering filigree shadows on the walls, and cautiously pulled out of Cam, guiltily lingering a moment at his entrance where Cam's flesh burned hot.

"You haven't come yet, have you?" Cam asked placidly.

Guy huffed a laugh as he added more lube to both his cock and Cam's, both slick with oozing precum. He inhaled sharply as Cam reached and clutched his cock, fascinated.

"It's wider now? Twenty-two or twenty-three now. Bigger than when you passed out. That explains a lot. Fuck *me*," he mumbled.

"Is that just an expression or a request?"

"Yes, porn star." Cam squeezed him tight, turning Guy's laugh into a brittle gasp. "You're too much, Guy. Do you even know how much you are?" His swimming eyes conveyed he wasn't thinking in numbers anymore, but Guy couldn't even count, staring at Cam.

Guy removed Cam's hand and buried their entwined fingers in the sheet beside Cam's head as he lined up and slowly pushed back in, cradling Cam's lower back up on the bridge of his forearm. Cam's shivering became shaking, and he gasped each breath.

"My whole body. The soles of my feet... My *cheekbones* are humming, Guy. What are you doing to me, demon?"

Guy snickered. "Who's the demon?"

"You," Cam panted, "smash against my door on a moonless night in a thin black coat, black shoes, black suitcase, black hair, black eyes, h-heat incarnate, looking like a door-to-door soul salesman...and the sexiest guy I ever saw."

"Heat? I had hypothermia." He'd been closer to orgasm on drinking that coffee than he was at the moment.

"I'd pay," Cam gasped. "I'll pay, name your price."

"I thought you were an elf in a gingerbread house."

"I thought you'd finally come to kill me," Cam cried, burying his head in Guy's collar.

What? "Cameron," Guy said twice, forcing him to meet his eyes. Cam's were blown-out black, and his good foot dropped to the floor. *Don't be paranoid. Don't be delusional, please.* "Why would anyone come to kill you?"

Cam focused at last, which turned out to be the last thing either wanted. Fear poisoned Cam's expression—not of death, but of being found out. "They wouldn't."

Okay, he's not crazy, Guy tried to reassure himself. Discounting demons, what would justify paranoia? He didn't steal the manuscript, and De Carli was dead.

A long blink later, Cam reopened his eyes to reveal their pupils blown, too far gone to claim coherency. His gasp was one of ecstasy as he shifted infinitesimally, pleading, "M-move."

Guy could stay rocking gently and Cam would come. He leaned forward to grind more firmly against Cam's throbbing prostate until he jolted and constricted around Guy, painfully tight.

"Wait. I'm sorry." Cam winced as he worried, "Don't, stop, I can't... Not yet. You're not ready."

It appeared that, for once, he couldn't read Guy. The feeling of him hot inside and out, his body, his voice and expression, and the fact he was with Cam pushed Guy perilously close to the edge. He wanted to say *Please come*, but what wouldn't be a command?

"Do you want to come together?"

"I can hold o-on."

"When you do, I will, so..." Guy couldn't think. He sank deeper into Cam and, drooling so much he couldn't taste Cam's tongue, kissed him until he was lost, until nothing existed but Cam around him.

The pressure on his cock as Cam suddenly constricted upon him, seconds from coming, was too much. He gripped Cam's cock and pumped it as he pushed, hearing Cam cry out through the din of his own heartbeat, voice shattered, "Guy, I *can't* anymore."

Guy loosely covered his mouth and stole his velvety tongue, muffling, then silencing him. As he arched his back, Cam's right leg slipped off Guy's hip, hissing with friction as its bandage scraped the blankets and his foot hit the floor by the mattress with a bang. He came, shooting warmth onto Guy's stomach, clenching his nails into Guy's back so electrifyingly tight that Guy came, too. He might not have noticed the moan torn from him if not stunned by its echo as he suddenly focused, worried about Cam.

"What happened?"

"Ow," Cam half sobbed, half laughed, panting against Guy's dripping chest. "That hurt. You *are* a demon." He kissed Guy's creased forehead before wiping the tracks of tears from his own cheeks with the backs of his wrists. "Wow. That *really* hurt. Not you, but my ankle. I'm speaking up now, okay?"

Before Guy could catch his breath, Cam slipped out from under him, wrapping a blanket over his shoulders as he stood and hopped to the door. A warm draft swirled in, constricting Guy's throat so tightly he thought he might tear up too when Cam ignored his "Wait."

His legs ached during the few steps to the kitchen, but Cam had already made it to the kitchen by the time Guy stood shivering, naked, watching Cam hold the corners of the blanket in his teeth to stay covered as he stretched on his toes to reach the highest shelf of a cupboard. He retrieved one of the bars of chocolate squirreled there, tore it open, and munched listlessly. Guy moved behind him to rub his back, but he didn't react. *Is that it? Feeling time is over?*

"What about your ankle? Shouldn't you put pressure or ice or something on it?"

Cam took a canteen from beside the sink and drank from it while his mouth was still full. Guy's mouth fell open when Cam swirled a mouthful and spat the half-chewed mixture into the sink basin. Cam then flung the remaining candy bar blindly behind him, letting it skid across the floor as he rinsed his mouth out again, spitting water over and over until it ran clear. He balanced on his good leg, damaged ankle hung in the air.

Guy gathered the shattered chocolate with scrunched paper napkins and noticed glistening come and lube trailing down Cam's thigh, but still Cam didn't react. His eyes were squeezed shut in a grimace as he lay his chin on the cold sink rim.

"Disgusting," he mumbled.

Shit. Guy shuddered harder, breaking his shivering. *It's some sort of abuse conditioning.* He wiped Cam with more napkins and threw them all into the bin of burnable scraps.

Straightening, he turned Cam around and hooked his chin over the top of Cam's head. "*You* taste good."

"So stay." Cam's words were stickily sweet against Guy's chest. His voice shook like his body, but Guy's heart swelled, blood roaring in his ears.

"Stay?"

He almost missed the near silent "Like you have been."

Guy drew back. He bunched Cam's hair in his fist as his eyes fell to graze Cam's *No* tattoo.

Fatigued eyes flitted their gaze between Guy's, unused to focusing without glasses at this range. "You can go back to bed. I'm going to write for a while."

"Wrong." Grabbing a hair comb from the bench, and placing it between his teeth, he hefted Cam over his shoulder. He tasted Cam on the comb as he dropped him onto the mattresses, bouncing him clear off them a couple of inches as he landed heavily beside Cam.

It wasn't the laugh he craved, but Cam's giggle was enough to warm Guy before he pulled the blanket over them. Guy combed Cam's tangles gently, then massaged his hips.

"Do I look like I need maintenance?" Cam grumbled, showing a crack in his restraint by allowing a complaint to slip through. He scratched at his neck where the blanket touched it, and pulled it over his head to rid himself of its weight.

Guy didn't follow until he'd rewrapped the bandage around Cam's ankle and restored his socks. "Cameron."

Sealed close in the pitch-dark narrow corridor of blanket, Guy couldn't feel or hear Cam breathing. Perhaps he was holding his breath, awaiting an order.

"Thank you," Guy said.

At the magic word, Cam unlocked, melting beneath Guy's hands. His heartbeat soon slowed and his breathing evened, until Guy wasn't sure if he'd grown entranced again.

"Cameron," he said softly, squeezing Cam's shoulder...and drew back the blanket in surprise upon hearing the lightest of snores. Rising moonlight revealed Cam was indeed asleep before Guy, but not so deeply he didn't respond to another squeeze by nuzzling forward, his damp lips sweeping Guy's chest, beckoning him to sleep too, to join Cam in the sanctuary of their shared embrace.

Chapter Sixteen

"I HAVE TO tell you something."

"Is it important?"

"Yes," Guy said.

"Can it wait?" Cam reached up to peel off Guy's goggles and hat where he stood shivering in the doorway.

"Yes." *No. Yes.* Judging by his bird's nest hair and the tang of his breath, Cam had slept again, despite the music from his laptop speakers, imbuing the hut with a soft pulse. Its reverberations buzzed through Guy's boots before Cam had turned down the volume moments before opening the door. He'd greeted Guy without the makeshift crutch, a long birch tree branch, he'd had Guy liberate from an overhanging rafter at 5:15 a.m. when Guy had insisted he stay at the hut, if not in bed.

"You're so cold," Cam purred through a slew of kisses before a wide yawn had him weakly pull away.

"Should I get your glasses from the counter?" Guy asked, taking off his coat.

Cam buried his face in Guy's sweater and shook his head. "Don't need them if you stay this close."

"Then let's burn them." Guy scratched the scruff of Cam's neck and felt him hum contentedly. "I don't care how good you look in them. You look good all the time. No more boundaries."

"Just nonsensical hyperbole," Cam replied.

Hopefully. Cam's flash of paranoia the night before had preyed on Guy all morning, but he had no idea how to broach the subject since Cam really did seem fine and, as ever, honest, which contradicted what Guy knew about coping mechanisms.

"You can tell me anything. You can't scare me off."

"I can scare myself off," Cam muttered.

"Cameron, you know how you were...switched on last night?"

A pause broke with a sigh. "Yeah."

"You were worried about someone—me—hurting you. Coming to kill you, is what you said."

"Sorry about that. Forget about it."

"I can't just forget things," Guy said. "Was it, like, a flashback? Because I've been wondering, have you ever switched on in a bad situation?" With his father?

Cam chewed the inside of his cheek. "I don't know. Seems like the kind of thing I'd have tried ten years ago. Not tried twice. Oh, but let's do what *we* did again." He perked up. "That was great, and I'm fine."

"You know, with your ankle, you should come home with me." Guy changed the subject, hating that he wanted to make it a command Cam couldn't refuse.

"Ha! You should stay and see my rabbit." After collecting his glasses from the log coffee table, Cam followed Guy to the kitchen.

"You can publish under your own name now," Guy said. "You don't need to find a rabbit to name it after your mom."

"And you don't have to stay."

Guy caressed Cam's cheek, easing the frown that marred his forehead. "I might."

Cam lifted his own hand and clutched Guy's loose fingers.

"But you haven't heard what I've got to say yet." *Talk. Tell him about yourself.* "You might not want me to."

"Ha." Cam raised Guy's fingers to his mouth and nibbled the tip of his forefinger. He moved onto Guy's third finger and did the same, sucking past his second knuckle, pupils blown so wide he couldn't be held responsible for biting. Guy closed his eyes as Cam moved to his fourth finger, rolling his tongue against it as Guy stroked his face with his thumb.

Cam bit down upon the base of his finger hard enough for Guy to open his eyes and see Cam's teeth were bared as he twisted Guy's hand around, cutting an impression of a circle. A ring.

Guy's heart didn't skip a beat; it stopped altogether. He pulled his hand from Cam's and stared at him, reeling as he slipped it into the short hair at Cam's nape and cupped his thin neck.

"Why do you want to get married so badly?" *To his sister and now me?*

"Be married to you, not *get* married. Why don't you?"

"We don't know each other that well yet..."

Cam laughed. "True, but we're each other's best hope for finding the other out."

"Cameron, look. I know you have a lot to tell me to scrape the surface of what you *do* recall. And—" He swallowed hard. "—I need to tell you."

Cam vanished from beneath Guy's hands, appearing to apparate by the front door in the space of a blink. Guy opened his mouth, but Cam raised a hand without looking at him, signaling just as he did on the trap circuit. *Stop. Silence.* His other hand hovered over the rifle propped against the locker. Outside, the porch floorboards creaked and an impatient knock rapped the door.

At least his ankle's better. Guy was shaken by Cam's sensitivity bordering on precognition. He hadn't heard a thing.

After a glance out the frosted window, Cam's white knuckles relaxed. He released the toolbox and opened the door through which a short woman bustled. Though he shivered at the blast of cold air, he was now no tenser than Guy had seen him around people in the bar in town when they'd gone to get supplies. As then, Guy could tell Cam's guard was up, but he seemed as wary of himself as of the stranger.

Did I set him off like this? Guy tried to remember meeting Cam. He'd been too frozen to focus but superficially on Cam's beauty.

"Cameron Campbell! You're damn near impossible to find. This place is nearly an hour's walk from vehicle access." No sympathy from either of them met the woman's complaint. She carried only a small backpack and was sensibly dressed for the subarctic.

"You're not a journalist," Cam said blankly. He walked to the kitchen and poured coffee for three, the water having coincidentally boiled. The woman didn't remove her coat and paid the price, flushing deeply, but Cam said nothing and left it to her to work out she needed to remove it. After she had, he pressed a steaming mug into her frozen gloves for warmth, bidding her to sit on the couch. He sat beside her on its armrest.

"I'm from Ames." The woman peeled off her gloves and stuffed them in her jacket pocket. "I've been trying to call for two days. Nice to meet you in person at last."

"Claire, right? And sorry. Reception comes and goes here." Cam shook her hand, ignoring Guy's small huff at the lie to which he, too, had been subjected before arriving.

So Cam *did* have a book under submission with Ames, despite the company's nixing the suggestion to Huw. Guy hadn't thought he'd doubted Cam about that anymore, so the mixture of relief and renewed distrust in himself formed a lump in his throat. Ames had contributed to Cam's suffering as a kid. It wasn't like they would have known about De Carli, but still, Cameron was clearly on edge, kneading his fingers together the way Guy kneaded his own warm mug, his cold-roughened palms by now inured to its surface burn.

"Do...you want me to talk now?" Claire shrewdly side-eyed Guy. "Who's this?"

"Guy Sutton, my research assistant at the moment and an editor with Fairbanks."

"Never heard of him," Claire sniffed, turning her back on Guy.

Guy's eyebrows shot up. "Hello."

"Hello," Cam repeated belatedly. "You do know of Fairbanks, though, right?"

"Yes," she admitted.

"I'm only here volunteering," Guy lied.

"Good!" she said with genuine sincerity. "I was worried about you all alone out here, Cameron!"

"I'm fine." The furrow between Cam's brows deepened, but his eyes remained wide as he appeared to concentrate, summing her up. "But thanks."

"Anyway, I'm obviously here about *Close to Home*. You never replied to my messages after saying you wanted to pull it."

"I said to cancel the submission," Cam corrected. "That one email had everything legally necessary for that to occur with no problems."

She hefted her small backpack onto the log coffee table, displacing several books onto which shards of ice—quickly melting to water—fell from the pack she opened to remove a plastic binder.

"Oh, sorry," she said as Guy and Cam both leaned forward to rescue the books. "This is the marketing package I've put together."

Cam drew back, his mouth tight. It pained Guy to step back rather than clasp a hand on his shoulder, but Cam hadn't glanced his way once since Claire had arrived, so he wasn't sure how to convey his support.

"I know, I know. It says Cameron Campbell. But there's really no point bothering with a pen name when your real name and your dad's is going to come out sometime. It's too good to fly under the radar." The smile she flashed flickered on seeing Cam frown. "Of course, that's after the first push to get it noticed. Think, Cam, how else are we going to sell it? It's so different from your dad, and from anything out there right now or coming out, that I know of."

Don't call him Cam, Guy growled internally at Claire. He was struck with surprise when she reacted to him at last, blanching after catching his anger in the corner of her eye. He...*showed* his anger?

She quickly recovered, tugging another set of papers from her bag. "Just sign this, and you'll get the advance you need."

"I revoked the submission!" Cam argued. "As soon as I sent it in!"

"I know, it's been a while, hasn't it? So I think you should resubmit it. Resend me your latest draft. And Ames will make a schedule to release it alongside the other one." Claire eagerly leaned in.

"What are you talking about?" Cam reluctantly took the bait.

"Look, I understand. It even explains why you're out here, living rent-free, according to the girl I got gas from earlier. You have money problems. You sent me the other draft, so I know you're still interested in Ames, and *we* are very interested in you, Cam." She kept her eyes trained on Cam, avoiding Guy altogether while maintaining the sort of false confidence befitting her clumsy stab at developing trust, yet all she'd have seen if she'd glanced at him was a mirror of the confusion painting Cam pale.

"What are you talking about?" he repeated.

"The one you sent by USB because the net crashes all the time out here, right? The cover letter was your pen name, even the envelope showed you sent it—but listing your New York address, because this here doesn't count, does it? No mailman," Claire chuckled.

"*What* book?" Guy asked.

She turned as regally as four layers of sweaters allowed and curtly addressed him. "*The Heart of Salt*. A cross-country—well, cross-realm road-trip fantasy, about a wizard and page escaping a political marriage..."

Cam's complexion turned from already pale to stark white, illuminating for the first time a constellation of nude freckles Guy had never noticed. It wasn't the book he'd sent Fairbanks, but Cam recognized it. "That's not even finished. It's abandoned."

Claire cast an eye over him and nodded to herself. "Yeah, I knew it. Be honest, Cam, that was your dad's, right? With your pen name, but it was his. I mean, it's totally unlike *Close to Home*. Your writing style's inimitable." She sought to reassure him of his talent. "It's even unlike your dad's last book, and the doc hadn't been modified in five years. But I'm not mad, not at all, quite the opposite. We can keep it between us—" Her steely gaze flicked an unspoken warning to Guy. "—but you know we can't publish *The Heart of Salt* until it's locked in as belonging to you after probate's settled. Which I'd already told Serena to hurry up before you even sent it."

Cam's voice shrank as much as his body folded into itself upon sliding from the arm of the couch into its mess of blankets, unwittingly encouraging Claire by moving closer. The contract documents he held slipped from his loosened grip, scattering on the floor.

"What?"

"A month ago."

When Huw received the injunction.

Claire continued, "I figured worrying about that was stalling your progress on *Close to Home*, like signing it, and I wasn't—I'm still not letting that go without a fight. So I asked her where you were at with your dad's estate, since I couldn't get a hold of you, and because you need to move on with your new career as Cameron Stewart."

"You told her my pen name." Cam lost his gaze in the flickering fire. Guy pressed a water bottle into Cam's hand, and he blinked at it a couple of times before sipping from it.

"She said you already stepped aside regarding all liquid assets after you discharged yourself from Bellevue."

"Manhattan," Guy snapped, the strain in Cam's voice reverberating in his spinning head. "Not Bellevue."

"Yeah," Cam murmured, shooting a wary glance Guy's way at the revelation he knew about Cam's hospitalization.

"Well, not challenging is mad." Claire seemed to notice her undiplomatic slipup, pressing her lips together, but blustered on. "You're entitled to a fair share of his bank accounts *and* property, and everything else. I think you should get a lawyer. It's what your dad would have wanted—he was one, after all. But what Serena did confirm was you never excluded yourself from ownership of his past works."

Does she know they're Cam's, anyway? It wasn't the first time he'd wondered, but Guy's curiosity turned urgent at the sight of Cam hooding his eyes. *Hold up.* He'd thought Cam and Serena had a good relationship.

"Which is why, I gather, you sent me that new-old manuscript of his last week. Turns out it was quicker to take two days just to get here than it was waiting for you to pick up your phone, so I'm glad I came because

I'm thinking of you! I want you to get on with your life, too." She leaned awkwardly to collect the contracts Cam had dropped, bundled them together, and clicked the ballpoint she retrieved from her backpack's side pocket before handing it to Cam. "So now you can sign properly to get your advance for *Close to Home*, and this one, too"—she nodded to the contract beneath the top one—"promising *A Heart of Salt* to us. We know how to best manage De Carlis, after all. I agree with you that it's what your dad would have wanted."

She'd employed typical negotiation tactics and flattery, burying the one item she was truly desperate to secure amid the *Close to Home* paperwork. Guy glowered, aware the "De Carli" book, even unfinished and "posthumous," represented a six-figure boon to Ames. It was a complete game-changer in how they'd push forth with Cam's *own* book.

Cam stared at the pen in his hand. He clicked it, hiding its ballpoint, and raised his chin, adopting a cold, corporate tone.

"I am sorry for sending you *A Heart of Salt* prematurely. It was very irresponsible of me. Please consider it revoked as well as *Close to Home*, which remains revoked."

"Ah, no. It's fine, Cam. You don't have to do that," Claire blurted, her pitch climbing.

"And I'm sorry about your computer virus," Cam said.

Her panic stayed, she cocked her head. "What virus?"

Handing her back the documents he still hadn't looked at, Cam stood. "Can you excuse us for a second?"

"I don't think you should talk it over with Fairbanks..." Claire buried her suspicion under a ruefully cheerful "Take your time!" considering Cam grabbed Guy's wrist and dragged him up the hall, into their bedroom.

The closed door wouldn't do much to block out sound if Claire wanted to listen to their conversation, but Guy heard her immediately start speaking on her phone.

"A USB," Cam muttered, dropping Guy's arm to pace in the small space. "And she just opened what was on it. Jesus Christ. And Huw told you I went to the hospital?" He turned to face Guy.

"Yes." That was the only reason Guy had agreed to hiding the purpose of coming to Nunavut in the first place.

"I'm fine now." Wringing his hands, Cam contrarily sought to reassure Guy. "And I'm not cheating on Fairbanks. You guys can take everything. I've spent the past month vetting you personally."

So have I.

"If you even want my stuff. *A Heart of Salt*'s not worth mentioning, and *Close to Home* was just vomit. I meant to bury at a boutique press who'd shove it out quickly so I could get some cash and move on...and I meant to send *Distant* to Ames because I know what they like, but I was nervous and drunk and I fucked up...but then Fairbanks bought *Distant* and gave me more money than I expected. I wrote my father's old editor at Ames to delete that mistake submission, but he'd retired and Claire doesn't understand the word no." Cam's hand flew to his chest, scratching the site of his tattoo beneath his woolen sweater, but flew out to keep Guy at bay when Guy stepped forward. Guy moved back again, shuffling out of the path of the doorway in case Cam felt the urge to leave.

"Cornell has my real name, so Serena would have known where I am. She never came."

She couldn't have simply been trying to protect her father's reputation. "She wants to keep exploiting you?" Guy asked.

"Ha!" Cam's usual laugh was soaked with bitterness. "She doesn't want me to publish fiction at *all,* in case I ever...and she must know what I sent Ames doesn't really count. But knowing my pen name, too, she would have called every midsize-plus publisher in the country to find out what else I was selling. But she still never came." He stopped pacing before Guy to clench his fingers in the fabric of Guy's knitted shirt, face contorted. Did he want Serena to come or not?

"Cameron." Guy cleared his throat, wishing he could clear his conscience as easily. His throat too stuck with a lump. "Fairbanks got an injunction before I came. Saying you plagiarized *Distant*."

"*What?*"

"That's why I came here." He couldn't hold a poker face at all anymore, he realized. Yet being expressive meant zilch as long as he perpetuated the lie clouding the air worse than the smoke permanently strung among the bedroom rafters, having seeped throughout the house for months. "I don't work for Fairbanks, exactly."

He closed his fingers around Cam's trembling hands, prizing them from his chest, then let go to alleviate the pressure visibly crushing Cam like he was an empty can.

A waver permeated Cam's voice, though not his stare, which still held a beacon of hope. "You're a contractor?"

I'd better not do this when it really happens. I'll tell him in better circumstances. It was like he was watching himself from afar, appalled, but charging ahead regardless. Was this what it was like for Cam when he dissociated? Which he only did because he'd been used so badly, deceived by people he should have been able to trust after giving them all he had.

"No. I'm not an editor. I'm a writer, a researcher. I want to help you… I'm a psychologist. Registered, not practicing. Huw sent me to evaluate you and your writing, and you don't get more thorough than a month-long, round-the-clock doctor's evaluation."

A dozen emotions sieved through Cam, in the twitching in his fingers as he slowly unfurled his fists, and the fierce focus trained on Guy's eyes, until a sorrowful smile ghosted across Cam's face like a shadow of a cloud and nothing replaced it.

Cam's low monotone matched his blank expression. "I…know. I know what month-long evaluations are. I've cheated one of them before. Did I p-pass this one, too?"

"*Yes.* You didn't steal a thing, right?" Guy knew Cam hadn't, so why was he asking?

Because he wasn't talking to any Cameron Campbell he'd met to date. The Cam that felt in overreactions was at one end of the spectrum Guy knew existed. Rambling Cam occupied the middle of the scale, and mornings' dead-eyed Cam sat at the lower end of a diurnal seesaw. *This* Cam was light-years away from all of them. He was a shell who slipped past Guy and out the door so silently it was as if he'd floated away on a draft.

Chapter Seventeen

Already in the hut's doorway, Claire hung up her phone and slipped it into her coat pocket. "Oh, good, you've changed your mind. I told you Fairbanks was too small. But my driver's waiting by the, er, *highway*, so if you could just sign..." She stepped aside as Cam took his coat from the hook behind her. "Oh, you're coming with me?"

Cam's dislocated laugh cut Guy deep. *He couldn't join anyone even if he wanted to.* Cam was forcibly alone. He was the only being in his existence, and he was far away on a different plane. Shrugging into his coat, he slung a scarf around his neck while placing the last of the kitchen's fruit stocks—a red apple—into a bag, then shoving it and two water bottles into his pack.

"Ames," Cam said poisonously casually, no longer on name terms with Claire. "I never signed a single thing with you. Not myself. And I never will."

"Think of the money, Cam," Claire urged.

"You know what? I really don't like your company. Nothing professional." He dismissed Claire's gape, turning to Guy. "Fairbanks is off, too, rescinded on your side. *Arrivederci.* I'll go sell my future books in Europe." Cam took a deep breath and released it, mechanically emptying his lungs, then hefted on his pack. His sinuous frame shook beneath it, but his arms were loose and fluid as a practiced waiter at whipping up his toolbox. His eyes held no such control when he turned to Guy, expression blank. "Fairbanks had its reasons. There's nothing to forgive."

"Don't," Guy begged.

Cam tugged open the door and didn't close it behind him. Claire and Guy followed him off the porch, into the snow.

"Cameron!" Guy shouted, already struggling to breathe in the cold, wading in unlaced boots through snow, which spilled down his shins and burned like acid. Perhaps if he made it a command— "Cameron, *stop*," he yelled with all the fortitude he could muster, drowning out the desperation in his voice Cam would probably catch, anyway. Cam knew him better than he knew himself. *No, he doesn't, and that's your fault.*

Airy Cam waded through the snow at only ankle-deep, his white coat blurred against the trees, more an apparition than ever. Guy was horrified to see him limping on his injured ankle, but when his vacant eyes focused at last, trained entirely on Guy, they petrified the blood in Guy's veins and all manner of thought flashing through his skull.

Cam appeared as an angel again, like the first time they'd met, only now he was a *real* angel—absolutely terrifying. He looked like danger incarnate, poised to launch himself and maul Guy limb from limb. Guy's body seized, paralyzed with fear, before Cam told him what he already knew he ought to do.

"Run," the wraith commanded.

No. No more fairy-tale bullshit. He's not a monster, he's not on a pedestal, he's flawed Cam. Who, even in his state, understood Guy had to return to the hut or suffer hypothermia in minutes. Yet the instinct to obey overruled Guy's rationalization, and he shook so hard he struggled to stand up straight.

"Cameron, I swear I've been honest with you. About e-everything else," he chattered.

Cam appeared to flicker in and out of otherworldliness, furrowing his brow as if he was trying to believe or even hear Guy, but was confounded by the task. "Me, too. It's my fault for assuming too much."

"Remember I'm sorry."

Cam spun on his heel and kept walking.

"Don't just not think about me because it hurts. *Cameron,*" Guy croaked.

Agile as a flurry despite his limp, Cam vanished into the sparse woods.

"This isn't over." Claire hung on Guy's shaking arm, panting after jogging to catch up, clouds of her breath obscuring her glare but not her scorn. "Do you have any idea how much a lost De Carli is worth? And you couldn't manage to charm it away from him even after staying here, though I can guess how you tried!"

"He d-does this, but he'll be back," Guy chattered.

"Plus there's his own writing. You haven't read whatever he sent Fairbanks, have you? If you had, you would've run faster, either at him or away. *Close to Home* is a fucking masterpiece." She fumbled the phone from her pocket and held it before her chin as she tugged at her scarf. "I don't know. Campbell's *in bed* with another company," she yelled into it, stamping her earlier footprints to dust as she stalked down the trail to the road.

A frost migraine turned the porch floorboards beneath Guy's boots to glue, and the sight of the living room to splinters as if being seen from outside through the iced windows. Everything was too loud—the popping embers in the hearth, the sloshing kettle in his shaking hands, blood rushing in his ears—stopping him from hearing Cam coming back. He fell back onto the couch. When his tears abated a while later, the stacks of books blocking the firelight rose above him like skyscrapers back home, protecting shaded streets from the setting sun's glare.

When he came to his senses, he downed a bottle of water before setting out, armored with enough heavy clothing to search for Cam until darkness fell. He followed small boot prints for miles, Cam's crumbs of churned snow, until encountering a shallow bank which had slid off an overhanging granite crag, erasing Cam's path. Cam was alone in the mountain range, injured, without a gun.

PERHAPS HE WOULDN'T return until the hut appeared empty from afar, Guy thought, painfully aware he wouldn't last long inside it without smoke issuing from its chimney. Huw called, wanting to speak to Cam, as Guy was shoving recovery planks, found in the back of Cam's truck, underneath its wheels to let the car crawl out of its bogging snow. He refused to believe Guy had thrown Cam's phone into the fire two days earlier in a fit of passion.

"I'd be more likely to believe you killed him to plagiarize his book, and now you're burying his body," Huw joked over Guy's grunts as he finished digging and clambered into the truck's cab.

The helm rattled like thunder beneath his gloves, far from its purr at Cam's ministrations. Guy had never driven in these conditions—*No one should. No one should even be a passenger.* He'd weighed the risk of Cam returning and needing the truck immediately to get medical treatment with Cam's own assertion he was safe enough with the satellite phone in his toolbox, which could summon a chopper on a clear day if the worst came to pass. It was indeed a clear day. The most sensible thing Guy could do to ensure Cam's safety was get him more food. The hut's cupboards were nearly bare, and though he'd walked the trap circuit earlier and seen every trap closed and folded, all of them tied in bundles with neon ribbon for collection later, Guy refused to believe Cam's survey was over. Surely, Cam would return and keep searching for his rabbit as before.

He believed it a little more as powder snow began to fall on the truck's windshield. Since these could well be his last words, he made a full confession to Huw, telling him everything. Huw was understandably tense about Guy having lost Cam, literally as well as his novel, but also worried enough about Guy to try to reassure him all would work out.

"You don't know Cam well enough to make that judgment," Guy said.

"But I know you," Huw replied. "Think of something."

With hands gripping the wheel and eyes peeled for moose, Guy ruminated all the way to town. From what he'd pieced together in the last month and online the night before, Serena was in New York, off social media, and a mundane corporate solicitor who occupied their childhood home. She must have known Cam was their father's golden goose, but did Cam know she knew? If Guy had the timeline right, Cam had proposed to her just before De Carli died and Cam went on suicide watch at a hospital for a month. Had De Carli heard about the proposal? From whom, and why? Who had committed Cam?

The injunction had failed to rein him in and bring him home, but then, that didn't seem to be the object if she didn't want Cam publishing anything under his new pen name. Guy remembered all the pockmark scars covering Cam's back. Did they routinely drug him to make him write? Tranquilize him to subdue him? His delicate form was aesthetically perfect to Guy and didn't seem to bother Cam, but was his growth stunted by years of abuse and neglect? Was he often in pain but suppressed it, as with his ankle? And the damage to his foot, missing a toe. Guy was furious at himself for not pressing Cam about it. He wanted to know every gory detail. Only now he had no right to ask.

Of course, he'd had no right to before. But Cam hadn't known that.

Caitlyn, the taciturn general store's clerk, thankfully remembered Guy—or his attitude.

"Oh! Volunteer!" she greeted him. "Flying solo today, eh? Joey said Brendan just messaged him. He picked Cameron up on the road way north of you guys' hut. Did you have a fight or something?"

Thank Christ. The ranger, of all people, would certainly carry a gun. "He's okay?" Guy asked.

Her gloating eased, with a flash of confusion at seeing Guy's frown. "Yeah, they would have said if he was weird. Don't think too hard about it. Cabin fever gets to everyone. You can settle over beer when he gets here." Suddenly she was welcoming, helping him find the food and gear he needed, and cheerier still when Guy paid with a credit card, not wanting to bill Cam's tab. She lifted Cameron's wicker post box onto the counter, burbling, "Here's your mail! I opened the *Vogue.* Cameron always lets me."

Besides the magazine, the box held a letter from Cam's former college, a package from Huw, and one unregistered letter envelope containing no letter, from the feel of it. Instead, it held a small, rectangular object, unmistakably a USB, delivering to Cam files free of any ISP tracking. The envelope was addressed *To the Cornell researcher's cabin,* its sender *Cameron Campbell,* with Serena's address, all written in neat handwriting distinct from Cam's illegible scrawl. Guy took only that from the box, stuffing it safely into his jacket's inner pocket.

"So he isn't that writer's son," Caitlyn had decided. "He must just know him." He still went by Cameron Stewart in town, Guy remembered.

"Hey, do me a favor and I'll get you your own *Vogue* subscription when Cam leaves town," Guy promised, collecting up his bags of food.

"He'll be here forever," she retorted. "There is no rabbit."

"Tell Brendan and...Joey, was it? To keep Cam close for a few days." Until Guy knew what was going on, Cam would be safer surrounded by a lot of people.

"How close?" Caitlyn teased, until confusion returned to her face on seeing Guy's fall. "That'll happen, anyway. There's meant to be heavy snow coming in. It'll probably block the road to your cabin by the time Brendan gets back here." Checking her phone, she said, "I think they're planning dinner and darts. The food will freeze if you put it in the car while you're having a drink, waiting for them, so you can just leave it behind the counter if you want."

"Thanks, but I'm going home." Guy absently bid her a farewell, heading out the store's front door to Cam's truck.

HAMLET WOULD HAVE more easily made a decision as to whether to dig into the USB, and Guy was well aware he himself was no prince. He didn't allow for a second that the USB was addressed to the hut, not Cam specifically, so legally he could open it. He tried to believe that after his betrayal, he'd be so worthless in Cam's estimation that Cam wouldn't care what he uncovered. The memory of his empty eyes haunted Guy, leaving him cold no matter how close he sat to the fire, blistering his back with chilblains while shielding its heat from the heavy laptop he'd retrieved from a cupboard. If Cam had been right about Claire's USB hosting a virus, it only made sense to insert it into a computer that had been discarded by a hiker.

In the end, what won out was the fact—not just Guy's desire—that Cam needed to be protected. Guy's self-loathing was moot; someone needed to know the real reason behind Cam's fear, and by Cam's own reckoning and willful denial, he probably couldn't defend himself alone. Under a cloak of dusk light that turned bloody the hut's usual fireside rose-gold aura, Guy inserted the USB.

It contained a text file titled *You forgot a lot*, and a video file *Let me remind you*. Guy sucked in a stilted breath, clicked open the document, and saw *Close to Home* set out as a submission for publication.

Far from Cam's usual florid style, either when writing as De Carli or on *Distant*, this story's language was brutally concise, and the setting contemporary. As always, however, Cam's prose both stood alone and elevated him. It told of three siblings exacting revenge on their sadistic babysitter in such stark scenes, littered with disorienting details, that it reminded Guy at once of case files he'd researched years before when he'd still had the stomach for criminal psychology, because the violence it depicted was unprintable as fiction.

The kids' murder plan was cold and surgically precise, and kick-started the book with a controlled bang made sicker once it was contrasted with the increasingly chaotic way they mutilated her corpse, imitating what she'd allegedly done to each of them. Perpetrating violence corrupted the kids' psyches further, whirling them into a devilish dervish of escalating violence incorporating one another, until the last remaining survivor—the numbest, arguably most broken but resilient kid—was left alone, feigning amnesia, if indeed he'd had any siblings or a babysitter to begin with. If Guy hadn't read it as autobiographical, he'd never have sympathized with the character, and recognized that casting that kid as an unreliable narrator was the only way to make the book salable. Most significantly, the text stressed the kid was an unreliable witness because he chose to be, thereby compromising his own morals, being selfish to survive. That there was no justice in the book, or the world, was its message.

The moment Guy read the kids repainting an already red wall with the blood of their exsanguinated victim, he considered the book a vivid personal fantasy of Cam's, because Guy knew De Carli had died straightforwardly of a heart attack...hadn't he? Had De Carli's body been untouched? Or had Cam and Serena both...

The dying of the sun made the flickering light from behind more apparent, though Guy shivered as if the fire had died. He poked another log into the hearth, stalling, until his clammy fingers found the laptop's trackpad behind him and set the video on the USB to play.

Chapter Eighteen

A HALOGEN GLOBE drenched the center of a large room with stark light, casting deep shadows in the grooves of Cam's rib cage. He looked thirteen, but could have been eighteen. Loose jeans hung from his hips as if the camera subtracted ten pounds, and he put his hands in his pockets to pull them up as he rocked absently on his bare feet. He looked like he hadn't slept or eaten in days.

The room was so barren its purpose was unclear until the camera zoomed in and out of focus for a moment and offering the view of a single pipe-metal bed pressed to the wall in a far corner. Scattered around the room's periphery was an old laptop as chunky as the one now playing the video. It sat on a chair between two bookcases, every inch of their space crammed and overflowing with books. Stacks of books scaled the peeling wallpaper. An antique tallboy perched over a single pair of worn trainers, unfashionable lace-up high-tops as high as they were long to fit Cam's small feet.

My son is a simple boy. He wants for nothing," De Carli had said.

I like clutter. It feels like a home, Cam had told Guy. And, *I didn't know there was more to want.* Guy's unblinking eyes stung, and he gripped the sides of his tablet screen so hard the border's pixels blurred as he noticed the walls of the room were painted burnt orangey-pink.

A short girl-next-door-type teenager strode into frame, wearing fitted jeans and a T-shirt. Serena. Her hair, in a loose ponytail, was as long as Cam's was when Guy had met him, though onscreen Cam's was shorter than after he'd cut it and idiosyncratically ragged. Otherwise, the siblings bore an uncanny resemblance to each other in body and face shape and size. Their mannerisms were also similar, but while Serena's half smile appeared eerily familiar to Guy, hers was malevolent.

Immediately, Cam kneeled. The steadiness of his actions—no timidity—along with the sparse furnishings and bare light made the scene look staged. The fact he'd moved fluidly meant he wasn't disassociated like Guy had seen him in the mornings, but he was detached, and seemed to read his sister like one of his hundreds of spine-damaged books, reacting to her requests before she spoke, before she knew them herself. Guy established she bored him. She was chilling, but transparent. One-dimensional. Her smile spat vapid giggles Guy imagined were shrill while she wrapped a studded belt around Cam's throat. Guy couldn't hear the mechanical gasps that billowed Cam's frail ribs, but faithfully imagined their desperate wheeze.

You can't consent to grievous bodily harm, the lawyer's son, another lawyer's brother, had told Guy.

I know, I'm not stupid, he'd also said when Guy told him abuse wasn't his fault. But did he really think that?

Have you ever self-harmed? Guy had asked when he'd first seen Cam's tiny scars. Cam had said no.

Cam's eyes often betrayed flashes of presence, causing rippling shifts in power as Cam played tug of war with his mind, debating whether to fight back. But then he turned back into a lost kid again, nothing but skin on ribs, bloodshot eyes unseeing.

He waited for her to finish strangling him with the belt, its spikes facing his skin, breathing in and out in snatched opportunities he granted himself, distinct from when she relaxed the binding. Endurance was all he had control over out there in his self-imposed space, and he managed it expertly, deliberately removing himself from Serena.

But his young body, dripping in blood from the neck down, was undeniably vulnerable. His shoulders, bony as wings, steeled as though he knew what was coming. Guy recalled with horror the precise surgical scars peppering his skin, Cam's unease at bondage on the porch, and his pulse spiked while the pause dragged on. Still, he was unprepared.

A spoon and plate were placed before him on the floor, bearing a lump of cake covered in chunky pink frosting. Cam's mouth fell open—he must have needed water, or sugar to alleviate the shock of his bleeding, but still he hesitated, spoon poised above the cake before plunging it down. He stabbed awkwardly, pressing hard until it seemed to burst, spilling rice—

Hundreds of maggots writhed on the porcelain and spoon Cam brought to his mouth to listlessly chomp, but worse—the "cake" itself jerked. Guy glimpsed gray feathers as a section of it flung out, flapping, the bird flopping over the side of the plate onto the floor where its wings twitched in a heap. Instead of red blood, black-and-green ooze spilled from its disemboweled torso.

How the *hell* had she kept a body that degraded still alive? *Cam would know. Cam could somehow*, Guy realized, having read his book about the babysitter, knowing his interest in biology. He was clever enough to, and so too was Serena, probably, if her depiction as the babysitter in the book had been accurate. De Carli might not have abused Cam beyond stealing his books. Serena might have done it all. But there was nothing in Cam's book about forced feeding, nor a bird...nor a camera.

Serena shook a pointed finger at Cam, a pastiche of chastisement. She stalked to the camera, retrieved from behind its view a...shotgun, spun it into her hand like a baton, and silently blew a hole in the plaster wall behind Cam's head. He didn't blink, but blood poured from his ear down his neck, dripping from his sunken collarbone onto his prominent ribs. His eardrum had burst.

A storm of emotions danced on Serena's face—*Just like Cam, when he's okay. Like Cam described me*—but her enjoyment clearly held while she reloaded the gun, poking the bird with her toe. It jerked and she jumped, blasting it, but in her haste she clipped Cam's foot, leaving his little toe hanging by a thread of skin. Flesh, frosting, and goo sprayed the splintered floor.

He, too, jolted with shock, a mouthful of bile splashing from him as his stomach heaved out of rhythm with sudden hyperventilating. An ominous premonition threatened to crystallize, and before he could conjure up the words to make form of it, Guy begged aloud of his brain and the old scene playing out in real time.

"No, don't."

Cam disappeared into himself. His eyes turned to hollow abysses, resistant to plundering, as Serena stripped his shrunken, outgrown jeans from him.

"Don't, Cam," Guy pleaded, but Cam was farther away than simply stranded in the past. He was imprisoned inside his head as well as in that room.

Guy had read the books Cam had written, the coded messages in bottles that were never answered. He'd liked them. He'd discussed them with friends, raved about them with lovers, looked forward to collecting each one. His fingers smeared the screen as he touched them to Cam's back as it writhed into a greater haunch. His young, hairless chest beat visibly, bare where a tattoo now scarred him with the strongest word Cam knew, the one he'd adopted as his talisman at ten years old.

"*No*," Guy yelled. He didn't know if it was due to Cam the neat freak's anger over the ruined floorboards, the disintegrated bird, or because his body became asymmetrical—none of those things could be cleaned by the worn broom standing sentry by the window—but it was as if the silent film grew more silent. Cam hadn't flinched, but he'd snapped and it was clear that if he launched himself at Serena, they'd both die.

He'd never appeared more scarily alike his sister than right now, but she became nothing compared to him, a mad bug next to a towering beast, and Guy held his breath, despite knowing Serena was still alive. The reality playing out onscreen was so warped by the monster that was Cam that Guy half expected him to demolish her. He chose not to, instead exhaling and disappearing back into himself.

Relieved, Guy exhaled raggedly too, and his hand flew to his clanging chest where, on Cam, a tattoo reigned.

Cam requested something and waited still as a statue until a minute later a pair of scissors were pelted at him, missing his eye by pure luck and splitting the skin on his cheekbone. He sawed their blunt blades through the remaining tendon connecting his toe to his foot, face glassy as a doll's whose red lips cracked open to say a silent, "Thank—"

Serena silenced him with a kiss, then spat on his wounded foot the aftertaste of vomit she'd taken from him, cauterizing it with acid. He winced as he hobbled, led by her to the small bed—he was feeling pain again as she lay him on his stomach and set an alarm clock on the bedside table...next to a bar of chocolate. His dead eyes closed, blood weeping from his foot onto the pristine sheets. *Sleeping beauty*, Guy thought for a second before Serena produced a handful of syringes—and the film cut to a newer scene on the same stage.

The light was brighter in this one, another overflowing bookcase added to the far wall, including textbooks and first-edition De Carli spines, which Guy recognized. Cam was in the center of the room again, hunched in a crouch on the floor, hands on his knees, covered in blood and bruises. His eyes were so blackened they looked like sockets in a skull. Guy couldn't tell if they were open, let alone if Cam was mentally present or not. He hoped not.

His lips were blackened by a bruise on one side, their flesh white on the other, but appeared to have been scribbled across in pen... No, his paled mouth was sewn shut with black string, so tiny dots of red lined his lips. Snow White again.

No. It wasn't string. It was hair, *his* hair, drawn from behind his ear. If he opened his mouth, the stitches would rip his lips, or tear out those strands of his hair, or both. Breathing through his nose, then, Cam's chest heaved like mechanical bellows. He panted as hard as he had during sex with Guy, and Guy could almost hear the impatient clicks of their tongues over and over in the gaps between his *own* gasps, which made Guy realize he kept holding his breath, watching, waiting.

"I'm sorry, I'm sorry, Cam," Guy said, ghostly white knuckles clawing the tabletop next to the screen, the inch of distance between them and Cam's image a million miles. Cam dropped to his knees as he wretched, Adam's apple lurching to swallow back down the glob he coughed up, refusing to tear his mouth's stitches. Drops of clear liquid fell before him instead, darkening the floor where it wasn't already stained. Whether or not Cam was feeling, his body was crying.

Serena sauntered into the frame, clad in a bikini, kicked Cam's shoulder with her bare foot, and mouthed, "Get up."

Cam tried so hard to stand. Guy stopped the video. It was only a third elapsed.

"No. No way," he heard himself say with finality, not incredulity. "No." *No, period.* Already his mind was rejecting what he'd seen; he couldn't recall how the video had started, and he didn't want to try. Not right then. His stomach continued to lurch with revulsion, and he got to his feet, needing to move. He wanted to hurl the tablet into the fire, but hurled his own self away instead, outside, thrashing his arms into his coat as he stumbled down the trail and into the woods. He retraced the path he'd traveled the day before in pursuit of Cam, knowing the soul he craved to see wasn't at the end of it, having to imagine small boot prints beneath his own fresh ones as unseasonal snow fell in buckets upon him.

Quivering icicles threatened to drop from branches overhead each time Guy stumbled, throwing out his gloved hand to steady himself. He'd never be domineering again. He'd only be kind, only be honest, be there for Cam however he needed him to be. He'd do his best to read and understand the cluttered, warm, illuminated works Cam built piece by salvaged piece, word by word, so Cam would never think himself voiceless again.

Stopping on the highest promontory of a ridge, Guy looked back across the valley at the distant hut. An unbroken sigh spilled from its pipe chimney, the rippling smoke the only movement for miles. The glow of its undying fire pulsed with its flickers like an arrhythmic heartbeat. From where Guy stood, it looked like a minimalist illustration of a fairy-tale tableau. Its solitude amplified its solace. In his tragic wisdom, Cam had chosen a fantastic fortress in which to sheath himself.

Guy had thought he'd known what cold was before coming there, and been proven wrong his first night. He thought he knew De Carli, then he thought he knew Cam—wrong again. *Forget fantasy. I don't even know the real world.*

Even so, he couldn't deny knowing what the towering clouds spilling over the ridges of mountains to the west preceded. Caitlyn had warned of heavy snow, but he knew what an incoming blizzard looked like in Iowa and in New York, and what he faced right then promised a dark night ahead, trapped inside the hut with only books for company. If he hadn't heard earlier that Cam would be safe in town, he'd be about to go mad.

He understood now that compartmentalization was important, necessary, and he trusted Cam to know how to keep his sanity intact; he honestly did. But as he ran to the hut against a wind that threatened to turn him to stone before he made it, he decided that, for himself, dissociation was damning. Silence could go to hell. He bound the USB in a bandage and placed it inside the first aid kit, belatedly realizing he'd ejected it too late; if there was a surveillance mechanism triggered on it, it would have been activated and running the whole time thanks to Cam's reliable internet connection.

Guy only got one phone call in before the blizzard knocked out Cam's makeshift receiver on a nearby mountain and, with it, all reception, so he made sure it counted.

Chapter Nineteen

AT 3:56 P.M. on the fourth day after Cam left, the distant but unmistakable sound of ice and twigs crunching beneath the weight of one hundred twenty-eight pounds beneath forty-four, or as Cam would put it, fifty-eight kilos plus twenty, broke the silence in the hut. At last, the sound wasn't a dream.

Fifteen degrees Fahrenheit was fine weather, so Guy slipped on only his coat, gloves, and boots over the two layers of sweaters and pair of jeans he wore before stepping out onto the porch. Firelight streamed through the windows behind him, stirring shadows on porch pillars, which framed the empty trail ahead like a church aisle. Cam's crunching footfalls slowed before his familiar white hood broke the monotony of snow-laden branches, and stopped completely the moment Guy became as visible to Cam as Cam's glasses, glinting in the last of the sunlight, did to him.

Cam swayed with the force of his pack's momentum after pulling up short, but looked straight at Guy, braced to withstand Guy's apology. "I thought you'd gone to Arviat. And further. Caitlyn said you'd gone home."

Funny how he remembered names of some people and not others. "I know. I've only just come back online, and when I called the store, she said I just missed you."

"The road was so snowy that Brendan dropped me a ways up the highway, and I walked here." Now he was remembering everyone's names.

Guy trudged toward him, watching Cam's hesitance change to slight alarm as he raised his gloved palm high to halt him. The beginnings of a beard, slick with iced sweat, covered Cam's chin above his scarf.

"Stop, I'm disgusting."

Undeterred, Guy swooped to peck a welcoming kiss on Cam's cheek. Cam flinched as Guy leaned in, and his hunching threw him off-balance, toppling him backward onto his pack like an upturned turtle. Giggling at the shock of his fall, his limbs relaxed as Guy kneeled in the snow beside him and unclipped the fasteners compressing Cam's chest and waist so he could breathe.

Cam slid down the base of his pack to sit cross-legged next to Guy, and Guy pulled a glove off and pressed his fingers against Cam's colder neck beneath his scarf, feeling his pulse race as his circulation was restored. It continued to pound hard and fast as Cam visibly reeled, giddy with the flood of blood warming his body.

"It's not the pack. It's not heavy," Cam excused himself, leaning forward into Guy's hand. "It's your fault."

"Sorry." Guy took back his hand and replaced his glove.

"I fucked up," Cam began.

Guy flicked Cam's collar. "That's not true and you know it," he said firmly, and witnessed a crack in Cam's armor, evinced as a twitch in his eye.

"I chose not to look into you," Cam elaborated. "Your face has a high stock value, you know? You're so bad at hiding feelings, I figured facts were the same. Your next book better be inscribed 'To dear Cameron' with exes and zeroes filling at least two pages. Blot out the whole damn text with them. And don't you dare use a pen name."

Guy twisted a gloveful of powdery snow against Cam's coat. Cam packed a snowball in his hands but failed to land it on his target before Guy caught his hands and bent back Cam's fingers, stopping short of inflicting pain, aware Cam would never cry mercy.

"I'll write two books by the time your next one comes out to piss Huw off with more work. I'll write a psych book that outsells yours." Cam panted beneath Guy, watching his face. "Slow down. You're thinking too fast."

Guy had no idea what expressions Cam was reading. He freed him, and Cam took off his glasses and dusted snow and ice particles from his long lashes. The frozen nose clips had burned red marks into his nose.

"Forgot my goggles," Cam muttered.

Guy stood, tugged Cam up by his gloved hand, and waited until Cam hefted his pack into his arms, not bothering to put it on to cover the hundred yards to the hut. Then he picked all hundred and eighty pounds up in his arms and started walking.

"Yuck." Cam pounded a glove lightly on Guy's chest. "I'm gross and heavy, Guy." He clutched his pack, as if to bear its weight himself, and wriggled free of Guy the moment they crossed the hut's threshold. His pack thudded against the closed door.

"But..." Cameron gestured at dirt specks on his coat as Guy steered him to the couch, protesting the mess he might transfer to it, but slunk onto the nest of blankets. Guy retrieved a water bottle from the kitchen, and Cam unscrewed the bottle cap with his teeth while peeling off his gloves. His coat was folded as neatly as the puffy material could be and set on the log table.

"Drink the whole thing," Guy ordered. "Whether you're thirsty or not. You're dehydrated."

Cam closed his eyes as the water infused into him. The smacking of his tongue and lips against the plastic, his sigh as he slumped, surrendering to the cool nourishment, was obscene. Guy was sick for the distance dividing them, two feet of vacuum drawing him toward Cam. *Goddamn that beard*. Rivulets dripped down Cam's chin and neck into his scruffy collar, which was bleached white in patches with salt from his sweat. Each drop cleaned tracks in the dirt caking his skin, luminous against the dark hair plastered to it.

Now that Guy knew him, Cam was no less magically frayed at the edges by the light he exuded. He was a tiny, kind, perfect prince, fine features complementing wizened eyes that locked on Guy's, overcoming Cam's own fear like the warrior he was. He was strong but flexible, a controlled wildfire immolating Guy's body with no more than a breath.

He drained the bottle and looked past Guy for a space of floor where he could drop it. Guy took it and lobbed it into the fire.

"That was recyclable," Cam criticized, twitching his nose, which had begun to run, making him sniff.

"*You're* recyclable. Take a bath," Guy commanded.

Wincing as he stood, Cam did as ordered with a hint of relief in his expression. If there was one thing Guy knew he liked to do, it was procrastinate.

The sounds of sloshing began as Cam dumped saucepan after saucepan over his body, and Guy thanked Christ for sunshine and solar power, which let him keep the boiler warm indefinitely while awaiting Cam's return. Guy removed half-frozen canteens from Cam's pack, which thankfully hadn't spilled when Cam fell. He placed Cam's undamaged laptop and notebook on the dining table, and was gratified with Cam's wan smile when he exited the bathroom, naked, and glimpsed his possessions were safe.

Cam reappeared from the bedroom dressed in shirts, socks, and jeans, his thumbs hanging from the belt loops of his self-tailored pants. Tendrils of hair hung by his freshly shaven chin, too short now to cover shoulders raised high with tension. His face had fallen, dragging Guy's heart with it, and yet further at seeing he limped slightly. The walk from the highway had troubled his sprained ankle badly enough Guy was glad he'd carried him earlier.

Cam shrugged into a dark gray sweater he retrieved from the laid-out contents of his pack and faced Guy, extending his arms as if for a hug, but made no move forward.

"Four days sitting in that bar without the internet, and I think I finally got the hang of knitting. You didn't like my Christmas sweater, but what do you think of my second attempt?"

"You *made* that Christmas sweater?" Guy scanned the room for a glimpse of the familiar red, and rummaged through blankets on the couch to turn up the ugly sweater, which he held before him.

"Mm... I missed you," Cam said. He'd let himself think about Guy, then. "It'd be logical to hate you. But I can't." Looking down at his own gray knit sweater, Cam focused for a second on the emblem stitched into it on the left side of his chest—a sideways triangle and lowercase B. Something written in Inuktitut. "I knitted myself a boyfriend sweater, wanting the curse of doing that to come take away my feelings. You know, if you knit something for someone, they dump you. Maybe it's my fault, too, that I knitted that one"—he lifted his gaze to the red sweater—"before we met, not knowing who it was for."

"I didn't know." Guy balled his fists in the scratchy red wool.

"I thought I wrote books for me, but it turned out they were love letters. I still like what you said about writing being a dialogue, even though I don't believe it." Cam's gaze reached Guy's face, where it lingered despite Cam's anguish. "You have to go. If I'd known you were here, instead of hoping, I'd have made Brendan wait and collect you. I'll walk with you to the highway. Can I use your phone?"

"Cameron," Guy said.

"Caitlyn said you... I got an envelope. From home, with something shaped like... Was it a USB?"

Guy nodded.

"After the third day without internet, I went stir-crazy enough to try calling my sister. I couldn't reach her." Cam jutted his chin forward to recover composure over his crumpling face. "You need to leave, because I don't know what'll happen next. My imagination's not that good. But I'm not so dumb I believe in…happy endings…" He trailed off as Guy approached and stood before him, then leaned down to meet the lips that parted in a quiet gasp.

Cam tasted of water. Not water in the city, but melted snow here. The name Guy had called Cam in his head for a month escaped him as their kiss ended, the name of best fit, blunt and breathy, small and strong. "Cam."

It was as good as an incantation, melting Cam with a slow shudder, and he kept his eyes closed as he shook his head. "No."

"That's what your sweater says, isn't it?" Guy guessed the script written over Cam's tattoo.

Cam nodded.

Whether his return here had been to enter into a last stand against his feelings for Guy or against Serena wouldn't change how things were already unfolding. "I know Serena abused you."

"Yeah, I figured you would."

"And I called the cops, Cam," Guy said. "On her."

"No!" A convulsive twitch rocketed down Cam's back. He leaped back. "You can't do that!"

"I did. You can do what you want to me for it. You can already deregister me from the American Psychological Association for a lot of things. You should. But I had to turn her in. You don't have to do a thing now; you don't need to testify. There's video evidence, and it doesn't matter how old you were or what she made you do, you can't consent to grievous bodily harm."

"No, no." Cam shook her head. "She *always* recorded us. That doesn't matter. She has a contingency if I ever talked. I know. I wrote it."

"I know. I read it," Guy said.

Cam reacted to the sound of light footsteps outside, but having spent the past four days listening intently for just such an approach and with both ankles fine, Guy beat him to the door and wrenched it open.

Against a lavender-bruised sky, in a white coat and white-gloved thumbs hooked under the shoulder straps of her pack, with a long black fringe sweeping over a broad forehead and an expression of undiluted surprise on her fine features, Serena looked even more like Cam in person than Guy had anticipated. She stood with one foot before the other, having stopped short ten yards from the boundary of the porch and curled her hand over her eyes to make out Cam standing behind Guy in the rosy light, Cam's eye line blocked by the hand with which Guy gripped the doorframe. He squeezed its smooth wood, massaging his fingers against it, keeping them warm.

A grin further lit up Serena in the hut's spilling glow. "Don't move," she spoke in a normal volume, trusting Cam would hear.

Guy didn't trust that, feeling in the stillness of the freezing air that Cam had seized up entirely behind him, no longer breathing. It was possible he *couldn't* move. He was switched on, and Guy couldn't tell which way he was going to break. He was a living bomb, destructive energy contained, and a split in him would destroy them all.

"Don't move," Guy repeated to him, left hand stretching out behind the doorframe to clasp the hut's rifle, which stood balanced upright on a book stack by the locker beside the door.

"Ha!" Serena thought he'd spoken to her. She swung her backpack around to front and unzipped its top pocket, withdrawing a large handgun made to appear bigger in her small hands.

Gutsy placement, Guy reluctantly thought, unable to doubt that exposure to the cold in that pocket might have affected the gun's mechanism. He wanted to believe she was that stupid, but couldn't. Choosing to arm herself right then with that gun over the shotgun Guy suspected she still owned showed she'd come here seeking close combat. He refused to contemplate what else was in her pack.

"You're not supposed to have company." She peered at Cam incredulously, ignoring Guy. "You? Ahhh." She sighed in a singsong melody. "Now I have to change plans slightly."

Tell me about it. Guy tightened his grip on the rifle he'd removed from its bag days earlier.

She'd only raised her arm to half-mast before flicking her wrist and firing, catching Guy off guard, and knocking him off-balance with a lightning bolt of pain that pierced his upper arm. The solidness of Cam's body gave behind his elbow as Guy jerked for the second time to spin the rifle to slap the trigger into Guy's half-numb hand, the trigger guard slipping over the index finger of his warmer hand like a loose ring made for him alone to wear. Before Serena's arm completed its arc to aim at Guy front-on, Guy already saw nothing but her, and squeezed the trigger as coldly as he knew he used to always look.

The blast of pressure the bucking stock kicked against his shoulder overwrote the pain in his bicep by snapping his collarbone. It threw him back on unsteady ground he realized was Cam's body only as he was falling, and shrank into himself, bracing for collision, desperate to minimize the damage he'd inflict by falling on top of Cam.

Hearing them late, Guy noted the two shots came in such quick succession their cracks overlapped, and continued overlapping in the pulsing echo reverberating through the valley. Silence settled in the vacuum as the ripples of sound dissipated outward, all animal life, which was usually lively at twilight, holding its breath, no wind to rustle evergreen leaves or creak branches, no movement anywhere around Guy but for himself scrambling to sit up in the doorway of the hut.

Chapter Twenty

SEEING CAM BLINK shot such relief through Guy that his elbow buckled again and his hand slipped from Cam's hip, landing on his good shoulder on the floor with a thud. *Thank Christ*, he nearly cried aloud at seeing Cam's ashen complexion regain its color. His skin was as stoic to the freezing draft as he was himself, staring out the open door, coherency flooding gradually back into his wide eyes. Guy struggled to straighten up against the locker, to see out the doorway over Cam's shoulder.

Serena lay on her back in the snow. The furrows of the snowbank covering the trail, carved by the wind, obscured her pants from this angle, leaving her coat, a loose snake of ebony hair, and the bottom of her chin visible. Thin stripes and flecks of color were flung behind her like paint. The night sky seemed to fall upon her like a thin veil, turning her skin blue, the lacy blood spatter violet, and her white coat another's sky's midday blue.

By contrast, pain clouded Guy's vision with static while Cam wriggled out from under Guy's legs and jolted to his feet, continuing to blink rapidly as he offered an outstretched hand to Guy. Guy tried to lift his left hand to grab it, only for the static to be blown away by a sudden flare of sharper pain. He took Cam's hand with his own right one, too focused on its warmth to register the strength with which Cam hauled him up with one pull.

"You're not hurt?" Guy asked. The bullet that passed through his arm didn't look to have landed...except to have lodged in a far wall, its halo of splinters distinguishing it from other knots in the wood.

Cam shook his head, tugging Guy's hand closer to his body, ignoring Guy's letting him go. "You are."

"I need my fingers back," Guy pointed out, nodding at the rifle. Cam dropped Guy's palm, letting him carefully pick up the gun, but his arm darted out to grab Guy's sleeve the moment he crossed the threshold.

"I'll be right back." Guy waited for Cam to release him, finger by finger, then stalked slowly off the creaking porch boards into the footprints he'd left scattered in the snow earlier. Avoiding them, he went wide to approach Serena from the side, gun cocked with its stock against his breastbone. If she moved and he had to suddenly fire now, he'd split his rib cage straight down its center.

Cam didn't leave the doorway, but a quick glimpse showed his eyes behind the glasses he'd straightened were as wide as the lenses themselves.

Encouraged by the amount of blood denoting a considerable exit wound, Guy quickened his approach, his ankles burning as snow breached his unlaced boots, his lungs tightening in the cold now his adrenaline was wearing off. He relaxed enough to lower the gun, balancing it in the crook of his arm to awkwardly latch its trigger safety into place with shaking fingers as he trudged through the snow to stand in front of her, blocking Cam's view.

Serena's eyes were half-shut, their pupils vacantly gray. It wasn't just her hood or snow that made her head sit so deeply and oddly in the snow; Guy surmised the back of her skull had fractured into gravel by the pressure of the rifle bullet's entry, then vacuum as it exited her. He squatted beside her and pressed two forefingers to her jugular. A full thirty seconds elapsed before he could confidently cancel out the effect of his own irregular shivering, and of using his nondominant right hand, to believe she had no pulse.

Her hair didn't feel like Cam's. Unlike his cloudy down-like strands, hers was as thick and slick as the body of a black snake, unnaturally glossy, clearly often-treated. Guy supposed that, boasting that face, she must have a lot of admirers at her law firm, but upon drifting into wondering whether she'd roped any into the sort of bizarre scenes she'd made Cam— *No. Stop.* It was possible to pull his own mind up short as long as there were other more pressing actions to consider. It wouldn't last, but he relished the distraction of simply being cold while he could.

As he stood, Guy's teeth broke free of the tension with which he'd clamped them shut, suddenly chattering so hard he bit his tongue. Tasting coppery slime, he tried to swallow but coughed instead, then reflexively spat a gob of thin blood into the virgin snow at Serena's feet. The cold air filling his nose and throat threatened to seal his airways shut with blades of ice despite the dryness also claiming them—he still couldn't swallow, and spat once more, clearer now, as he trod on his own footsteps to circle back to the porch. Stamping the snow off his boots, he shut the door behind him and sighed at the shift in temperature, his coat already sliding off his drooping shoulders before he'd begun to remove it.

"How?" Cam asked, baffled. Guy didn't understand. Cam continued, "You didn't disarm her? Just...in the forehead?"

Guy nodded, already only shivering as normally as if he'd simply come in from the cold, too frozen on the surface to feel anything but pain and pulsing at his core.

"Come here," Cam beckoned.

Guy realized he was in shock, mental as well as physical, only after obeying without a thought. Operating on a delay, it occurred to him he'd equally thoughtlessly kicked the door closed behind him, knowing without considering it that what was best for Cam was to keep them both warm. *On the plus side, I'm not hypothermic*, he thought nonsensically.

"Strip," Cam demanded.

Guy laughed, earning an electric shock of pain. As it eased, he found the throbbing in its wake radiated from just below his neck, and less sharply from his bicep on the same side. His collar felt like it had an invisible arrow still lodged in it. His arm, like a three-inch-thick sword was being forged in its muscle. Looking down, however, neither of them bled much...

No, wait. His arm was gushing blood the same color as the straggling yarn glued to its exposed flesh. Rivulets dripped down the rifle barrel he was still clutching and fell on the floor, their tiny splashes hitting the covers of books strewn on the floor. He peeled his fingers from the gun one by one, feeling pain flow into each of them as they were freed. They all flexed easily enough, meaning no tendon or nerve damage, though depending how the muscle swelled, that might still occur.

"Think I broke my collarbone. But I'm fine. I just need to sit down." He did while talking, letting his legs give way for him to slump on the floor, leaning back against the closed door.

Cam opened the first aid kit and advanced toward him with a thick wad of bandage padding and scissors. "We need to cut off the sweater."

"Stop." Guy finally caught up to the present. "Toss me the bandage. Stay there."

Cam cocked his head slightly, but did as bidden. Satisfied Guy could apply pressure to his wound, Cam turned his attention to the bullet in the wall for just a second before he retrieved a water bottle, candy bar, and blanket to pass to Guy, keeping his distance as Guy had asked.

Guy tore into the candy, ravenously choking bitefuls down in between gulps of cold water that tasted as syrupy. He hugged his left forearm to his chest until his right hand was free to hold the bandage against his bleeding bicep, and found in that short interim his collarbone had started to numb and resisted him moving his left arm at all anymore.

"Can you get me an icepack? Or anything frozen?"

"Snow?"

Even if he'd been able to easily move from the doorway, he didn't want Cam to go outside. "Is there anything in here?"

From Cam's blank look, Guy gathered nothing came to his mind, either. There was nowhere in the hut to freeze anything; they did without foodstuffs that needed freezing, as they couldn't leave anything outside for fear of attracting bears. Shit. Guy hoped no bears or wildlife would set upon Serena soon.

"Oh! Here." Cam took a bottle of water from the pack he'd worn outside not half an hour earlier. Its contents were still cool enough for Guy to sigh with relief when able to press it beneath his chin and shoulder like the body of a violin.

"The setting's different, but I can work with this," he told Guy, starting their conversation in the middle of a thought. "Here's what we do. Take off that sweater and shirt so I can stitch your arm. There's plenty...well, enough antibiotics." He fished in the first aid kit, withdrawing scissors, more cotton padding, and the bandage roll containing the USB Guy had hidden. Thankfully he placed that bandage on the table, not unraveling it. "Your bone injury will be more difficult to hide, but there's nothing to do for a clavicle break but wear a sling after resetting it anyway. The bullet I can get with tweezers"—he nodded at the wall—"but the ground's too hard to dig. We can't leave remains in a cave, or for bears, that's uncontrollable..."

He bobbed down and disappeared behind the kitchen counter, to draw from cupboards beneath it an array of knives, a small meat mincer powered by a manual crank, and cleaning products. Bolting upright like a jack-in-the-box, he became visible to Guy again, inspecting the labels of bottles he'd stacked on the counter.

"Commercial bleach, 25 percent ammonia. It was more economical to carry here than household stuff."

Guy had seen Cam distill capfuls of it into water before swabbing the floors.

"Carpet shampoo for the couch. Ammonium hydroxide...can't mix these two," he instructed Guy, pushing the bottle next to the bleach. "Dishwasher detergent, chlorine. Drain cleaner, hydrochloric acid. Acetone fire starter liquid. People used it for barbecues in the summer."

Finally Guy recognized Cam's cleaning compulsion, and his rattling off Serena's weight and the milliliters of cleaning fluid he'd amassed in an equation accounting for available bottles and liters of water, as the product of his boredom and need for control during whatever solitary confinement bouts he'd been subjected to in the past. That and plotting.

"I can write the equation down— No, no drafts, no proof," Cam muttered to himself. "No antifreeze. Won't work... I'm not going to put this many chemicals in a lake... Ecological impact of releasing it in the stream?" He paused for a second, rounded the counter, and pointed to a rolled-up tarpaulin stretched between two of the overhead rafters. "I'll pick her and all the bloody snow up, and carry the lot to the stream. Open her jugular and brachial arteries, do CPR to circulate her blood to bleed it until it's too frozen to pump."

It. Guy shivered.

"Then this—" Cam tapped the manual mincer, then waved toward the gas stove. "And boil that, all of it into these bottles and anything else that seals—a coffee container?—along with all this." He gestured to the cleaning equipment. "While I'm gone, you burn everything that's flammable. Her clothes, pack, equipment. She won't have a phone on her, or receipts for gear, which'll all be common brands. Untraceable. Her car, too; she can't have walked here but from the highway. It'll be the most common make and model for this region."

"How do you know?" Guy asked.

"Because that's what I'd do." Cam climbed onto the couch, found he couldn't reach the tarpaulin, and stepped down to move to the table instead. "The mix I make won't be flammable and we can't bury or release it anywhere near here, but in these bottles, it'll be easy to carry. Fifty-eight plus twenty-odd of liquid, ten, twenty bottles...two trips to the truck," he estimated. "You drive my car to town after transferring it all into her car, which I'll drive. Put her unburnables in the center of the bar's hard waste dumpster, the one with the orange lid. It won't be chained. Don't tell anyone about your arm, but if anyone asks why you're alone, we had a fight. You, I don't know, thought I cheated on you. That'll do. Return to New York by bus to Arviat, then rental car, don't fly. No, that'll be too hard with your arm and shoulder. Okay…" His gaze traveled as he reworked his plan. "After I empty the mix into the Hudson Bay—I'll minimize the environmental impact by doing it at a few spots—and after I bury the handgun's pieces in sand far from the storm surge line—gotta file the serial number off," he reminded himself. "I'll get rid of the car, hitch to Arviat, meet you at the bus depot at 4:00 p.m. tomorrow, and I'll drive. By the time we arrive, she'll have been noticed as missing. So I'll have to be there, anyway. If she's gone, I gotta go home. I'll have to."

He lifted his eyes to meet Guy's, inviting scrutiny, then clapped his hands together at spying a hole in the plot he concocted. "You don't have an alibi for the last few days. Mine's fine, but your cell phone was out, so it couldn't log your network location… Never mind. She will have handled that by giving herself an alibi far away. And the shot in the hut wall?" he asked, as if repeating an interruption from Guy. "Easy to sterilize and fix, but reckless of her… She would have needed to frame us as having fought instead of"—his will to imagine ran out—"anything else."

Guy swallowed hard, tasting copper again. *And they call* me *cold.* Shifting on the hard ground through which cold seeped from outside, he wrapped the blanket he'd been given tightly around his shoulders, ensuring it didn't come into contact with the front of his sweater. Cam's Christmas sweater.

"I'm sorry about your sweater," he said.

"Oh, forget about it." Cam shook his head. "God. We'll burn it. It's embarrassing. Like my first novel."

A smile pricked at Guy's lips. "How old were you when you wrote that one?"

"Eight. I didn't burn it, but there's no *way* you're reading it."

"I don't know, *Close to Home* was pretty good. Is that your first contemporary book?"

"Second. Wrote one when I was sixteen. You're not seeing the first." Cam gave up trying to reach the tarpaulin, dropping his arms to his sides. "But following that pattern, I think my second sci-fi's going to be good enough even for Fairbanks the first time around. And this"—he gestured to the equipment on the kitchen counter—"will work."

"Have you done it before?" Guy asked.

Cam looked down at him. "Not...actually."

He has a future in crime fiction, too. Most importantly, he has a future. Guy pressed the blanket against his tender arm, displacing the sopping wadding that fell on the floor by his leg with a wet smack. He spoke seriously, trying not to sound imposing, but with no room for argument nonetheless.

"Okay, Cam. But this is what I want. Don't touch me. We have to preserve the gun's residue on me as much as possible. Call Brendan. Have him call the sheriff or whoever's in charge out here."

Cam's mouth fell open and he alighted from the bench seat he'd clambered upon, flinching as he put too much weight on his ankle. "In Arviat? No, Guy. I know how the law works. It'll go badly. I have motive."

"She has motive, and she shot first. And *I* shot her. There's probably a warrant out for her back home, anyway."

"She could have dealt with that. We can deal with it."

Guy shook his head. "Make the call. Just one thing. You never mentioned a plan. You never thought of one. Everything else was as it happened. Self-defense."

"No. People won't believe that. No!" Cam stepped closer to Guy, but stopped two feet away, giving his likely compliance away.

"Otherwise you'll never be able to rest. You'll live in fear forever, no matter where you are. I can't allow that, and I can't let you pay for something I've done."

"I can," Cam promised.

Guy looked at him, beholding him, seeing everything Cam was at once. "Trust me," he said quietly.

"That's illogical," Cam retorted, his brows crashing together as he fell to the ground, feet splayed before him, like his strings had been cut. "Why would I?"

"My phone's on the table."

Without standing, Cam crawled on his knees to snatch the phone off the tabletop, and his mouth fell open again on seeing the lock screen set on it. "No," he whispered. Tears instantly filled his eyes, and he swiped roughly at them with the sleeve of his new gray knit sweater before they could fall. "You didn't. Really?"

"I followed one home," Guy explained the picture. "To its den or warren. One of the exits, or entrances, depending on your orientation."

The photo of the rabbit he'd taken with his phone was worse than pictures of Bigfoot, but it was proof nonetheless. *He didn't make it up. He wasn't just hiding.* Guy hadn't realized he still doubted Cam's story until he saw the damn thing's smoky tufts of gray fur stand out so much against the snow he wondered how it could exist anywhere, let alone survive in the freezing woods. It stood out *so* much from its background, it was impossible to miss, and it was by far the cutest bunny he'd ever seen in his life. It looked hand-drawn. It couldn't have suited Cam more if it tried.

"You got the GPS?" Cam's voice cracked.

"I got coordinates for the whole mile I tracked it," Guy said.

"All I need is DNA. Fur, scat, food it's chewed. Oh, my God, Guy, I can go *home*." Cam fell back upon the ground in a daze. His stare lost its steeliness as everything that had unfolded hit him. He could go home anyway. He could preserve his mother's name any way he wanted.

"They're going to split us up for questioning," he warned Guy. "Even though we'll have had two hours to get our stories straight."

"So reduce that time length." Guy released his arm to grab the bandage Cam rolled to him, stuffing it in his pocket. He pressed more padding to his wound. "Reduce the possibility of us coming up with something sophisticated. Don't let anyone hang up, and if the battery runs out, have them—the station wherever—call you on your laptop so we're never off the line. You record it, too. So they know we're not talking."

Cam closed his mouth and dialed.

They were given an estimate of two hours until someone would arrive, and told by the emergency services responder to not touch anything. The order was repeated by the officer to whose desk they were transferred.

Real shock set in amid the silence. Cam buried his shaking body up to his neck beneath two blankets pulled from the couch, but didn't zone out, and Guy wanted nothing more than to break more bones hurling himself at Cam to warm him up with a hug.

"If she'd come half an hour earlier," Cam chattered, cold despite the fire.

Emotions too large for words filled Guy in place of the blood escaping his arm now in a trickle. When faced with the limits of the three-letter label identifying himself and Cam to the world and each other, or the books full of words they wrote that failed to express everything they were, Guy found it easier not to think about it. Psychotherapy that sought to uncover the bare bones of experience wouldn't work for either of them in the near future. It was maladaptive, fine, but all he planned to do for as long as he was able was support Cam however he could.

His shoulder and arm grew too stiff to react in spasm as the coldness outside bled through the door into his back, so his chest took up the role, crushing Guy's lungs and pulling his head down low until his chin crackled the plastic of the sweating bottle still propped against his clavicle. Dizziness overcame him for a spell, and his hand cramped where he wrapped it around his wound. Serena's gun was large, but its caliber wasn't; the entry hole he tentatively mapped was pea-sized, and the exit hole at the back of his arm as large as a silver dollar. The swollen flesh between them pounded with throbbing.

The vivid memory of Serena's blank face blurred with his memories of Cam in the mornings, and he tried to overwrite it with images of Cam animatedly pacing, plotting, or better yet laughing, kissing him, since right then Cam was disturbingly silent, his eyes closed, his composure too relaxed, making the false peace of the moratorium eerily pregnant with anticipation. Blessedly, a soft snore let Guy know Cam had drifted off, sitting up.

I love you screamed through Guy, melting the walls and floor beneath him, bathing the room in gold, pelting his brain with stars, the impact of the admission overloading his mind so he couldn't see anything from Cam. He was roused from his stupor by voices shouting outside. Cam awoke with a start, taking only an instant to refocus on Guy.

"Sleep well," Guy said while being led away by the first of two sets of attending officers. "Wake up okay," he called more urgently. "You don't have to remember this."

"I've remembered everything I've ever done in the last two years." Cam clutched at the embroidered word on his sweater. "I love my life. I love my life," he repeated, tears streaming down his face as Guy's futile request for one more minute together was denied.

Chapter Twenty-One

"THE DEATH OF a US citizen near Manitoba's Caribou River Park Reserve is no longer being treated as suspicious. In other news out of Nunavut, Cornell University researcher—"

So they've claimed him back. Guy scratched his signature into a property release form at a side desk in Iqaluit's police station, wishing he faced the same direction as the receptionist and could watch the TV suspended from the ceiling. *Cornell let Cam come in from the cold.*

"—spotted the rabbit last July and spent fall and winter searching for it, only to stumble upon a warren where enough DNA material—and this footage!" The announcer could be smiling, perhaps even honestly at whatever was playing. "—was collected to verify it as a species unknown to the region, and the world. Unlike the outgoing rabbits, shy ecologist and discoverer Cameron Campbell refused to be captured on camera, but the US native had this to say."

Foolishly, considering what the newscaster had just said, Guy turned to face the TV to catch a glimpse of Cam. The screen showed only two rabbits bounding over snow, their bodies whiter in full than the one he'd photographed last week. Armed with Guy's GPS, Cam must have found a whole family of the creatures.

"I'd like to extend my gratitude to Cornell; the volunteers who assisted with fieldwork; to the township of Arviat; and to the community of Ipasila for kindly putting up with me. And of course, to the good people of Nunavut, and Canada." His stiff voice was turned yet more mechanically tinny over airwaves.

The poor guy was even camera-shy when it came to voice recording, but to have pushed through DNA testing that fast, Cam must have called up heavy favors at his alma mater or from people he'd worked alongside. *Or blown. Good for him.* He was able to get what he wanted dealing one-on-one with people, and he'd managed to make it back out into the field, so he clearly hadn't been shaken up by questioning...or everything else.

And from the look of the rolled-up, knotted bandage in the plastic baggie Guy removed from his tray of belongings, it hadn't unraveled either, meaning the USB survived the 800-mile journey from Arviat to Nunavut's capital city, Iqaluit, unseen. The blood covering it couldn't have deterred a dedicated investigator. They must just not have gotten to it, so Guy's telling of the video he'd seen remained unconfirmed.

Cam had been right. On a road relatively close to the hut, police had found a 2012 Ford F-150 truck registered in Minnesota but wearing Ontario plates, which looked at home in Nunavut but for its being abandoned. Serena's backpack contained another gun and weapons of torture. Her passport and immigration records placed her in the Caribbean. All of that evidence still would have put Guy on a twelve-month track awaiting trial by jury, which even then granted him only a fifty-fifty chance of winning a not-guilty plea by way of self-defense, had Serena not been wearing a hidden camera in her jacket. *She always recorded us*, he'd said. If Guy had shot her in the chest where he'd been aiming, instead of luckily hitting her head, he'd have blown away his chance of being released within a week. As it was, the eager prosecutor's case against him had no strength and was dropped. The fact the footage Serena recorded had no audio, and his looking so harmless, secured Cam's release from Arviat's local police station within twenty-four hours. The property Guy now stuffed into a plastic bag didn't include any message from him, however.

But at least he got released fast. And further hoped, *At least he's okay.* Guy had no idea whether Cam would pick up if he called, if Cam had a new phone number, or had kept Guy's phone, since it wasn't amongst the items in the tray. He didn't know if he had the right to even contact Cam, having abandoned him in his darkest hour—well, *a* darkest hour—the moment Guy had gotten himself locked up.

Hmm. Guy was going to need a new coat. He wondered if his stuff had been collected from the hut...and whether he'd get Cam's Christmas sweater back from forensics if he wrote a request. At the moment, he was wearing an itchy black sweatshirt given him by the police, under an equally fetching black sling. Though his bicep was coming along fine after two-dozen stitches, it was going to take another two months for his collarbone to fully heal.

Huw's voice from the overhead TV jerked him back to the present. "We knew we had something special as soon as we read it," Huw lied.

"My colleague immediately pegged Mr. Stewart as the next De Carli—but he's the old De Carli. The young one!"

Oh, no. That news had broken, then, as the price to pay for being honest with every cop they'd encountered who asked the right questions. A murder case, discovering a new species, and "the resurrection" of De Carli. In the space of just a week, Cam was making a splash in the world, but it sounded like his accomplishments were still being partly obfuscated by attributing them to different names. As soon as someone circulated a photo of him, it'd be game over. Unfortunately for them both, Cam's face belonged on front pages. On billboards. On the outer jacket, not even the inside sleeve, of hardcovers.

"Hey, stranger!" a familiar voice called.

Guy whipped around to see the TV, thinking its volume had jumped, before he saw Huw standing inside the reception door. Reaching him within three long strides, Guy nearly knocked him over with a one-armed hug.

"Whoa, whoa," Huw cried in surprise. "Hugging? Is this a late April Fools' joke? Because I thought the one you pulled off was good enough."

"I'm happy to see you." Guy grinned harder at Huw's obvious shock of seeing him grin in the first place.

"Yeah, but is that a gun in your pocket?" Huw asked, then pressed his lips together in self-admonishment upon spying the receptionist's reaction. "Whoops. Too soon. Come on, let's blow this Popsicle stand for civilization."

"What? A Tim Hortons?" Guy chuckled.

Huw let the heavy glass door creak shut behind them before retorting, "Sure you didn't shoot *yourself* in the head? God, I would have. It's so chilly."

"You came all this way to pick me up?"

"Now, that'd be stupid," Huw said. "I'm taken. And Sean's a handful, you know? With a difficult past? I don't think you could possibly imagine what that might be like to deal with..."

"Ha!"

Huw laughed harder than Guy at his unexpected response and, after ushering him into the back of a waiting cab, sat shivering in the front passenger seat, pressing his bare hands to the heater vents. There was no partition between the driver and back seat. *Just like home... Wow.* Guy pulled himself up short. He hadn't thought of Iowa as "home" even when he'd lived there. All the country air he'd taken in lately *had* gotten to him some. *Or the water.*

"Your real bag's in the trunk," Huw answered his unasked question. "And you can forget about lifting it, you invalid. It weighs forty pounds...which is eighteen kilograms, apparently. I swung by that cupboard you were staying in to help Cameron pack. All right, all right, mainly out of curiosity, but not all of it perverse. How 'bout that rabbit? Cutest thing I've ever seen! The, uh, *town* by there is having some ceremony or festival for it in July. Cameron's been invited back, so I bet you will be too."

Invited back? "Isn't he still there? After finding the thing comes a new survey, mapping, tracking, behavior studies, breeding programs," Guy repeated the plans he'd heard Cam outline.

"No, someone else can do all of that. Cameron wants to sleep in." Huw craned his head to look out the windshield. "Wow, the northern lights!"

"It looks much stronger out of the city," the cab driver said. They were already leaving the town's limits, heading for the airport, which could only send them as far as Ottawa.

Guy twisted in his seat to see out the back. The aurora looked like rain falling in sheets, far closer than he knew it actually was above the barren land speeding past the window. Shimmering neon blues and greens much brighter than he'd imagined lit up the vast sky, mocking Guy's memory of flying into New York and considering it an endless lake of light. In Iqaluit, the sky was on fire—a gas-blue, steady, slowly dancing fire. *Christ*, he wished so much that Cam were here to see it with him that the ache in his shoulder flared. Those electric colors reflected in his icy-pale irises would really...make him look like his father did in old photos.

"What else has come out about Cam?" Guy asked. Whatever had, he figured it wouldn't matter at this point if the cab driver listened.

"Not that you banged him," Huw said, proving Guy wrong. The driver raised an eyebrow through the rearview mirror, failing to feign disinterest as Huw continued, "Not much, really. He was neglected, beaten up sometimes or something, and his sister came to get him so she could keep cashing in."

"She was a finance lawyer," Guy said.

"He's a walking dollar sign. Nancy at Rival's acting like she won the lottery instead of just a promotion so far. The big five publishers have been screaming down my inbox for days, and I bet Cam's getting worse from them and agents alike. He managed to sneak through La Guardia after the Toronto consul finished processing his sister's ashes, and he braved Brooklyn to go expedite a name change, but he's going to need to hole up for a while."

"He wasn't that attached to his old name," Guy said.

"Of course, the forms were sealed immediately, so I don't know… Does this look forged to you?" Huw passed back his phone. Guy tilted its screen to avoid the glow from overhead so he could make out the document it showed. He scrolled down, then up, and down again, checking he hadn't mistaken the lodged and stamped name change order for a Cameron Sutton, listing Guy's address. Dropping the phone on the seat, Guy fished in his pockets for keys he knew he hadn't been carrying on him the night he was taken from the hut…

Huw laughed. "So you *didn't* know."

"You could tell from my face?" Guy asked, unaware what expression he wore. He still didn't know if he ought to dare to hope that Cam had taken his name with a view to reconciliation. *Christ*, was Cam at his apartment? Guy wasn't exactly messy, nor a clutterer—in fact, his shelves mainly held up dust, and there were manuscript drafts on his desk he really didn't want someone of Cam's writing caliber to read.

"That little thief," Huw said.

THE HUNDRED THINGS Guy planned to say to Cam started to evaporate amid the scent of bleach and vanilla permeating the hall where Guy stood alone, wheeled suitcase by his knees, knuckles trembling just short of his own front door while he built up the courage to knock. It opened, anyway, before he could do so, and all the words Guy had practiced fled him.

He entered without saying anything, letting Cam close the door behind them. The cleaned and straightened living room smelled strangely unfamiliar without the woodsmoke he'd grown accustomed to, and had begun to link to Cam's presence. The whole place—even the landscape of buildings outside the window—looked too wide and empty but for Cam blotting out the worst of it by standing between Guy and the outside world. His raven hair was cut short, wolfish and feathery all at once, making his jutting chin seem sharper and his graceful neck even longer. From shoulders to knees, a loose blue dress draped across his small form. It was the same color as his eyes, which stared intently at Guy from behind large glasses. His feet were bare, his nine toes curling into the floorboards as his fingers stretched out ahead into the cool morning air.

Cam nervously nibbled the side of his lower lip. "Welcome home."

"It's your home. You can have it. Say the word and I'll leave, move out, at any time, now or in the future," Guy promised. "You're in complete control here."

"I'm ve-very far from it," Cam stammered, and a surge of love rocked Guy forward to claim his mouth.

With one arm, Guy lifted Cam and lowered him back on the long couch, then lay upon him with all his weight crushing them together whilst Cam defied gravity to rise against Guy, drawing Guy closer still with nails sunk deep into Guy's back. His tiny form was all-encompassing, his thin calves and arms like steel jaws sprung with tension, but he rolled as best he could to avoid brushing Guy's injured shoulder. Wrapping his right hand as far as it would go around Guy's straining right bicep, he hung from it as he pressed his chest to Guy's. Spreading his legs around Guy's thigh, he rolled his hips upward to rub the length of his erection against the bulge swelling painfully behind Guy's unforgiving fly.

"It's not going to work here, we need to move," Guy growled.

Cam nodded, mouth agape to chase Guy's tongue with his own as Guy leaned back out of reach. Cam whisked his dress over his head, but Guy struggled to undo the Velcro on his sling. Cam stepped up onto the couch's cushions and pressed his lips to Guy's while first unclasping each button of Guys shirt, tearing at the last one, which had the audacity to stick, and then peeled both shirt and sling off him before pushing a lock of his own hair back from his forehead, furrowed with impatience.

"*Short* hair's not supposed to get in the way," he muttered, taking Guy's good hand in his and leading him to Guy's bedroom. He hadn't worn underwear so was already naked, *of course*, and slipped across the floorboards as lightly and soundlessly as he did through snow, as though he were wearing the woolen socks he'd never been without until now.

"I missed you," Guy breathed. The apologies he'd intended to deliver threatened to surface in his mind, but sank again upon seeing Cam's earnest longing, his creamy skin turned mauve by pollution's hazy glow streaming in from the window. Guy closed the bedroom door to seal them both up, as alone in near-silence in the city as they'd been in their bubble at the end of the Earth, and slid his jeans off to pool at the foot of the bed on which Cam lay, his cock bobbing full and pink as a rose. Cam ran his nails lightly down his own chest and stomach, shivering while circling them around his balls, and slowly slid free the lubed plug he'd kept inside him, waiting... *Jesus Christ, for how long?*

An incoherent moan escaped Guy where he stood.

"I missed *you*," Cam said, his voice thick with lust, his eyes shining with need that grew in intensity as Guy kneeled beside him and wrapped his hand around Cam's cock, hooking his thumb over its end. Throbbing ridges rose fiery hot beneath his fingers. Cam's mouth was swollen, his lips flushing redder as he worried them with his front teeth.

Guy bade him lie down with a nod, hungrily, as Cam unraveled when Guy drew a dewdrop of melted lube from Cam's ass to the tip of his twitching cock. Ignoring the pain in his shoulder, with his other hand Guy pushed a finger smoothly inside Cam's slick ass, twisting it and inserting his thumb too to stretch Cam's entrance wide enough to send a shiver rolling down his own spine. Blood pooled in Cam's cheeks and his breathing turned ragged.

"Ready when you are," Cam murmured.

Guy had never seen anything as pure as Cam was at that moment, nor felt as singularly consuming an emotion as the need he had to give Cam everything. Was this what it was like for Cam? To feel too much?

"Are you okay?" Cam asked, his pupils swelling with concern, making them stand out like lit coals against his skin, and the stark blank canvas of the tousled sheets. "We don't have to."

Guy's throat tightened, strangled by adoration. He slid his leg over Cam, reaching to slip a pillow beneath Cam's head, and traced the contours of his face, hypnotized at the way Cam leaned into his palm, refusing to give up contact.

"Cam." The name itself was a balm, soothing the pain wrought by Guy's bursting heart. "I love you so much."

More wondrous than Cam's concern was his relaxation at the sound of Guy's voice, and glow as the words sank in.

"You're breathtaking," Guy said, blessing Cam's praise kink, stoking it as he stroked Cam's cock alike. "Strong. Beautiful. Never leave; I'll want you around me forever. I want you to always..." Cam smiled as Guy kissed him, until it turned too lustfully deep, the pair of them shifting together until Guy was deep within Cam and hung over him, balancing with one hand, the other loosely brushing Cam's short hair. They both panted, breathlessly swelling in unison, inebriated with heat.

Guy had some knowledge of what Cam reacted best to, but could never have anticipated the joy he felt at Cam's surrendering to him. His complete trust in spite of everything tore at Guy until it sunk in that he was the same. *This isn't me making up to him. It's not a matter of reassurance or healing. It's just natural. Inevitable.*

"You make me strong enough to handle you."

Cam quailed beneath Guy's gaze. "You're reading me." Goose bumps spilled down his neck, washing over a patchy flush that patterned his chest like stepping stones in an eddying river. "You can do anything you want to me, you know that, right?"

"I want what you want." Guy placed his hand over Cam's clamoring heart and stoked the crimson bloom on his skin until it stretched to Cam's navel. He sank his teeth around Cam's nipple and sucked, letting it rise before he abandoned it to kiss Cam's lips. Cam shuddered as Guy skimmed over the bud of his other nipple with his nails as he nibbled Cam's jawline. Cam's heartbeat pounded through his thighs as they gripped Guy's sides, nestling in the dents of his pelvis which arched into his weight. "You're perfect."

"You're my..." Cam began, but the wordsmith lost his words and trailed off, uttering, "You're mine."

Guy wrapped his hand around Cam's cock one finger at a time and massaged, steadily increasing the pace of his thrusts as the pressure of Cam's caresses climbed. Sweat pooled between them, and their breaths clouded in the cool air, forming a steamy haze that amplified their panting and fueled the sensation they were mercifully alone. They saw, heard, and felt nothing but the other, filling one another to the brim, about to overflow.

Cam's head fell back, the bottom of his jaw pulled tight, the arteries in his craned neck pumping blood as hard and fast as they could. Again, Guy pushed further, lifting Cam's legs back, higher up as he went. He scrawled with his nails on Cam's stomach, not resisting each time Cam grabbed his hand to kiss it, to beg both for mercy and for Guy to keep going. Guy couldn't read what he was thinking; his own thoughts no longer made sense.

"I've got you," Guy repeated to him, granted a moan each time.

Guy ran his sweating hand down Cam's shaft to cup his tight balls, digging his fingertips into Cam's taint. Cam's cock slid against Guy's abs, and he curled his stomach to bury its tip secure in his navel. Cam's sweat-slicked limbs smacked against Guy's skin where they locked around him, the sound competing with the boom of the pulse that matched the quickening of Guy's thrusts.

"I missed you," Cam blurted out.

"I love you, too," Guy misreplied, slipping away despite the chanted *No* in his head.

Cam toppled his restraint aloud, pleading, "Yes, yes." Guy moaned Cam's name, but doubted Cam heard as he begged, "M-more—*please.*"

Guy forced one last thrust deeper than ever and twisted his hips to screw in as Cam bore up into him. He held them united with all his strength, unable to think now as constriction wrung him out.

Cam's neck arched back as he let out a loud cry that banished the last of Guy's reason. Pleasure overcame Guy, quickly dissolving into darkness as he kept coming harder, pouring heat into Cam while holding him so tightly that, as Guy came to, he found he couldn't breathe himself. Suddenly aware he was crushing Cam, Guy released his grip but couldn't pull away as Cam kept pushing his disheveled bangs into Guy's neck, his hips stuttering as the last of his orgasm subsided.

As they pulled apart to meet one another's eyes, Cam giggled. Bliss overwhelmed him, and he laughed as Guy kissed away his tears, proud that Cam had allowed himself to be emotional. As he settled, Guy gave in to giggling himself and rolled over him, the two of them making a knot of frayed nerves sparking with joy. They quieted slowly, clinging to each other after rearranging their bodies into a knot considerate of Guy's aching shoulder, and stared into each other's clear eyes.

"It's five-thirty a.m.," Cam said without looking away.

Guy didn't doubt he was right, down to the second. He gathered he was about to discover a new perspective on the city through Cam. His apartment already seemed like a different place, a home at last. A stream of dustless sunlight pooled in Cam's open palm, which Guy cupped in his hand in the air above them. Cam's hands had softened since he'd stopped trapping each day, and his skin grazed Guy's only as lightly as a shadow, so Guy clasped his fingers to reassure them neither were dreaming. The blankets were damp and smelled of Cam, and Guy had never been more comfortable in his life.

"You said I had nothing to worry about, but that's not true," Cam said wistfully.

Guy met his eyes. "Tell me."

"When I think about how I don't care about gender or notice the gender of who I like, it's a totally different kind of gray feeling, but when I stop myself from thinking, it's like sensation takes over, and after a certain tipping point, I can't feel anything. You've seen me feel everything when things are good, and you've seen me feel nothing, but I think maybe I could go both ways at the same time. I have no idea what would happen if I allowed that, or if it just happens one day. That was my plan two years ago. To trigger it."

Frenzy, Guy caught on. Cam could break both ways. When he *let go* in a negative situation by retreating into nothing, he got lost in a contained implosion. If, while he was in danger, he decided to feel everything instead, he'd explode outward. Guy knitted their fingers together and lowered their clasped hands to rest on his chest, glad Cam could anchor himself in the red crescents he dug into Guy's skin.

"First, I was going to get her off-balance by proposing. Make her doubt I had any sanity left. I wasn't sure myself, because no matter how I looked at it, it didn't make sense to continue being a doll and a ghost anymore, not even poetic sense, but I thought I'd never be free of my past. So logically, the only way to break from it was to break with my future...by killing her, then myself. But I love writing. I *love* it, Guy."

Guy squeezed Cam's hand to his throbbing chest.

"And it turns out love is, like, *Fuck logic.* Right?" Cam's other hand touched the tattoo on his own chest. "So I hid out at the hospital and applied to all these remote wildlife projects. We'd never been anywhere before. Beyond the five boroughs was beyond her reach, especially if I went north. We hate the cold. We hate clothes. Me slightly more," Cam added, as Guy frowned at his blurring of his self and Serena.

"None of it was your fault. You know that, right?"

"I think she accepted the proposal because she knew it would kill my father. I asked her not to tell him, but it doesn't matter. He would have committed suicide later anyway if I'd gone ahead. He wasn't... He wasn't a good man, but he would have done that. He wouldn't have willingly survived me murdering Serena. I really think he loved us, but only because we were what he had left to remind him of my mom." Cam's mouth twisted into a smile. "Hey, does Fairbanks cover my therapy, or are you going to charge me direct?"

"I'm already calling the last six weeks a writers' retreat for my taxes."

"I wrote a book for you while I was waiting. Just a novella," Cam corrected himself when Guy reared his head back to look at him.

"You didn't have to do that," he said, crushed with gratitude, too blank to notice he'd stolen Cam's past catchphrase until Cam laughed.

"Ha! It poured out as easily as the one I did when... The debut one. When I was ten."

Guy had a copy in the other room.

"That one took two weeks. Then it took the whole summer to edit, which dragged on forever, and was such a waste of time until I got this huge hardback." Cam scratched Guy's chest in jagged lines, then clasped its hair in his fingers and tugged gently in apology. "My father ruined it by writing an inscription in the inside cover. He'd changed the dedication in it, too, to me, thinking I'd be happy my name made page two. I'd dedicated it to my mom. So I burned it." He dragged his lower lip along the red marks he'd left on Guy's skin. "I wish I hadn't done that, but not as much as I wish he'd left it alone. A whole summer, Guy."

"Summers don't come cheap," Guy agreed. He'd spent his tenth summer being temporary best friends with a kid who'd turned out to be gay, too, though at the time their sexuality was irrelevant. All they'd done was build unstable forts in sandlots, explore the woods, and hang out at a public pool. There was no talk of sex, no pressure to grow up, no need to remember details. Its ease was why it had stuck with him. "I promise the next one will be fun."

"We probably can't share a bed in the hut alone again when we go see the rabbit."

"Probably not," Guy agreed. The hut and its walking trail was about to be hit with heavy tourism this summer.

"That's when I knew I was in trouble. When you put the mattresses together."

"It took that long?" Guy asked. "I think I was ruined from the moment you laughed in your truck."

"Ha!" Cam giggled. "The first night we shared a bed, you pulled my back to your chest and held me, and when I tried to move, you growled into my neck."

"Yeah, I'll bet that was scary. With my nasal voice?"

"Guttural, not nasal," Cam responded. "A puma gargling magma. Fucking evil Aslan, you should apologize. I nearly died in your arms.

Hey, tell me." He poked Guy's ribs. "Were you really asleep the whole time while I jerked off?"

"*Cam*," Guy spluttered.

"You *growled* at me." Cam was wracked with giggling again and ran trembling fingers over Guy's features. He pinched Guy's lips, and Guy missed when he playfully snapped at him. "And you said you assumed the risk for my jerking."

"Because you jerked in your *sleep*."

"I should have jerked you in your sleep."

As revenge, Guy leaned past Cameron's soul-penetrating stare and murmured against his neck. "How did I growl?"

Cam twitched, playing it off as a shrug. "Lower."

"Cam," Guy growled, only half feigning aggression as lust built in the pit of his stomach once more.

A shiver rippled down Cam's spine. "Fuck."

"Soon. Anytime."

Cam fumbled his fingers around Guy's waist, pressing the length of their bodies together.

"Lower," Cam whined hoarsely. Guy bit his earlobe and Cam gave a shuddering sigh. Guy stopped playing and rubbed Cam's back, firming out the knots in his muscles until they turned pliant.

"You're so cool," Cam murmured. "It isn't fair."

"Life's not fair." After everything Guy had done, Cam still loved him. "Cam? Thank you."

"L-love you." Cam's heart fluttered beneath Guy's fingertips.

"Mmm," Guy rumbled contentedly against him, an unintentional growl, and felt Cam's heart skip a beat.

"Will you kiss me?" Cam mumbled, voice thick as honey, and Guy obeyed.

Epilogue

GUY

Guy closed his eyes, the rocking motion and swishing sounds of brushing his teeth lulling him to relaxation near sleep again. Home sweet home never lost its appeal, especially their en suite, even in the sweltering summer. An approaching shuffle alerted him to the reflection of Cam slumping in behind him. He wasn't braced to receive the head butt right between his shoulder blades, and jabbed the toothbrush into the inside of his cheek.

"Ow."

Cam slid his arms around Guy's neck and crawled up Guy's back, relaxing as Guy bent forward and slipped his free hand beneath the legs wrapped around his waist. It wasn't enough, so Guy spat and tossed the toothbrush in the sink, then flung his other hand back to support Cam's ass.

He hunched as he stood, knowing that in this state Cam couldn't grip if he were tipped back any farther. He was still a wisp of a creature, but had gradually grown heavier since they'd returned to New York. Guy wasn't sure if it was because Cam was putting on weight or because he'd started to relax more in these sorts of vulnerable positions...and in general, Guy supposed, staggering back to the bed and laying Cam down. Cam nestled back into the quilt, but when Guy lay beside him, he mustered the strength to roll over and burrow into Guy's chest.

"Back to...bed?" he murmured.

"Yeah." Guy had nothing urgent on. Cam hadn't come to bed until sometime after Guy had woken at two in an empty bed. A bleary recon found Cam outside on the balcony's hammock, relishing the late breeze instead of what he called "recycled fridge air," his saucer-eyes dry all the same, thanks to his staring competition with his laptop screen. He was winning it.

He smelled like stale sweat now. Guy ran his fingers up Cam's back, entangling them in hair that now reached Cam's shoulders, its tendrils as soft as water but ensnaring as vines.

"I might not sleep. Might watch you."

Cam dragged in a few deep breaths. "I watch you all the time."

In replying at all, he was more awake than he was giving away. "Might blow you," Guy tested him.

Cam's closed eyelids twitched as he fought to keep a straight face. "I blow you all the—"

Guy tipped him over, rolling Cam onto his back as he curled up, giggling, squinting against the sunlight streaming in through the window. A lazy kiss was all Cam could return before losing his place in their game and his expression melted back into neutrality. Guy rolled the pair of them once more and arranged Cam's dead limbs so he could sleep stretched upon Guy like a cat, feeling Guy's chest rise and fall beneath him. Resigned to his fate, Guy pulled a corner of the quilt to block the sunlight. Cam was too far gone to hum acknowledgment, but he curled his fingers against Guy's arms.

"I love you, Cam," Guy said in time with the rhythm of Cam's breathing so as not to disturb him.

A brush of soft flesh against his chest was the matching reply. Cam had managed to kiss him, as always.

CAM

Cam had grown comfortable enough tangling himself with Guy to become a dead weight when asleep, free of the tension that had always forced him to sleep lightly. Unfortunately, it made it hard for Guy to slumber when Cam lay completely on top of him, compressing his chest, and he was likely to wake up if Cam shifted. He therefore lay still, eyes at half-mast, listening to Guy's heartbeat hasten the instant Cam flexed his fingers by their hips.

My husband's a seismograph, Cam thought with pride. Forgetting his resolution to stay still and not disturb Guy, he gulped a yawn, scraping his morning shadow on Guy's chest. *I'd bring him coffee in bed, but he'll follow me out to the kitchen and end up serving me while my head's flat on the counter. It'd be nice to wake him up with a blow job, too, now that he lets me do that, but I'm too tired. If only I had coffee in me already. We need a butler.*

For long minutes, Cam languidly scrawled with his nails in Guy's chest hair, avoiding his saliva pools, then took responsibility and licked their patches clean as his hand strayed south to the bramble of hair he loved to pull. He swallowed hard, conditioned as a Pavlovian pet at the sight, scent, and taste of Guy's body, and at the coarseness of the hair he nuzzled into.

A robot butler that doesn't complain or judge us. Cam had only recently started seeing a therapist, and though he'd initiated it, he was unsure whether the process was worthwhile. He didn't feel judged, per se, but he wasn't comfortable talking to anyone but Guy about the memories he never knew for sure were true or not. Unfortunately, he wasn't comfortable burdening Guy with them, either, but Cam quite liked using sessions to learn about and adapt coping strategies she proposed. And it was nice chatting with a girl; nearly all of Guy's friends were men, and Cam didn't go out often enough alone yet to make firm friends of any (or no) gender. He wasn't there yet.

A sexbot would be cool...but I'd smash it, Cam thought placidly, *if Guy ever used it alone, when he knows he can do absolutely anything to me. I wouldn't think, I'd just come to and see the robot in shards. Guy would be fine. I wouldn't touch him in a rage.* It was really nice to have reached that level of trust in himself. He still feared tipping the wrong way into nothingness. Belatedly, he realized he'd woken up clearly, twice in a row, just this morning. It was becoming a habit.

Even if I did hurt Guy somehow, he'd forgive me. I'm allowed to do anything but hurt myself, and he's become pretty liberal about that. Cam idly pressed Guy's nipple, his lips curling into a smile as it rose. *Ha.* Guy was conditioned to him too... *He doesn't care if I stay up late as long as I sleep late. And he liked my tattoo.*

Three small letters sat squarely between Cam's shoulder blades, traced from Guy's neat signature. Having the central letter—*U*—etched over his spine hurt less than the hammering of his first tattoo on his sternum, which had played havoc with his heartbeat before he let himself tune out. Cam got the second tattoo the first hour Guy left for a few days, so it healed for Guy to discover while stripping him.

At the inevitable pause, Cam turned, expecting a lecture on the dangers of infection, how he shouldn't have subjected himself to pain. Guy was cross-legged on the bed. He was white as snow, his composure shot.

"Sorry," Cam said.

"Cam, will you marry me?" Guy asked. His voice was steady, but his mouth wavered. All his features were in their right places, but looked stranger than a moment before.

Cam had never seen Guy's eyes look like that. After a moment, he realized it was because they were stiller than they'd ever been, his mind locked on just *one* emotion, his expression saying one thing. Entranced, Cam traced Guy's face, running his thumb over Guy's parted lips. Guy kissed it as it passed and Cam jumped.

"Say yes," Guy said.

Duh. All of him was Guy's, all Cam's flaws, with the addition of a brand for life, a life that was Guy's to do with as he wished. What was Guy's was Guy's. What was Cam's was Guy's. He trusted Guy to take care of him, but if he couldn't, Cam would take care of them both.

"Campbell" would live on as a pen name and as *Lepus campbelli* for a few millennia. Cam was an optimist when it came to humanity's longevity. Humans had tenacity. He cleared his throat. It didn't dislodge the boulder in it, put there by the earthquake currently rocking the bed. Legally, he had Guy's surname. He had Guy's first name tattooed on his back, opposite the *No* he'd had done while on a frog survey in Cambodia, after getting out of hospital—opposite that one on purpose...which Guy knew. Guy knew nearly everything about Cam, and he still loved him.

"Okay. Yes, please."

Cam lost count of how many times Guy swore he loved him with his arm hooked tight around Cam, holding him securely as a brace, kissing his tattoo. Tears dripped from Cam onto the fists tangled in sheets below his face. When the usual tranquility flooded him, the first coherent word to surface from it was "husband." No longer "boyfriend" and skipping "fiancé," he already thought of Guy as "my husband." They already had the same name. It was official, Guy had granted his wish at last. Relief shot through his afterglow like a firework and exploded effervescence in him, making him burble as if revealing happy news, "Hey, Guy, we're getting married."

He wondered why his vision was so blurry, whether he'd come too hard. Then Guy embraced him and he found the saltwater covering Guy's shoulder wasn't just sweat but more tears that itched where they pooled in Cam's dimples and sealed him to Guy, making their skin squelch and smack along with the clicks of their kiss.

Marriage was no guarantee Guy would stay close. He could always change his mind, and Cam would drop back to stalking him until death did they part to ensure Guy's safety and identify the fleck of insanity in Guy that ever made him love Cam.

It was a puzzle for the scientist to crack. Guy wasn't staying out of guilt about Serena—he knew Cam could keep a secret, but still protected Cam by never discussing it. Why? If it was because Guy was himself unhinged, Cam would exploit that so they never parted. It was why Guy shouldn't be with him.

Or was it a *Fuck logic* situation on Guy's end? The way he loved Cam like Cam loved him, and like Cam loved writing, beyond reason, even when it hurt, especially when it hurt? If they were *both* mad, was that okay? Enough? It was for Cam. He trusted it probably was for Guy, too, but time would tell. Hopefully, plenty of time. Two lifetimes side by side.

'Course it meant he'd have to meet Guy's family. *Hmm.* He'd deserve a reward for that. Cam tensed every muscle, then relaxed them all slowly. *Forget a butler. I want to adopt a dog. We could train it to fetch...well, not coffee. Clothes? Oh, we could dress it up—*

Books, he interrupted himself. *It could fetch books. And the mail. Or it could just do what it wanted, be exactly what it is, and be loved unconditionally.*

Guy sighed beneath him and Cam drew himself up on his forearms, feeling better than usual. Dozing an extra few hours helped, but Guy's warmth beneath him relaxed him more. He said Cam hardly jerked in his sleep at all anymore, which Cam knew to be true, as long as he was glued to Guy from head to all nine of his toes.

"I love you, too," Cam said, voice clear as he responded to what Guy had said earlier as if no time had passed since. He peeled free of him, and Guy raised his forearm to cover his face, obscuring a yawn. "And I'll make coffee. Stay put."

"Can you turn on the recycled fridge AC?" Guy mumbled.

"You're still going to sweat, just wait," Cam flirted, heading for the window instead to roll it open.

"So then we'll shower, and shower again," Guy promised, exactly as Cam sought, and muffled another yawn in the quilt Cam had kicked aside earlier without a thought.

About the Author

After living in the UK, Vietnam, and Japan, Reece is currently based in Australia. She loves painting digital portraits and translating Japanese literature whenever she's not battling her cat for access to her keyboard to write romance.

She loves to talk all things books and can be found on social media and at reecepine.com.

Twitter: @reecepine

Website: www.reecepine.com

Also Available from NineStar Press

Connect with NineStar Press

www.ninestarpress.com

www.facebook.com/ninestarpress

www.facebook.com/groups/NineStarNiche

www.twitter.com/ninestarpress

www.tumblr.com/blog/ninestarpress